W9-BCC-735

Tachyon transmission was a marvelous invention. A man could send infinite replicates of himself anywhere in the galaxy—wherever duty called. If one of the copies got killed, so what? The original would still be alive and well back on his home planet, and he could always send replacements!

Such a man was Ben Pertin, who lived on Earth.

And then there was:

Ben Charles Pertin—stationed on Sun One, central headquarters of the intelligent races in the galaxy.

Ben James Pertin—sent to the probe ship Aurora after Ben Frank Pertin was reported missing on board.

Ben Linc Pertin—dispatched to the artificial satellite orbiting Cuckoo.

Ben Yale Pertin—one of several Pertins sent to explore the surface of Cuckoo. Some returned—many did not!

And most of them were in love with the same woman!

ALSO BY FREDERIK POHL AND JACK WILLIAMSON
Published by Ballantine Books

FARTHEST STAR

The Saga of Cuckoo

FREDERIK POHL
JACK WILLIAMSON

A Del Rey Book

BALLANTINE BOOKS • NEW YORK

A Del Rey Book
Published by Ballantine Books

ISBN 0-345-30700-3

Manufactured in the United States of America

First Ballantine Books Edition: February 1975
Second Printing: February 1983

Cover art by David B. Mattingly

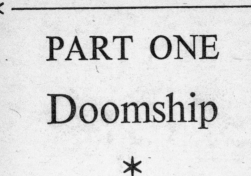

PART ONE

Doomship

*

ONE

*

    The place was called Sun One. It had begun as an asteroid, circling a young blue-white giant in the great dense cloud called the Orion Nebula. Over centuries it had been built upon, sheathed, and tunneled; and what it had become was the closest thing there was to a central headquarters of the loose association of intelligent races in the Galaxy that had made contact with one another.

    In one of the inner shells two members of a very junior race were meeting. They came from Earth. They loved each other. They were young. They planned to marry. All these things made them curiosities to the races that possessed personal curiosity, and they were widely watched, heard, or sensed as they came toward each other. They didn't mind. Ben Charles Pertin saw the girl and launched himself in a shallow three-percent-gravity dive over the heads of a thing like a dragon, a creature composed mostly of a single great blue eye, and a couple of scurrying collective creatures from one of the core stars. "Sorry," he cried down at them, caught the laughing girl's hand, and stopped hard beside her.

    "Ouch," she said, releasing a holdfast with her other hand. "I'd appreciate a little less enthusiasm next time."

    He kissed her and took her arm. "It's part of the image," he said cheerfully. "You know what the chief of delegation says. Make them know we're here. Earth may be the newest planet in the association but it isn't going to be the least important. We have a duty to

3

Earth to make ourselves known throughout the Galaxy, and a duty to the Galaxy to contribute our strength and our know-how."

"I think," the girl said, "that if you're going to talk like that you'd better buy me a drink."

At this shell of Sun One the curvature of the spherical surface they walked on was noticeably sharp. They found it was easier to leap than to stroll. To travel arm in arm, which is how Ben Charles Pertin chose to walk with his girl, required practice and a lot of discomfort—not only to them but to the other sentients in the concourse. Pertin and Zara shifted grips, so that each had an arm around the other's waist; then Pertin caught the holdfast webbing with his free hand and partly tugged, partly kicked them into the air. They shot past the dragonlike creature, narrowly missed a steelwork vertical strut, touched down again next to something that looked like a soft-bodied beetle with three dozen legs, and were in sight of the little refreshment platform they liked.

Pertin said "Hi!" to a thing like a green bat as it flapped by. It hissed something shrill that his personal translator repeated into his ear as, "I recognize your identity, Ben Charles Pertin." The girl nodded, too, although all members of that particular race, which was called the T'Worlie, looked alike to her, and in any event the T'Worlie did not have the custom of nodding since they had no more neck than bats.

As they waited for traffic to clear, the girl said, "How did your meeting go?"

"About as usual. Things are all fouled up on the probe." He was watching a tumbling boxlike robot that was coming toward them on a tangent, correcting its course with methodical jets of steam from the faces of its cubical body; but the tone of his voice made the girl look at him sharply.

"What is it, Ben?"

He gave her a caught-in-the-cookie-jar smile. "I'll tell you about it when we sit down."

"You'll tell me now."

"Well—" He hesitated, then cried, "All right, we can make it now!" But the girl wrapped her fingers around the webbing of the holdfast.

"Ben!"

He relaxed and looked at her. He didn't say anything, but he didn't have to.

"Ben! Not again!"

He said defensively, "I have to, Zara. The other one's dying. There's nobody from Earth on the probe now to represent us. So I agreed to carry the ball."

He looked appraisingly at the traffic of aliens, then back at her; then he looked at her with a sudden shock of surprise. The girl looked as if she had come very close to crying.

"Oh, Zara," he said, half-touched and half-annoyed. "What are you making a big thing about? It's nothing we haven't done before."

"I know," she said, and blinked hard. "It's only—well, it's sort of silly. But I hate the idea of your dying out there while we're on our honeymoon."

Pertin found that he was blinking himself; he was touched. He patted the girl's hand and said seriously, "Honey, one of the traits I like best in you is that you're not afraid to be sentimental at the right time. Don't knock it. I love you for it. Now let's go get that drink."

The little café was nearly empty. That was one of the things they liked about it. It had actual waiters, Purchased People. They didn't have much personality to display, but they were actually human, genetically speaking. Pertin and his fiancée enjoyed ordering in their rudimentary Italian—not their own language, to be sure, but at least a human language, and one for which they did not need the Pmal translators.

Pertin pulled his feet up, crossed them in air, and settled gently onto his chair. They looked about while waiting for their drinks to be brought. Pertin had been

on Sun One for more than two years now, the girl for
several months. Even so, familiarity had not dulled
their interest in the place where they were stationed or
in the work they did there. The girl was a newswriter,
broadcasting to Earth every week on the stereostage.
Pertin was an engineer. His job on Sun One didn't involve much engineering. It did involve an interesting
mixture of skills. He functioned partly as a sort of legal-
ized spy and partly as a goodwill ambassador from
Earth to the rest of the Universe.

The mere fact that a job like his existed was still se-
cretly thrilling to Ben Charles Pertin. He was not yet
thirty. Even so, he was old enough to remember the
time when the human race thought it was alone in the
Galaxy.

Space travel itself was not new. The old "nations"
had put up their chemical rockets and sent them chug-
ging to Venus, Mars, and the Moon in his grandfather's
time. They had looked for life, and come up empty every time. Nuclear probes a generation later investigated
the outer planets, the satellites, and even the asteroids,
with the same result. No life. By the time Ben was
twelve years old, the juice had run out of space travel.

There were still a lot of ongoing projects, such as the
close-orbiting satellites that photomapped the Earth and
relayed TV programs from Rangoon to Rochester and
back. An occasional plodding probe was sent out to sample a comet's gases or measure the solar flux. And of
course there was always the Farside base on the Moon,
where radio astronomy had retreated when the world's
communications systems had ruined reception for every
ground-based dish. But no excitement was generated by
any of that. There was not even any interest. If some
pollster had sampled the Earth's billions with a question
like, "Do you think intelligent life exists elsewhere in
the Universe?" he would have been likely to receive as
a general response, "Don't know; don't care."

Then came Contact.

It happened just as Ben Pertin was turning thirteen.

Something had been found on Pluto. An artifact, half buried under Pluto's mirror of ice. The Earth suddenly looked outward again. The stereostages were full of it: the first fumbling attempts to patch it together, the first daring experiment at putting power through it. Everybody talked about it. Ben and his parents watched the glowing figures on their stage, enthralled. Their evening meals grew cold because they forgot to eat. In school, the kids made the discovery the main subject of every class.

And when the ancient communicator came to life and the first alien face peered out of its screen and looked into the face of a human from Earth, the world went mad.

"I don't want to hear any more of that cockamamie Earthman's Burden talk," Zara Doy said. "I heard too much of it when I was a kid. I don't *want* you going out to die. Stay here with me."

Pertin said fondly, "You're sweet, Zara. But this is important. The situation on the probe is exploding; the beings are fighting. They're dying uselessly. I can't back out just for some sentimental ideas of—"

"Sentiment be damned! Look. When we get married I want you right in bed with me, all of you. I don't want to be thinking about part of you dying way off in nowhere!"

"I'll be with you, honey. All of me."

"You know what I mean," she said angrily.

He hesitated. The last thing he wanted was to quarrel with his fiancée two days before they were to get married—and less than two days before he kept his promise to go to the probe ship. He rubbed his troth ring and said, "Zara, I have to go to the probe. First, I said I would; and the boss has passed the word to all the other top brass on Sun One. Second, it's important. It's not 'Earthman's Burden.' It's simple logic. We're new and pretty far behind, compared to the Scorpians or the methane crowd or the T'Worlie. But look what we've done already. We have Earth people on every major planet, working in every big project, taking part in everything that's happening. The others are getting used to us. They consult us now. If I back out, who else is there to go? Earth won't be represented—"

"I don't care."

"It's not as if I haven't done it before—"

"The other time you went we weren't going to be married," the girl responded fiercely.

"All right, that's true. Now I owe you something. But I owe our planet something, too. We're just *beginning* to contribute our share of leadership in the Galaxy, Zara. I mean, look at that waiter! Half the Purchased People around are human beings, now. When the non-viables edit a copy for Sun One, say, what shape do they copy? Human! The human shape is as familiar in the Galaxy now as the Sheliaks—and all in twenty years!"

Zara sucked at the last of her drink and put it down in its cage. She stared at the waiter, who was smoking a cigarette and thinking whatever thoughts a blanked-out personality was allowed to think; then she shook her head.

"I'll lay it out nice and orderly like an engineer for you, Ben," she said. "First, if they copy human shape, is it because they respect us or because they have some crazy methane sense of humor? Second, if they buy our convicts for Purchased People, likely enough it's because we have more criminals to sell. Third, I don't like the whole idea of Earth trying to dominate the Galaxy. Fourth—"

"Dominate! I said 'leadership.' It's not the same thing at all."

"It's a prerequisite. Not sufficient, but necessary. Fourth, I still hate it all on personal grounds, and I'm not talking about idealism, I'm talking about sex. I'll get over it. I know that. But it's going to take some of the joy out of going to bed with you, Ben, thinking that at the same time somewhere else you're getting eaten by a Sheliak or dying of radiation burn. I'm sorry it's so, but it's so."

Ben said doubtfully, after a moment, "Would it be better if we postponed the wedding a little bit?"

"I don't know. Let me think."

He waited, finished his drink, looked cautiously at the girl. There was no anger or misery on her pretty face; she was simply staring thoughtfully out at the other beings in the concourse.

Pertin beckoned to the waiter and paid the check. "They thank you," said the waiter, staring appraisingly at Pertin and the girl. "Will there be anything else?"

"No, we're going." But still the girl sat there. Then she sighed, and smiled at him.

"Well. You want to go pretty badly. Feeling the way you do, I suppose you ought to go. I won't stop you, Ben, and it's silly to put off getting married. But there is one thing I want you to do."

He waited warily.

"Give me your ring. No, just to hold. When you're finished going to the probe I'll give it back to you. But I don't want you wearing my ring when you die."

Last-minute briefing was in the tachyon transport chamber, out at the far shell of Sun One, and heavily shielded. Dr. Gerald York Bielowitz checked Pertin out himself. He was a methodical man—one of the reasons he was head of the mission to Sun One; and he read from a soundscripted list.

"We've got about ten minutes, Ben Charles. Let's see. Object Lambda. You know as much about it as I do: it's anomalous, it's exciting, the only way to find out about it is this probe, and it's in Earth's interest to make the probe succeed."

He dropped his eyes to the page and went on: "There's no possibility of survival on the probe, of course, and this has undoubtedly had some effect on the psyches of all the beings there. To the extent they have what we can map as psyches, I mean. But in my opinion, the physical problems have caused the trouble. Some of the beings are dying—your predecessor among them, of course. Others are functioning poorly, probably because of ionization interference with their nervous systems—or whatever corresponds to nervous systems.

"At any rate," he said, checking off another point, "the beings on the probe no longer constitute an orderly system. There's violence. Some of the deaths are from fights or murders. This is seriously interfering with the operation of the probe, and threatening its very success. You know how important that is. If we blow this, it's more than a hundred years before we get another chance.

"And finally," he said, folding the list and putting it in his sporran, "your account here will be credited with double-rate pay for your services on the probe. Your equipment will follow, along with Doc Chimp here." He nodded civilly to the hairy little handyman who crouched next to Pertin. "And good luck to you both!"

"Thank you, Gerald York," Pertin said gravely. He stepped up to the transport portal, waited for the signal and entered, giving a half-wave to Bielowitz as the door closed behind him.

This was the fourth time he had found himself in a tachyon-transporter box, or at least the fourth time that he remembered, or that it had actually happened to *him*. They all looked about the same. On the inside they were featureless except for what looked like studded nailheads almost completely covering each of the six interior surfaces. He stood there for a moment, and felt nothing.

But something was going on. The sensors were counting, locating, and identifying every atom in his body, measuring their bonds to adjacent atoms, charting them in a precise three dimensional matrix. The information obtained they encoded into a string of binary numbers; whereupon the great tachyon generators glowed into life, transmitting the numbers at a billibit per second in the direction of a point outside the farthest spiral arm of the Galaxy. It took only moments.

Then Ben Charles Pertin stepped out of the box and shook hands with his head of mission. "You're the best man I've got," Bielowitz said solemnly. "Thanks."

Pertin then went back to his office and worked through the rest of the afternoon. He left a little early to meet his fiancée and take her to dinner. Over the coffee she returned his troth ring to him.

TWO

At about the same time that Ben Charles Pertin was putting his ring back on his finger, as much as time at two points separated by relativistic distances and velocities can be called the "same," Ben James Pertin pushed his way out of another, almost identical box on the probe ship.

He stopped just outside the portal, moving slightly to allow it to close behind him. His expression was grim. "Lucked out," he said aloud, looking around the unfamiliar chamber.

There was no one to hear, or to see the bitter and despondent look on his face. The chamber was deserted. The probe was in free-fall, and Pertin floated slowly away from the transport; but nothing else was floating in the room. There was no litter, no sign that any other being of any sort was within thousands of light-years and, as he listened, not even any sound.

He swore softly to himself and twisted his body around to face the crated personal effects that were nudging their way out of the box. There wasn't a great deal to come: some tapes, some changes of clothing, personal items. All his belongings were in a couple of crates, and at the end of the string of transmissions came his companion on the mission, Doc Chimp.

Doc Chimp thrust out a long arm and caught the handle of the door as he went by. He hung there for a moment, staring at his environment with an expression that was a parody of Pertin's own. "Oh, wow, Ben Charles," he said sadly. "What a place."

"It'll be 'Ben James,' I think," said Pertin.

"Sure," Doc Chimp said dismally. "Me, I'm not going to bother. If you want to call me something different, call me stupid."

Doc Chimp was Earthborn, but he was not human. He was five feet three inches tall, weighed more than two hundred pounds, and, in high-G environments, habitually walked on feet and knuckles. His parents had been chimpanzees, but Doc Chimp was something different.

For one thing, he had a sense of humor. He reflected it in the clothes he wore. Over his hairy barrel chest he wore a little red vest, open, with the coarse black fur sprouting through. He didn't need it for comfort or for modesty; he wore it to please his own sense of the comic, and for pockets to hold his automatic translator, the key to his private suitcase, and a supply of macadamia nuts, of which he was very fond. For modesty he wore shiny brown lederhosen. On his head he sported a kepi with a sand veil around sides and back, and over its visor a bright green plume.

Even the plume was sagging dejectedly as he said, "I think I'm going to hate this place, Ben James."

"We didn't come here to have fun. Where the hell is everybody?"

"Don't know, Ben James. Can't say."

"Stow our stuff then. This thing won't stay in free-fall long; we'd better find somebody before it starts firing again."

"Certainly, Ben James. But there's somebody coming now."

Pertin said, startled: "I don't hear anything."

"Neither do I. But I smell it. It's a T'Worlie, coming fast."

The probe ship was T'Worlie property, but fortunately for the other races of the Galaxy the T'Worlie didn't have a very strong territorial imperative.

They had been civilized for a long, long time. They

were an inquisitive race, in their unhurried way, and no doubt that was why they had been sending their probes out for hundreds of generations. Little T'Worlie rockets had radiated in all directions from their mother star, some of them aimed at other stars, some at nothing closer than the Great Nebula in Andromeda, ten million years' travel time away.

Only a race like that, deploying probes as lavishly and patiently as it had, could have discovered the curious astronomical object called Lambda. No other race would have been in a position to do it. Sirians, with their limited time-binding capacities that reached no more than a week into the future, wouldn't have bothered. Nothing that promised a remote payoff interested the Sirians at all—which made them unattractive partners, but inoffensive foes. Humans of course had no chance; their technology wasn't up to the job, and the farthest terrestrial probe was still climbing toward the turnover point on its now senseless journey toward 40 Eridani A.

But the T'Worlie thought long, slow thoughts, and they were gently but persistently curious about everything. If their race lived long enough it would learn everything there was to know. None of them seemed to mind that no T'Worlie now alive would be present to learn it.

Lambda had been discovered first by an unmanned T'Worlie scoutship and reported in a routine synoptic survey. It attracted no attention at all. When first observed, its great distance and low luminosity put it at the very threshold of detectability, and the traits that made it unique had not been noted.

Subsequent observations attracted more attention. Its weak spectral lines seemed to shift toward the violet, rather than the red—which is to say, it was moving *toward* the Galaxy instead of away from it. Curious. But the lines were so very weak, the point so very distant, and the orderly T'Worlie had many other things on their agenda to investigate.

Then, by accident, another scout turned up the same object in a survey.

It might not have been recognized if the computers of the T'Worlie had not been so patient and painstaking. The second scout had been launched five thousand years earlier, its vector several degrees away. From its point of view, Object Lambda was in a wholly different part of the sky, and its rate of approach, indicated by the spectral shift, quite different.

But the computers had sensed a possible match and had clucked over the figures until they confirmed it. There existed a specific, if hypothetical, orbit and velocity, which, seen from those two scouts at those recorded times, would have given exactly those readings.

From the estimated elements the computers made a prediction. They requested a special observation from still a third unmanned scout. Lo! It turned out as they had predicted.

Object Lambda was not more than twenty thousand light-years from the edge of the Galaxy, and was approaching it at about one-sixth of light-speed.

At this point the T'Worlie announced their discovery to the galactic civilization at large, and began a study of their existing drones in that general part of space.

The T'Worlie drones were as small as interstellar probes can be made: a scoop, a hydrogen ram, some instruments, and a tachyon installation. The T'Worlie had been launching them, thousands at a time, for tens of thousands of years. As they had never invented war, they were able to accumulate large quantities of surplus capital, and so the probes were not at first a particularly expensive project for them. Like most early-industrial races, they had energy to burn. They burned it. Their planet was largely water-covered; though they looked like bats, they were somewhat more analogous to flying fish. Their water was rich in D_2O, and they spent its fusion energies profligately.

The T'Worlie drone model was standardized early. A program was set up under which each drone, upon reaching a point suitably distant from all others, flashed a tachyonic signal to the T'Worlie planet, whereupon the tachyon transmitters scanned, encoded, and transmitted whole new drones to the mother drone's unit. As each new drone flashed into being, it signaled in to the T'Worlie planet, was given a course and program of its own and went onward. The effect was that of an enormous globe of drones, at the end thousands of millions of them, expanding outward like the shell of a dead supernova.

The program was fully automatic and economical of everything but the energy eaten up by the tachyon transmitters, and for ten thousand years there seemed to be an endless supply of that.

In the end even the T'Worlie began to realize that their energy resources, though huge, were not infinite. The drone program was cut to a trickle. But it was never stopped, and the great swelling bubble of drone ships expanded out, into globular clusters, out toward the neighboring galaxies, along the spiral arms, in toward the core of the Milky Way itself. It was a T'Worlie drone that had buried itself on Pluto and been found by the exploration from Earth. In fact, T'Worlie drones had brought into the galactic society at least a hundred races at one time or another, almost half of the total so far located. Another race might have thought of using that fact to establish dominance for itself, but the T'Worlie didn't think that way. They had never invented empires, either.

So when the T'Worlie began to be deeply interested in Object Lambda it was easy enough to find some hundreds of drones on courses and at points that were not too remote from it.

The next job for the T'Worlie computers was calculating which of these drones was on the course that would involve least time and energy in diverting it to the neighborhood of Lambda, with its huge Galaxy-ward velocity. Fortunately a handful of drones in that section had been redirected inward long before, to fill gaps in the global screen. Among them was one that was, by the best of luck, on a course that could match Lambda in less than five years.

After that there was no problem. The drone's matter receiver was put to work giving birth to automatic tools, hull sections, drive units, instruments, finally people. The tools went to work, assembling the hull sections, installing the drives, making room for the people. What had been a tiny kick-ram, no bigger than Earth's early Apollo capsule, was transformed and expanded into a thousand-meter vessel with room for a crew of several hundred.

There was, to be sure, one problem.

The rebuilt T'Worlie ship, now named *Aurora*, was big; but it needed to be big. It did not possess a great deal of surplus mass.

The ship was driven by the sequential explosion of hydrogen fusion charges, directional in a cone-shaped blast against a great battering plate at its base. Not much of the ionizing radiation from the fusion explosions seeped through the base plate, but enough did so that the members of the crew were constantly bathed in it.

T'Worlie and Sheliaks, Purchased People and Boaty-Bits, robots and humans—all responded to this in their individual and idiosyncratic racial ways. But few complex chemical or electronic processes can operate without damage in the presence of ionizing radiation. It didn't matter who they were. In the long run it came to much the same for all of them. They died.

Pertin and the chimp scrambled to the corridor entrance and peered out. The vinegary T'Worlie smell was strong now, and they could hear the sounds of something happening outside: a puncture-tire hiss, a faint high-pitched singing.

A circus procession was sailing toward them down the center of the corridor. First was a T'Worlie, a bat's head on butterfly body, no bigger than a pigeon but strong enough to be dragging with it a kitten-sized furry creature with enormous saucer eyes as it flew with powerful strokes of its green-spotted filmy wings. Behind the T'Worlie and the being it carried was a glittering cloud of steel-blue particles, like a swarm of gnats in the sun; and behind them, coming fast but decelerating strongly because of its mass, the square-edged form of a Scorpian robot, all fore jets pumping reaction mass.

The T'Worlie made its shrill whistling sounds, and the Pmal translator on Pertin's shoulder rattled into life. "I identify you as a Pertin," it said with mechanical precision. "I propose you transfer at once to high-G accommodations suitable to your structure, mode urgent."

"Why, Nimmie!" cried Ben James, suddenly, inexplicably, foolishly glad. "It's good to see you."

The T'Worlie braked with its filmy wings, and the five patterned eyes studied Pertin. "Verify your statement of identity," the Pmal translator rattled in his ear. "Query implications. Request clarification."

"Why, it's me, Ben Ch—Ben James Pertin. From Sun One. Why, just yesterday I saw you in the social concourse, remember?" But he stopped; this copy of the T'Worlie he had known would not remember.

The T'Worlie hesitated. It was some Nimmie or other, Pertin was sure; the key to recognizing T'Worlie was not the five eyes, or the small sphincter mouth with its cat's-whisker vibrissae, but the patterns on the wings. Green spots predominating on a pale yellow background; five of the bigger spots arranged in a sort of wobbly letter W, like the constellation Cassiopeia from Earth; yes, it was Nimmie, all right, Pertin knew. But perhaps a Nimmie he had never met, in some different line of descent.

The vinegary smell deepened; it was a sign of polite cogitation in a T'Worlie, like a human being's *Hmmm*. But Nimmie did not respond exactly. He was distracted by the swarm of tiny beings, who swept into the tachyon-transport room, swirled around Pertin and the chimp, and reformed under the T'Worlie's wings.

The kittenlike creature spoke, with a voice like a purr. The translator rendered it as: "No time kidding around, get hell out!" And the T'Worlie concurred:

"Mode urgent. Accept transportation via robot. Your physical safety at risk!"

Doc Chimp chattered: "I told you I wasn't going to like this place, Ben James. It isn't safe. Of course, I'm only a monkey, so it doesn't matter much about me. It's you I worry about."

"You're an ape," Pertin corrected automatically, his brain concentrating on what the T'Worlie had said.

"Sure, but an ape that knows what isn't safe. Come on, Ben James! Let's do like Bat-Ears says and split!"

Suddenly, the decision was taken from Pertin. The Scorpian robot hissed slowly by, still decelerating, came to a stop, reversed itself, and began to pick up momentum for the return. And as it passed Pertin and Doc Chimp it simply caught them up, each under a silvery tentacle, and bore thm away. In reverse order the procession steamed away: first the robot with the two terrestrial primates, then the swarm of Bit-creatures, then the T'Worlie and its passenger.

The probe was powered by huge nuclear thrusters; the power was only off for short periods, long enough to permit instrument readings or other work that could not be carried on during deceleration times, and the rest of the time the entire environment suffered under a surging uneven pulsing drive that averaged nearly seven gravities.

The welcoming-and-transport committee barely got them to a place of refuge before the thrusters started again. The Boaty-Bits had darted away at the first warning white-noise blast; they could not operate at all under thrust and had to find safety lest they be stepped on. The T'Worlie and his passenger were next to go, leaving only the robot to see to tucking Pertin and Doc Chimp in. The robot had no particular objection to high gravity—Pertin had noticed that on the trip from the tachyon chamber; when the robot had to change direction it simply braced itself with a few of the steel-coil tentacles, stopped against whatever was in the way, and pushed off in another direction. The sensation for Pertin was like being tossed around at the end of a cracking whip, but he survived it.

The thrusting started before the robot had finished sealing their cocoons, and it was even worse than the ride. The cocoons, meant to protect them against the thrust, were tailor-made to their dimensions, equipped with the best of springing devices and every comfort. But there was no such thing as antigravity, and that was what was needed.

The robot tarried for a moment. It could no longer jet about, but its tentacles held it easily off the floor, octopuslike. As the thrusts came the appendages gave gently, then returned to position.

The robot seemed to be trying to communicate. Pertin, looking out of the cocoon faceplate, shrugged and spread his hands. One Scorpian looked like another, but if this one had come from Sun One it might recognize the human gesture. The trouble was, there was no way to tell whether it was responding to it.

Then the Pmal crackled into life: "—not move. Prerequisite explanations to you. I am repeating this on all comm frequencies, will. Imperative you not move. Perequisite—"

The Pmal faded again, as the robot evidently shifted to another possible frequency. "All right," said Pertin, "we'll wait." But whether the robot understood him or not he could not say; it rested there on its tentacles, swaying under the thrust for a few moments more, and then slithered undulatingly away.

The probe was decelerating furiously now; a rollercoaster ride, multiplied by a hundred. There was a lot more noise than Pertin had expected, both the distant rumble of the nuclear explosions and the screeching of the torsion-bar shock absorbers that did their best to level out the thrust. But the cocoon was designed for it.

"Doc!" he called. "Can you hear me?"

The chimp's cocoon was only yards away, but the thuuud-*screech!* drowned out all other sounds. Pertin stared around. The room was half machine. Bright metal valves, gray plastic tubes coiling like dead entrails, colored screens where enigmatic symbols flickered and vanished. The walls were a sick, off-color green. No human would have designed a room like this, but of course it had not been designed for humans in the first place. It was a standard T'Worlie cocoon container, modified to take terrestrials; and the T'Worlie merely allowed them to use it.

The thuuuuud-*screech* went on and on. Experimenting with the cocoon, Pertin discovered that it would meter an anesthetic dose into his veins, or even a selective analgesic to deaden the auditory nerve for a time to block out the remorseless nuclear thunder. But he didn't want to sleep, and he wasn't tired; he wanted to get about his business. When your time is running out, he thought, you don't like to lose any of it.

Then he discovered that the cocoon had a built in stereostage.

The apparatus was not wholly familiar, but with any luck he should be able to reach Doc Chimp, at least. His first attempt was not a success. He gently turned a knurled pointer under the hollow silver hemisphere of the stage and was delighted to see it fill with the shining silver mist that indicated it was operating.

But when the mist abruptly condensed it was to show the image of a nude blond girl. "Mr. Pertin, sir," she caroled sweetly, "welcome aboard! Tonight for your entertainment, sir, you may watch me star in *The Belle of Bellatrix.* A thriller-drama of the love of a human beauty for a mutated alien and its fatal consequences. Feel the fear of the terrified girl! Share the wrath of her human lover! Feel the coils of the monster around her! Taste its dying blood! All these available by using the sen-sat foils in the small cabinet by your right hand.

We have many other stereostage fiches, Mr. Pertin, and—"

He finally got that fiche turned off, and the nude blonde vanished, still smiling. She dissipated as the camera zoomed in at her until at the end all that was left was a Cheshire-cat smile and the memory of her pale, slim figure.

Then the stereostage blinked, swirled with color, solidified, and Doc Chimp's homely face was staring out at him.

"Got you first time," Pertin cried, pleased. "I didn't think I would be so lucky."

"You weren't," the chimp said. "I called you. I want to volunteer for something." The chimpanzee face looked subdued.

Pertin said, "What?"

"I think I ought to take a look around," Doc Chimp said sadly. "God knows I don't want to. But most of the beings will be tied down to pressure cocoons and I'm not. Quite."

"Good idea," Pertin said, a little surprised. He hadn't known the chimp well on Sun One—it wasn't that he was prejudiced against mutated animals, but of course they didn't have much in common. But he had an impression of Doc Chimp's personality that was at variance with the act of volunteering for a solitary excursion into what might be trouble. Humorous, pleasure-seeking, a little lazy—that's how he would have described the chimp. "And thanks," he added. "Meanwhile I'll just send back a report to Sun One, if I can figure out how to use this sterostage."

"Ah," said Doc Chimp, the mocking light in his eyes again, "allow me to instruct you, mighty human. You know, I figured you'd be too involved with high-level considerations to take much interest in hardware. So I checked out all the instrumentation with the T'Worlie on Sun One before we left."

* * *

Pertin needed only a few minutes to learn to operate the component in his cocoon; it was not, after all, anything but a stereostage, and they were common all over the Galaxy. Then he lifted himself on one elbow against the surging thrusts of the drive, the cocoon's self-adjusting circuits buzzing busily to try to compensate for his unusual position; and he watched the chimp cautiously lever himself over the side of his own cocoon—timing his movements to the surging of the drive—drop clumsily to the floor, mutter to himself angrily for a moment, and then slowly, painfully lumber off on all fours. He did not look back.

Pertin felt curiously better, as if he had discovered a friend where he had expected only an inadequate tool. He worked the controls of the stereostage, got himself a circuit through to the recording fiches of the tachyon communicator, and spoke:

"This is Ben James Pertin," he said, "reporting in to Sun One. Doc Chimp and I have arrived safely. There was no apparent problem from the transmission; at least, we look all right, we're breathing, our hearts are working. Whether our brains are scrambled or not I could not say. No more than when we volunteered for this, anyway, I'd guess. We have seen very little of the probe, have contacted only a few of the personnel; but in general the situation appears much as we understood it. At present I am in an acceleration couch, waiting for the next period of free-fall for further investigation. Doc Chimp, who is performing very well and deserves credit, has voluntarily left on a scouting mission.

"I'll report again when I have something to say," he finished, "and—personal to Ben Charles Pertin: Have a good time on my honeymoon."

He snapped off the stage before he could decide to erase the last part of the message.

In spite of the best efforts of the cocoon, his kidneys were beginning to feel bruised. The noise was even more of a problem. Efficient soundproofing kept it out of the cocoon as noise—at least, as airborne vibrations—but there was too much of it, the amplitude too great, to be shut out entirely; and it seeped through as a continual thunder and squeal.

Pertin shut it out of his mind, thought of sleep, decided to brush up on his knowledge of the "hardware."

His first attempt at the fiche library of the stereostage was only half successful. He just managed to avert the appearance of the bare-skinned blonde and found he had secured a record transmitted by another member of the crew—race unspecified—apparently for a sort of public stereostage broadcast on its home planet. He shut out of his mind the public broadcaster he should have been getting ready to marry about this time—some thousands of light-years away, *was* getting ready to marry—and discovered that the name of the vessel was the *Aurora*, or *Dawn*—the sound was of course different in the T'Worlie tongue, and they had named it; but it had the same shared meanings of new day and bright glowing promise. He discovered that it had only limited facilities for recreation—well, he had known that. There were tape-fiche libraries for almost every known race and some special high-pressure atmosphere chambers for a few of the exotics. That was it.

This was not exactly what he wanted, so he tried again. But instead of getting a fiche on the ship itself, he got one on its mission, evidently a briefing record dubbed for humans. The narration was by a man Pertin recognized, about sixty, plump, freckled; he had been a minor functionary on Sun One. He spoke in a high-pitched voice, smiling emptily at the stereo pickup:

"We will show you all that is known about Object Lambda. First we will locate it, as it would be seen from Earth if visible at that distance."

Behind him another stereostage tank glowed, shimmered, and filled with a universe of stars. Two of the brighter ones pulsed to call attention to themselves as the man spoke.

"Those stars are Benetnasch, in Ursa Major, and Cor Caroli, in Canes Venatici. Those faint stars over

there"—as he spoke a faint line of light ran around an
area of the tank, enclosing it in a square—"are in
Coma Berenices, near the north galactic pole. Now
we'll take a closer look."

Benetnasch and Cor Caroli swam aside. The faint
stars of Coma Berenices grew brighter, spreading apart,
as the whole field of stars seemed to move. To Ben
James Pertin it felt as if he were plunging head-on into
a sea of stars. The bright points fled out of the sides of
the stage, and the few remaining ones became brighter,
until only a few were left, and beyond them ghostly
faint blurs that were no longer part of the Milky Way
but galaxies in their own right.

Then the illusion of motion stopped.

Another square of light formed around a patch of
blackness in the center of the stage, indistinguishable
from the emptiness around it.

The man said, "Now we've reached the limits of Sol-
orbiting instruments. Object Lambda is at the center of
that square, but it is invisible. It is slightly better in the
far infrared."

The pattern of stars shimmered; some became brighter, some dimmer, and in the center of the square there
was what might have been a faint and shapeless glow.

"This is not instantaneous," explained the lecturer.
"It's long exposure and image-intensified. It would never
have been detected in routine sweeps from Sol-based instruments. Even the T'Worlie scouts first detected it
only because of the chance occultation of some stars in
the Milky Way itself, seen from beyond. What we will
show you next is not an actual observation but an artifact as it would look from Earth, as deduced from all
available observations."

The object brightened half a dozen magnitudes as he
spoke.

"As you see, it has a sort of tipped-disk shape, like
certain classifications of external galaxies. However,
that's not what it is. First of all, it is far too small,

perhaps only two or three A.U. Second, its spectrum is wrong.

"At its apparent distance, as determined by its angular diameter—as if it were indeed a galaxy—it should be receding at a major fraction of the speed of light. Of course, we know from triangulation from the T'Worlie ships that that distance is wrong by a good many orders of magnitude. But according to its spectrum displacement, it is actually approaching the Milky Way at nearly relativistic speeds."

The image blurred and disappeared, and the plump human was standing there by himself. He said with satisfaction, "The T'Worlie scout has confirmed the speed as accurate, in the range of fifty thousand kps. Its position, relative to Earth, is some thirty thousand light-years from Sol, in the direction of a point near the northern fringe of Coma Berenices. It is not an object from our galaxy. There are no spiral arms in that direction, nor many isolated stars or clusters much nearer than Sol itself.

"The T'Worlie backplotted its position from all observations of their drones, as recorded over the past several thousand years. Most of the data are ambiguous, but they did establish a probable line of flight. Their hope was to find a galaxy from which the object might have been ejected, and then to try to discover the reason for its high velocity. The T'Worlie were only partly successful—I should say, only *possibly* successful. No such galaxy was detected. They did, however, find scattered star swarms which they believe to be the fragments of a galaxy that collapsed and then exploded more than half a billion years ago. It is the present working hypothesis that Object Lambda was ejected from that galaxy—by what means we cannot say."

The man's expression became enthusiastic. "Because of the anomalous nature of Object Lambda," he said, "the all-race conference on Sun One determined to transmit a full size scoutship through the drone equipment,

and to staff it with a crew of volunteers of all races."
Volunteers! thought Pertin, grimacing. "And after con-
siderable effort in negotiating, it was agreed to include
Earth humans as part of the crew. The political implications of this step are of enormous consequence
and reflect the true coming of age of Earth humanity in
the Galaxywide confraternity of civilized peoples.
Thank you," he said, bowed, smiled, and disappeared
as the fiche came to an end.

Not a minute too soon, thought Pertin. A little more
of that and he would have been ill. The cocoon had a
fine built-in waste-handling system, but there was no
sense in overloading it.

He began to see what Zara had been talking about
when she accused him of an "Earthman's Burden" complex. It sounded pompous, stupid, and faintly threatening, he realized, at least as expressed by the man in the
briefing fiche. Pertin tried to get his mind off that
track—because he didn't want to question the cause for
which he was eventually going to die, and because
above all he didn't want to think about Zara Doy. He
was in the middle of trying to get *The Belle of Bellatrix*
back on the stage when he became aware that something was scratching angrily at his cocoon.

For a moment he thought he was dreaming. He
glanced back at the fading nude on the screen, then
outside at the nude girl who stood there.

But Pertin was a pretty superior type, and he ori-
ented himself quickly. It was no girl. It was not even
human. It was a female young Earth person in shape,
but the stuff of which the shape was constructed was
not flesh and blood. It was silvery and bright, with a metallic hue. The eyes were orange and glowing. The hair
was not separate tendrils; it was a single solid piece,
sculptured slightly for cosmetic effect. The creature
was, he realized, an "edited" version of some methane-
breather or one of even more exotic chemistry, some
being who was structurally nonviable in oxygen-bearing
air and had had itself transmitted in an altered form to

take up its duties on *Aurora*. And it was holding a scrap of what looked like paper.

It was not right-side up. Pertin gestured, and finally the "girl" understood and rotated what she held until he could read its message. Then he signaled her to stop. It said:

> Sorry, Ben James, but you've got to get out of there. Things are worse than we thought. Aphrodite here will carry you to me. They guarantee she won't drop you and squash you; and, actually, Ben James, it seems to be a matter of life and death.
>
> *Doc*

The girl did not speak, but the orange eyes blazed imperatively, and the hands beckoned.

Pertin sighed, and opened the lid of his cocoon. "Okay, Aphrodite," he said. "Carry me off."

Astonishingly, being carried by the pseudogirl was actually worse than being toted by the robot; but this trip was slower, and Pertin had a chance to see something of the *Aurora*. It was roughly cone-shaped. At the nose and through the midsection were living quarters for the several score individuals who manned the ship. Since the crew varied widely, they needed a good deal of room. Space had been provided for methane-dwellers, space-flyers, and cold creatures, as well as for the more common forms based on carbon, oxygen, and water. However, most of the nonviables either stayed home or sent proxies or edited copies, so these spaces were mostly empty. "Below" the living quarters and the space for the exotics were the hardware-instrument sections. Below them still—in the sense of being stern-ward, toward the thrusters—was a layer of dense liquid for a radiation shield. It wasn't very effective; but of course, Pertin thought, the shield didn't have to be effective enough to keep them alive forever, since there was neither hope for nor point in that. Below the shield was

the tachyon-transmission deck, where Pertin and the
chimp had arrived. And beyond that deck, the shock-
absorbing gear and thrusters. Since the *Aurora* was decelerating, it happened that the "stern" of the ship came
first in line of flight; but that made little difference to
anyone aboard. It was "down." And down was the direction they were going. The pseudogirl had wrapped
Pertin in a thick blanket of something like heavy-duty
plastic foam. It was not as good as his cocoon by a long
shot, but it kept him from dying of the ceaseless grinding changes in gravity as the thrusters shoved and the
"girl" levered herself down a ladderlike series of pro-
jecting rods. She did not speak, nor acknowledge Pertin's efforts to speak to her. Either there was something
wrong with his Pmal translator, or she simply was not a
coversationalist. But she was considerate enough, and
when they reached the instrument deck Pertin was
bruised and sick, but alive.

"Ben James!" cried a familiar voice. "I told you
Aphrodite would get you here all right!"

Doc Chimp, thin lips grinning widely, scrambled over
to help the silvery girl put him down, propping him
against a sloping bulkhead so he could look around.
They were worth looking at, a nightmare crew if he
ever saw one. Besides the pseudogirl and the mutated
chimp, there was a Sheliak in its high-G mode, looking
like a flattened baker's bun on the deck, another web of
plastic foam that hid an apparently human-sized figure,
and a row of small cocoons. Two were empty; the third
contained a T'Worlie. From a speaker outside the cocoon a T'Worlie voice whistled a greeting, and Pertin's
Pmal translated:"I recognize your identity, Ben James
Pertin. It is advantageous to all of us that you are
here."

"Thanks, Nummie," Pertin said, but he was staring
at the other plastic wrappings. A human being seemed
to be concealed in them; but apart from himself he
knew of only one human being on the *Aurora*, one he
didn't really want to think about.

He said aside, "Doc, who's over there?"

Doc Chimp said, "Who? Her? Oh, I don't know her name. She's Purchased People for some low-G type or other. But she's on our side." The web stirred and a face peered out. It was human enough as far as features went, but the emptiness in the eyes told Pertin that Doc Chimp was right. "Anyway," the chimp chattered, "I better fill you in. Hell's really broken loose, Ben James. A bunch of beings tried to wreck the telescope. Not sure but what they've done it, too; the Scorpian's trying to see how much can be salvaged. If it and Aphrodite here hadn't come along, we'd be out of business until they could send new instruments through—and by then it would likely be too late."

The thuuuud-*screech* was a lot closer here; apart from everything else, it was making Pertin's head pound. "What beings?" he managed to croak.

"Didn't see them. I just saw somebody disappearing into a passage, and then the Sheliak here came hellfire-fast after him and saw me. For a minute he thought I was them." Doc Chimp cocked his head ruefully. "You could've found yourself short a monkey right there, Ben James, if I hadn't talked fast. Then the Sheliak commandeered me to help, and we came down here to hold the fort. Oh, how sore my soles and knuckles are, Ben James, against the pounding of those rockets! But I did my duty. Then we got the observatory deck sealed off—they'd used a chemical explosive on the telescope and sprung a port—and then I happened to think of my human master, off there watching *The Belle of Bellatrix* without a care, and I persuaded Aphrodite to fetch you."

Pertin frowned. "I don't quite see why," he objected. "I can't help."

"You can stay alive," the chimp declared. "I didn't tell you all of it. When they came for the telescope they had to get past the T'Worlie here. Well, you know T'Worlie can't do much against any being that can operate in high-G. But they tried to do what they could. And two of them got killed."

That was a shocker if ever there was one; the one cardinal rule among the races of the Galaxy was that no race could ever kill or seriously maim a member of another. Even on Sun One, what disciplinary problems arose were handled within the delegation of the race that produced the problem; there was some provision for a body of other races sitting in judgment if the offending race failed to deal with the problem, but that law had never had to be invoked. Pertin would hardly have believed the chimp if Nummie hadn't confirmed it.

"They're crazy, then," Pertin said. "All right. We'll have to get a report back to Sun One. Nummie, is your sterostage operating?"

"Confirm that it is operative," the Pmal sang·in his ear. "State that such a transmission has already been sent."

"Good. I'll have to send one too, and I think the rest of us should; but that can wait." Pertin tried to shift position as the floor surged particularly viciously, suppressed a groan, and thought: Since we're here, they probably won't try anything right away. Then he said, "What we need is a comb-out. Get every being on board to account for his whereabouts and try to identify the ones who did it. For that we need a little free-fall. Can we arrange that?"

The silvery girl spoke at last. Apparently she had heard everything, had simply seen no need to comment. "We can have a little free-fall. We can have a little comb-out. But we probably won't need to arrange it right away as the next observation period is only—" A meaningless sqawk, but Doc Chimp filled in:

"She means about fifteen minutes away."

It took a moment for Pertin to realize that the girl's words had been in English. He looked at her curiously, but there was no time to think about that. "Fine," he said. "How many were involved in the bombing?"

"Not less than three nor more than eight," piped the Pmal translator, responding to the T'Worlie's whistle.

"Out of how many in the crew?"

The T'Worlie hesitated. "There are in excess of three hundred thousand beings at present existing within the ship's hull. Of these, a large number are collective creatures."

"Not counting the Boaty-Bits, I mean how many individuals?"

"There are not less than two hundred forty nor more than two hundred fifty."

Pertin said, "So the troublemakers are a tiny fraction. That's good. We'll broadcast a shipwide alarm. Most of the crew will cooperate—"

He stopped, staring at the silver pseudogirl. "What's the matter?"

She had stretched out her fingertips toward the entrance port, almost in the traditional pose of a human sleepwalker. "The matter," she said in her incongruous colloquial English, the tones as deep as Pertin's own, "is that the tiny fraction of troublemakers is coming back."

A moment later no one needed the silvery girl's fingers to hear for them; the sound of a rush grew rapidly louder: a crackling electrical sound, like the patter of a collapsing charge field. Into the room burst what looked at first like a single huge blue eye. "Sirian!" Doc Chimp howled in terror, and tried to leap out of the way. But not even his simian muscles had the strength to leap, and the surging G-force of the rockets made him stumble and fall heavily on his side against the silvery girl. At one stroke, two-thirds of the beings able to move at all in the high-G field were immobilized; the T'Worlie, the Purchased Person, and Ben Pertin himself were wholly useless while the rockets were on. The Sirian, moving by electrostatic forces, was immune to mere ten- and twelve-G thrusts; and he bore with him something that glittered, carried under the great forward eye in a pair of crablike pincers, tiny and almost invisible.

Pertin, laid heedlessly just inside the portal, was first in the creature's path. He did not even have time to realize he was in danger before the Sirian was upon him. Then, queerly, the great eye stared at him and the Sirian paused, hesitated, and turned away. It propelled its glittering metal object at the bulkhead and at once reversed its field and sped away.

If that was another bomb, Pertin thought, they'd all had it now; beyond that bulkhead was empty space from the last attack. The rest of the ship might be saved if the automatic seals worked fast enough, but they would be boiled into outer space—himself, the Purchased Person, Doc Chimp, and the T'Worlie, at least.

Pertin had forgotten the Sheliak. The soggy baker's bun that slumped on the deck and had taken no part in the conversation was still in fact an able and intelligent being. It acted faster than Pertin would have believed possible. The bun shape elongated itself into a sort of stemmed sea anemone, flowed like lightning up and down around the bomb, surrounding it, drowning it in alien flesh.

It exploded.

The only sign the rest of them could see was a quick convulsive shudder of the Sheliak's tissue. Even the noise was muffled and almost inaudible, in the constant thunder of the rockets.

But the Sheliak glowed brilliant gold for a moment with a flash of the last light of its life, and died.

They had defended themselves, but at the cost of one of their allies.

As if on cue, the thunder of the rockets stopped, and they found themselves blessedly free of the crushing G-forces. Doc Chimp, struggling to untangle himself from the silvery girl, went flying across the chamber,

ricocheted against a wall, and was brought up short next
to where Pertin was struggling to disassociate himself
from the plastic foam.

"Are you all right, Ben James?" Doc Chimp yelled.

Pertin pushed himself free and caught the outstretched chimpanzee arm for stability. He ached in
every bone and muscle, and he was drenched in sweat—
from the heat of the plastic wrap or from fear, he could
not say which.

"I think so," he said. "Why do you suppose he did
that?"

"What? Who? You mean the Sheliak? Why, I guess
it's their nature, Ben James—"

"No, not the Sheliak," Pertin said, but he didn't say
out loud what it was that was perplexing him. He only
thought it to himself. Why had the Sirian looked at him
with death in his eye, then stopped and turned away?

THREE

*

    It turned out there were two things wrong with Pertin's calculations. First, the odds weren't quite as favorable as he had guessed; he had not remembered that the bombers might have allies who were as gravity-bound as himself, and so hadn't put in an appearance. Second, he had not realized that a large proportion of the beings aboard the *Aurora* simply didn't want to be bothered. They were apathetic, hopeless, detached, or in some exotic mood with no human analog; or perhaps, here and there, they just weren't about to take orders from an upstart biped jackanapes from—what was the name of it?—Earth.

    The other problem was that the work of the *Aurora* was in observing Object Lambda, not in tracking down aberrant entities. Not even the fact that beings of one or two races had killed beings of another race could change their minds. The Scorpian robot, when it returned from patching together what it could of the damaged optical equipment, would not even take time to talk to Pertin; it went at once to its assigned place in the instrument chamber and began to oversee the series of observations that was what the thrust stoppage was for.

    Pertin could not even get the free-fall period extended to permit a full-scale search of the ship. The T'Worlie pointed out to him, reasonably enough, that as they were all going to die anyhow the first priority was the errand for which they had all undertaken to give their lives: to complete the observation of Object

37

Lambda. And the laws of celestial dynamics were remorseless. A certain quantum of delta-V had to be applied to *Aurora*'s course. There was only finite time in
which to do it. If they failed to put in the necessary
velocity change the probe would fly by Object Lambda
too fast to accomplish the mission to which it was as-
signed. So the T'Worlie were going to work on their
instrument observations and nothing else, although they
certainly wished him well, they indicated, in his search
for the guilty ones.

The search team turned out to be a party of five:
Pertin, Doc Chimp, the pseudogirl, the Purchased-
People woman, and the little kittenish object who had
joined the party to greet them on arrival. They couldn't
even recruit the Boaty-Bits to their cause. As soon as
the collective creatures had learned of the bombing attempt they had departed en masse to swarm in some
obscure corner of the vessel and unite all of their intelligence in the problem of deciding what to do about it.

Pertin saw a great deal of the ship, but found no
criminals. The one being they had certainly identified,
the Sirian, eluded their search. If a being the size of a
horse, emitting an electrostatic crackle every time it
moved, could avoid the searchers, what chance had
they for locating a party of unidentified marauders? No
chance, answered Echo; and they found nothing.

About all they really accomplished was to move the
acceleration cocoons for the low-G beings they had
come to think of as friends close enough together so
that they could watch out for each other when the
delta-V thrust immobilized them. There were many
such periods. By the nature of things, there had to be.
It was thuuuuud-*screech!* at least eighty percent of the
time, cut up the individual portions as they would. The
Aurora had thousands of kps of velocity to shed as it
overtook Lambda, if they were to avoid overrunning it
too fast to orbit their package. It made little difference
how it felt to the members of the crew.

To Pertin it felt like being kicked in the kidneys four or five times a minute, for hours on end. With allowances for variations in anatomy, it felt very much like that to most of the beings. Frail little creatures like the T'Worlie were particularly hard hit, or would have been if not for the fact that the *Aurora* was their own design, cocoons and all, and many thousands of years of thought had gone into reducing the damage to a T'Worlie frame in a cocoon. It was an advantage of a sort, but against it was the overpowering debit that on their native planet the surface gravity was less than a quarter-G. They were not creatures designed for strain.

It was the unfelt pain that was the worst. Every explosion produced noise and thrust, but it also sleeted a few more curies of radiation through their bodies and brought them a few hours nearer to death. As it was not felt, and as there was nothing that could be done about it, they seldom spoke of it to each other.

For half a dozen periods there was no further violence from anyone on board, and the *Aurora* went on about its business. Pertin reserved the time in the cocoon for taping his endless reports to Sun One, and for inspecting and studying the observation results on Object Lambda. When there was the blissful floating surcease, for half an hour or so at a time, he used it to roam around the ship. His announced purpose was to watch out for trouble. As time passed and trouble did not come, he stopped talking about it, but continued to roam. He was interested in the ship on its own merits. Simply by its novelty it helped take his mind off the growing number of things he didn't want to think about. This was the first real spaceship he had ever seen. That seemed strange to him, when he considered how many tens of thousands of light-years he had traveled since he volunteered for tachyon transmission from Earth. It was normal enough, though. Sun One was thick with beings who had crossed and recrossed the Galaxy a dozen times, and never seen a spaceship at all.

Object Lambda was getting perceptibly closer—not

to the eye, to be sure. No eye on the ship was in a position to see it anyway. But the cameras were able to make out more and more detail—not easily or well, because its intrinsic luminosity was so very low, and in the low-energy long-wave part of the spectrum at that. They had even discovered that Lambda was not alone in space. Huge as it was, nearly two A.U. in diameter, it carried with it little orbiting fleas. The biggest of them was not much more than a mile through and the distance was still enormous; but the T'Worlie instruments managed to detect them, even identify them. The longest periods of free-fall were when the T'Worlie deployed their photon mirrors at the end of a tether, far from even the vibration of a footstep or shifting weight of robot mass in the ship; then their optical emulsions greedily drank up the scant flow of photons from Lambda and converted them into images.

If they had had a great deal of time, they could have answered all questions from there, or nearly all. They were in intergalactic space, and there was no such thing as haze, beyond the advance scattering of their own rocket ejecta. But they had no time: the delta-V equation still ruled them, and one of its tricky parentheses said that deceleration early was worth twice as much deceleration late, since it gave them more time for deceleration before they reached the neighborhood of Lambda. And then there was the mere fate of their rapid approach. The image did not remain still in the T'Worlie mirrors. It grew. Minutely, to be sure, but enough that an exposure for more than an hour or so began to fuzz.

Even so, they learned. The nearest thing to pleasure Pertin ever found in a T'Worlie was when a particularly fine series of photographs had been taken, and it was discovered that they showed a hint, a shadow, finally an orbital line for the biggest of the objects that circled Lambda. The pleasure was spoiled for Pertin when the calculations of orbit and time turned out to be impossible; Lambda would have had to have the density of the solar wind to have so slow a satellite. But the T'Worlie didn't mind. Explanations would come. If not then, later. If not to the present generation, to the next. Meanwhile they were accruing information.

Between the hours of thudding acceleration and the briefer periods of frenzied activity, darting about the ship, Pertin was nearly always bone-weary and aching. Sleep did not rest him. Communication with Sun One was more and more an effort. The twelve-hour wait between transmission and reply—often it was more, when the other beings on the ship had queued up for their own transmissions—destroyed the rhythm of the communication; by the time he had a response to his report of the attack on the instrument chamber, he was already relaxing in the continued comfort of the experience that the attack had not been repeated. Once it was himself, or anyway that other self named Ben Charles Pertin, who reported to him. That put him in a tailspin that only a carefully metered dose of tranquilizers from the cocoon's store could deal with. From the expression on the other Ben Pertin's face, it was some strain for him, too. But the worst from Sun One was not from his other self, it was from Gerald York Bielowitz, who acknowledged a report, suggested some additional instrument readings that would be desirable, started to sign off, hesitated, and then added: "Oh, you'll be interested, I think. Zara Doy and Ben Charles were married three hours ago."

Pertin did not remember cutting the stereostage or seeing the little figure collapse. He lay there for a long time while the cocoon stroked and soothed him, lifted him, lowered him, gently massaged what pains it could from his limbs. At some point he fell asleep. In his dream Ben Charles Pertin married Zara Doy, but he was Ben Charles, and the two of them, intoxicated with the wine they drank and with each other, spoke sadly and wistfully about the other Ben Pertin who was busy about the task of dying on an alien spaceship a Galaxy away. When he woke up and discovered he was the other Ben Pertin he was in an instant unfocused rage.

It was Doc Chimp who woke him. "Boss," he whined. "Listen, wake up. I've been limping around this hellhole of a ship looking for the Scorpian robot, and—"

"Shut up," Pertin snarled through the outside communicator of his cocoon. His tone took the chimp aback. He slumped on his haunches, staring at Pertin's cocoon. He was in bad shape, Pertin saw, unwilling to care about what he saw: the bright green plume was sagging under the thrust of the rockets, the paws and knuckles were scarred and stained. That was why he was there, of course: feet and paws, he could withstand the constantly varying G-force of the thrusters with only a good deal of pain, so it was his job to do what Pertin could not when he was bound to the cocoon. A part of Pertin's brain told him that if he tried he probably could find ways of making the job easier.

The chimp's expression was no longer woebegone, it was angry. "Sure," he said thickly, "I'll shut up. Why not? We'll all shut up before long. Dead beings are all pretty quiet."

Pertin fought to control his own anger. "We'll be dead all right. What difference does it make? Do you think this is a real life, what we're doing here? Back on Sun One we're alive and well; this is only a dream!"

The chimp wailed, "Ben James, I'm tired and I hurt. I'm sorry if I said something wrong. Look, I'll go away and come back, only—"

"Do that," snapped Pertin, turning off the outside communicator.

The agitated hairy face stared dolefully in at him. Doc Chimp was by no means a jungle primate. The shape of his skull was different, the structure of his respiratory system was different, the very chemicals that flowed in his blood were different. But he was not human, either. Doc Chimp—his formal name was not that, but it was all Pertin had ever called him—was one of the mutated animals who had been constructed for special purposes in the molecular biology plants on Earth. His quadrudexterous hands and feet made him particularly useful even in free-fall, where he could fling himself about with perfect ease from toe rest to handhold, while humans like Pertin clumsily sprawled and spun. But he had his drawbacks.

A chimpanzee is simply not a human. His physiology is one count against him. He cannot develop the brain of a human because his skull is the wrong shape, and because the chemistry of his blood does not carry enough nourishment to meet the demands of abstract thought. He cannot speak because he lacks the physical equipment to form the wide variety of phonemes in human language. The molecular-biology people knew how to deal with that: things like widening the angle of the cranium called the "kyphosis," thus allowing the brain to round out full frontal lobes, restructuring tongue and palate, even adding new serum components to the blood like the alpha$_2$-globulins that bind human hemoglobin.

In practical terms what had been done to Doc Chimp and his siblings was to speed up evolution. But that was not quite enough. Two generations back Doc Chimp's ancestors could form only one or two of the simplest words and learn rote tricks; they lacked conceptual thought entirely. Doc Chimp had capacity. He did not have background or tradition. His sixty-degree kyphosis was close to the human average, so that his skull was domed; he possessed a forehead; he could remember complicated instructions and perform difficult tasks; he was capable of assimilating the equivalent of a trade-school education in skill and of conducting the equivalent of cocktail-party conversation in performance. What he lacked was ego. His psychological profile was high in cyclothymia but also in ergic tension; his moods shifted drastically, and he was always adventurous, always afraid. His emotional index was about equal to that of a human five-year-old. Frightened, he ran. Angered, he struck out. Baffled, he wept.

Staring back through the cover of the cocoon, Pertin relented. "Sorry," he said, snapping the communicator back on. "What were you trying to tell me?"

"I've lost the Scorpian," the chimp wailed.

"Well? Are you supposed to be his keeper?"

"Be easy on me, Ben James," the chimpanzee begged. "I hurt all over. The robot was supposed to be getting ready for some new instruments that were coming in. He isn't there. The stuff's piling up in the transmission chamber and nobody to do anything about it. I'm afraid it'll get damaged."

"What about what's-her-name, Aphrodite? Can't she store it?"

"She is trying to, but the Scorpian is a specialist in this stuff and she isn't. None of the other high-G creatures is, as far as I can tell, and, oh, Ben James, I've traveled so far trying to find someone who can help!"

He was a pitiable sight, his fur unpreened, his gay clothes smudged and wrinkled. Pertin said, "You've done your best, Doc. There's nothing I can do until the thrust stops—half an hour or so. Why don't you rest up for a while?"

"Thanks, Ben James!" the chimp cried gratefully. "I'll just take a few minutes. Wake me, will you? I—I—"

But he was already clamberinig into the cocoon, his spiderlike arms shaking with strain. Pertin lay back and closed his own eyes, allowing the cocoon to do its best, which amounted to increasing its rate of stroking his back muscles, trying mindlessly to calm him down.

It had seemed very easy, back on Sun One, to volunteer for a task even though the end of it was his certain death. He had not counted on the fact that death did not come like the turning of a switch but slowly and with increasing pain, or that he would be watching friends die before him.

*　*　*

Pertin didn't wake the chimp when he could finally move; he thrust his own way to the tachyon-transmission chamber, hurling himself down the corridors carelessly and almost diving into what turned out to be the silver pseudogirl. He didn't recognize the creature at first, for she had unfurled enormous silver-film wings and looked like a tinsel Christmas-tree angel as she drove past him.

In the tachyon chamber he found Nummie supervising an octopoidal creature from one of the Core stars in transporting crated equipment to an empty chamber. "What's happened? Where did Aphrodite go? What's this stuff?" he demanded, all at once.

Nummie paused and hung in the air before him, balancing himself against stray currents of air with casual movements of his wings. He whistled a methodical answer, and the Pmal translator converted it to this stately and precise form of speech in English: "Of those events which have occurred, that which appears most significant is the arrival of eight hundred mass units of observing equipment. A currently occurring event is that this equipment is in process of being installed. A complicating event is that the Scorpian artificial-intelligence being has elected to engage his attention in other areas. There are other events but of lesser significance. The being you name Aphrodite has gone to bring the Beta Boötis collective beings to assist in the aforesaid installation. The reason for this is that they are cataloged as possessing qualification on this instrumentation similar to that of the artificial-intelligence Scorpian. The precise nature of the stuff is tachyar observing equipment. I offer an additional observation: the purpose of it is to map and survey Object Lambda. I offer another additional observation: it will add to the radiation load by a factor of not less than three nor more than eight."

The T'Worlie hung silently in front of him, waiting for him to respond.

It had a long wait. Pertin was trying to assimilate the

information he had just received. *A factor of not less than three.*

But that meant that his life expectancy was not a matter of months or weeks. It might only be days!

Tachyar was simple enough in concept. It was like the ancient electromagnetic radar sets of Earth; the difference was that it used the faster-than-light tachyons to scan a distant object and return an echo of its shape and size. It was expensive—all tachyon transmission was expensive. Its only justification was that it was indispensable.

If you wanted to get a man, or an instrument, from one point in the Universe to some other point across interstellar distances, you had only two choices. One was to build a rocket—preferably fusion-powered, like the *Aurora*. You then had to launch it, set it on its way, and wait anywhere from a decade to a geologic era for it to reach a nearby star. If you wanted to go farther than that, you would wait forever. A voyage from a spiral arm to the Core, or from any point in the Galaxy to the deeps of intergalactic space where they now were, was simply out of the time consciousness of any race but the T'Worlie.

The other method was faster. It dispensed with attempting to transport matter at all. Instead of sending an object, you sent a blueprint of the object, and had it built from plan at the destination.

It was not a simple procedure. It required enormous expenditures of energy to generate the tachyon stream that carried the blueprint. It required complex scanning devices to measure every atom and molecule in the object to be transmitted, and to encode positions and relationships for transmission. Above all, it required a tachyon receiver at the point to which you wanted to go.

But granted all those things, you could "travel" at the speed of the tachyons, those particles whose *lower* speed limit was the velocity of light, and whose upper limit had never been measured.

Of course, the original object remained behind. It

was scanned and its blueprints were encoded, and then it was returned unharmed. The man who volunteered for a tachyon trip also stayed at home. What flashed across space was a description of himself, and what emerged from the receiving chamber at destination was a new-built identical copy. There was no detectable difference between original and copy. It would have been a foolproof method of counterfeiting or of duplicating rare art objects—if it had not been so expensive in terms of power consumption that there was little worth the cost of duplicating.

Tachyar was only one use of tachyons. Like ancient radar and sonar, it generated a beam and measured reflections. The problem in using tachyar was the magnitude of the beam. Vast energies were used, and the fraction that was wasted because of the natural inefficiency of the process produced ionizing radiation in large amplitudes.

Sun One must be taking the question of Object Lambda's satellites seriously if it was sending tachyar equipment to study them. The cost was high. It would be paid in the lives of those aboard.

The single planet of the golden-yellow star Beta Boötis was like a cooler, older Venus. Because it was farther from its sun, it was spared the huge flow of heat that cooked Venus sterile; but it possessed the same enormously deep, enormously dense atmosphere. It was spared the loss of its liquid water, and so its surface was covered an average of thirty miles deep in an oceanic soup. That was where the Boaty-Bits had evolved. Aquatic in origin, they could survive on Sun One or the probe ship only in edited forms adapted for air-breathing; they could not live on high-gravity planets at all, since they had only the feeblest mechanisms for propelling themselves about their native seas. An individual Boaty-Bit was about as useful as an infant jellyfish, and not much more intelligent. That didn't matter; the Boaty-Bits never operated as individuals. Their swarming instinct was overpowering, and once linked together they had a collective intelligence that was a direct function of their number. A quarter of a million Boaty-Bits equaled a man. On their home planet they sometimes linked up in collectives of four or five million or more, but those groupings could be maintained only briefly even in their oceans and were never attained in their air-breathing edited forms.

When they arrived in the tachyon-receiver chamber, they immediately took command. They were not specialists in tachyar gear. They were generalists. The skills required to assemble and install the crated instruments were built into their collective intelligence. What they lacked was operating organs, but the T'Worlie, his octopoidal assistant, Ben James Pertin, and every other being who came nearby were conscripted to be their hands and legs. It was slow work that would have been impossible in a gravity field for the T'Worlie, or even for Pertin himself; but in free-fall they were able to tug and guide the components into place, and the T'Worlie had mass enough to make the connections and calibrate the equipment. When they were nearly done Doc Chimp turned up, angry because he had been left behind, and his muscle finished the job quickly.

As they were finishing up, there was a blast of white sound from the tachyon-receiving chamber and warning lights flashed. Doc Chimp spun around, his wide jaw gaping. "Something important coming in?" he guessed.

"I don't know, but let's go look." They thrust themselves toward the chamber, got there just as the portal opened.

Three Sheliaks emerged.

They flashed out of the lock with a hollow hooting, long black shapes that rocketed toward the watching terrestrials and bounced down on the green metal surface of the chamber. They clung in spite of the lack of gravity, and flowed abruptly into a new shape, black velvet globes, thigh high.

Three more emerged, and three more. When fifteen had come to rest on the floor of the chamber the transmission stopped. Without a detectable sign, all of them moved in synchronization. From flattened spheres, like baker's buns set in a tray, they suddenly turned luminous, flowing with patterns of soft color, then elongated themselves and stretched up tapered necks that rose as tall as a man.

The tallest of them, the first through the chamber and the nearest to Ben James Pertin, made a noise like escaping gas from a compressed-air cylinder. In Pertin's ear his Pmal unit translated for him:

"Take notice! We are under the direction of the collective council of Sun One. We are to take command of this vessel, and all other beings aboard are to follow our orders!"

Pertin's curiosity was suddenly transmuted into anger, a radiant rage that flooded his mind and overruled his inhibitions. "The hell you say!" he shouted. "I've had no such instructions from the Earth representatives, and I deny your authority!"

The Sheliak paused, the long neck swaying back and forth. "Your wishes are immaterial," it stated at last. "We can destroy you."

Doc Chimp chattered nervously "Don't make him mad, Ben James. You know how Sheliaks are." Pertin did; they were among the few races that had built-in weaponry. On the infrequent occasions when the Galaxy found itself troubled by unruly barbarians, it was usually Sheliaks who were employed to quiet the opposition; they were the Foreign Legion of the Galaxy.

The long neck swayed toward the mutated chimpanzee. From the narrow orifice at its tip the sound exploded again, and the translators shouted at the chimp: "Your name! Your function! Reply at once!"

"I am Napier Chimski, technician," the chimp replied bravely.

The vase shape swung toward Pertin. "Your name and function!"

"Oh, Ben James Pertin," he said, distracted by hearing Doc Chimp's real name for the first time. "I'm an engineer. But don't go so fast! I've just come from Sun One myself, and I know there's no authority for one race to impose its will on another. I will certainly report this at once!"

The Sheliak swayed silently for a moment, toward him then away. At last it said, "No orders for you at present. Go about your business."

Pertin drew himself up, holding to a wall brace. "You're my business!" he shouted. "There are murdering beings aboard this ship. If you're here by order of Sun One, as you say, why don't you go find them and leave us alone?"

The Sheliak did not reply. All fifteen of them were swaying silently now. Perhaps they were conferring with each other, Pertin thought; Sheliaks had learned vocal sound only to talk to other races of the Galaxy, and the riddle of how they communicated among themselves was still unsolved.

"I certainly will report this," Pertin added.

There was still no response. The pointless confrontation might have gone on, but it was interrupted by the bright thrice-repeated flash of white light that meant the thrusters were about to go into operation again.

"Oh, hell," Pertin groaned. "Doc, we'd better get back to our cocoons."

"Never too soon for me, Ben James," agreed the chimp fervently, staring at the Sheliaks. "Let's go!"

They raced for the cocoons. The warning had caught others short; the corridors were full of low-G beings hurrying back to safety before the fusion rockets began again. The Boaty-Bits arrowed past them at top velocity, like a cartoon drawing of a swarm of wasps. The octopoidal creature launched itself from a wall at the end of the corridor with a multiple thrust of its legs and spun, tentacles waving crazily, past them. There was a thundering roar, and three Sheliaks raced past them, then another three and another, in Vees. A being like a six-legged spider monkey bounced back and forth, scratching and clawing for footholes, whining irritably to itself in a high-pitched tone. And abruptly:

"Ben James! Look!"

Doc Chimp was staring down a broad transverse corridor as they soared by it. Pertin looked, saw a creature like an enormous blue eye, at least a foot across. It swerved as he looked, revealing the body behind it, a tapered torpedo shape, glittering with patterned scales like blue glass. A stubby wing spread on each side, the leading edge thick and scaled, flowing smoothly into the body, the thin trailing edge a flutter of blue. And beyond it was something bright, metallic and angular.

"It's the Sirian, Ben James! The one that tried to kill us all. And wasn't that the Scorpian robot with him?"

Pertin reached out, grabbed a handhold, and checked himself. The chimpanzee reacted a moment later and also stopped himself, a yard or two farther down. "What are you doing, Ben James?" he chattered.

"I'm going after them!" Pertin snapped. "The Sirian's one of the murderers. And the robot's up to something, too."

"No, Ben James! You can't take the G-force. Let's let the Sheliaks take care of them, that's what they're here for."

The featureless green light of the corridor faded and changed to a dull crimson glow. That was the short-term warning; they had less than thirty seconds now before the rockets began.

Pertin cursed. The chimp was right, of course, and he knew it; it didn't make it any more enjoyable, though.

"Oh, hell," he groaned. "All right, let's go!"

They made it—not with any time to spare. They rolled into their cocoons just as the first giant thrust struck, and a moment later the regular repeated sound of the rockets reached them. The webbing spread itself over Pertin; he fell into the warm, receiving shape of the cocoon, but he resisted its comfort. While it was still adjusting to his shape, he was already stabbing at the controls of the stereostage, trying to summon all the cocoon-bound beings on the ship into a conference call. The automatic dialing circuits were equal to the job; it was not something that was often done, but the physical capacity for it existed.

But not this time. All lines were busy. Every being on the ship, it appeared, was already using his stereostage for purposes of his own—most likely for trying to transmit a tachyon message to his own people at Sun One, Pertin knew.

He fell back and let the cocoon massage him as soothingly as it could.

Thuuuuud-screech. Thuuuuuud-screech. The thrust felt more powerful than before, the tempo a bit faster. The thunder and groan of the drive made it nearly impossible for Pertin to think, but he had to think.

The problem on his mind was not any of the obvious ones: what to do about the Sheliaks, how to deal with the murderers, the completion of the mission. His mind worried at those a moment at a time and then let them go; they required action, not thought, and action was not available to him while the fusion rockets roared.

Instead, he thought about an unpleasant discovery. The discovery was that there wasn't much in being a hero. His heroism had been entered into lightly enough, but he supposed that was not in itself rare; how many soon-to-be Medal of Honor winners had volunteered for combat patrols simply because they were bored with sitting in foxholes, and found themselves caught up in events that made them immortal reputations?

But his heroism was not even going to get him a medal. No one would ever really know what was happening on this ship, because it was absolutely certain there would be no survivors. Either *Aurora*'s mission would succeed, in which event the Galaxy at large would accept their sacrifice complacently, or it would fail. Then they would all be thought of, when they were thought of at all, as that sorry bunch that wasted themselves for nothing.

With the thud and rasp of metal roaring at him, his cocoon seesawing to the violent deceleration of the rockets, tired, half-sick, angry, and hopeless, Ben James Pertin faced the fact that there was nothing left in his life anywhere that would give him one moment's joy.

Another Ben Pertin tens of thousands of light-years away was trying to soothe his bride. He said, "Honey, I knew what I was getting into when I volunteered. I was willing to go through with it. That other me on the ship doesn't feel any different about it."

Zara Pertin said harshly, "That other you is going to die, Ben Charles."

"But I'll still be alive!"

"And he'll be dead. Don't you understand me? *I love you*. And he is you, and I don't like to think about what is happening to him." She turned over, giving her back a chance to collect some of the UV tan from the lamps overhead, and took off her goggles. She said, "What's it like there now, Ben?"

"Well—" he said.

"No, I want to know. Tell me."

Ben Charles looked around the little simulated beach beside the great water tank that was their "ocean." There was no one around but themselves. They'd come here for that reason, but Ben Charles found himself wishing for an interruption. She turned her head and looked at him, and he shrugged.

"All right. It's bad," he said. "The sensors in his acceleration cocoon report some destruction of the white corpuscles already. Pretty soon he'll start having nosebleeds, then he'll bleed internally. He'll be getting weaker, running a temperature, and before long he'll die." He paused, then answered the unspoken question. "Probably within a week."

He propped himself up on one arm—easily enough; even here the effective gravity was only a fraction of

Earth-normal. He looked out at the thousand-foot cusp of water, curving upward to meet the bulkhead at its far end, and added:

"That's if he dies as a result of radiation, but he might not last that long. Some of the beings are getting violent. The electronic ones are malfunctioning, because the radiation affects their synapses. Insane, really. A lot of the organic ones are sick. All of them are scared. There—there have been deaths."

"I should have gone with you," Zara said thoughtfully.

"Oh, now, really! That's stupid! What would be the point?"

"I would have felt better about it, and so would you. He." She stood up, smiling, her mind made up. "If you have to go again, dear," she said, "I'm going too. Now I'm hungry. Race you back to the apartment."

FOUR

    The tachyar verified the orbits of the little bodies orbiting Lambda; the mass estimates were right, thus the density estimates were right. Object Lambda's average density was about that of a high vacuum. Nevertheless, it appeared to have a solid surface.

    Pertin greeted the news with apathy. There were more immediately important developments on the ship, and the ultimate purpose for which the ship existed didn't seem particularly interesting anymore.

    For one thing, the tachyon-transmission chamber was shut down. For better or for worse, there would be no more imports, no additional beings, no new crew members, no nothing.

    Its last function had been to bring in new structural members and drive units. Inside the former receiving chamber of the *Aurora* they were being assembled into a new, small ship. It took form as a squat, dense object, all fusion drive and instruments, with no living space for a crew. It would have no crew. It would carry nothing but itself, and the tachyon-receiving crystal that had been the *Aurora*'s.

    Pertin had no part in the construction project. The Boaty-Bits directed it, and the metal pseudogirl and a few other high-G types carried it out. He looked in on it once or twice. Besides the new members brought in on the tachyon receiver, before it was rehoused in its new body, the small ship used bulkheads and beams from *Aurora* itself. It seemed to Ben James Pertin that vital structural parts were being seriously weakened. As an engineer, that interested him. As a living human being whose life depended on the structural integrity of the *Aurora,* he didn't even think it worth mentioning. Whatever was happening was planned. If the life of the *Aurora* was being shortened thereby, it was because the beings doing the planning had decided the ship was wholly expendable.

The only nonexpendable part of the *Aurora* now was the little drone being put together in its belly.

The drone comprised only three elements: a tiny tachyon-receiving unit, built around the crystal from *Aurora*'s own, in a globular body fitted with weak handling propulsors, suitable only for correcting minor errors in the elements of an orbit. A thick half-shell of metal-bonded ceramics on one side, an ablation shield designed to flake and burn away, disposing of excess heat. And, outside the ablation shield, the enormous fusion-propulsion engines.

It was a high-deceleration drone. It would be launched from the mother ship at some point near Object Lambda. Its fusion jets would slow it radically. Stressed as it was, with no living creatures aboard, it could endure hundred-G delta-V forces. But Pertin's engineer's eye recognized the implications of the design. Even those forces would not be enough. The drone would make use of Object Lambda's enormously deep atmosphere as well. It would dip into it, shedding velocity by burning it off as friction, blazing like a meteorite from its ablation surfaces. That frightful crunch would slow it to manageable relative speeds; as it came out of its first skip into Lambda's air it would be near enough to orbital velocity for capture. Then its handling propulsors could take over the simpler job of neatening up the elements of the orbit, and a tachyon receiver would be in place around Object Lambda.

What about the mother ship?

All the evidence Pertin needed was there in the construction of the probe. If such forces were needed to put the probe in orbit, there was no hope that *Aurora* could join it. Its kilotons of mass were simply too great for the forces available to deal with. Even if the forces were available, its living cargo would be pulped by the delta-V.

Aurora would drop its cargo, flash by Object Lambda, and continue through intergalactic space. It would no longer have fusion mass for its reactors. It would stop decelerating; to all intents and purposes, it would be only another chunk of intergalactic debris on a pointless orbit to nowhere.

Its course would continue to take it toward the Galaxy itself, and in time, perhaps, it would approach some of the inhabited worlds within mere light-years.

But that time would be too late to matter to anyone. It was a matter of thousands of years from even the fringe stars of the Galaxy, and by then there would be little left of even the dust of its crew.

They had been written off.

Meanwhile, the deceleration phases were getting longer, the zero-G pauses for observation shorter and less frequent. Sun One had lost interest in the observations that could be conducted from *Aurora*. They were only waiting for the probe to go into orbit.

All through the ship, the living crew members were showing the effects. They were weaker and less rational, less capable of fine distinctions. The automatic machinery was running the ship.

As it poured the last of its fuel reserves into space to brake its flight, it manufactured enormous clouds of radioactive gas. They were not a hazard to the ship's crew; it was too late for such trivial affairs to matter to the doomed beings. But they had caused some concern to the planners on Sun One. A thousand generations later perhaps they would be a pollution problem, as the newly manufactured clouds of gas preceded the ship in entering well-traveled portions of space. But by then some of the deadlier elements would have burned themselves out, their short half-lives expended. In any case, that was a problem for the thousandth generation—by which time, no doubt, tachyon transport would itself have been superseded, and no one would any longer trouble with such primitive concerns as the crude slower-than-light transport of mass.

The gas clouds as they departed did leave some trace of ionizing radiation, added to the larger increments from the blasts themselves and from the tachyar. The combined radiation was a witches' brew of gammas and alphas and betas, now and then primary particles that coursed through the entire space of the ship from hull to hull and did little harm, except when they struck an atomic nucleus and released a tiny, deadly shower of secondaries.

It was the secondaries, the gammas, that did the dirty work. They interfered with the electronic functions of the computers, robots, and metal beings. They damaged the instrumentation of the ship. Above all, they coursed through the organic matter they encountered, knocking out an electron here, loosening a molecular bond there, damaging a cell nucleus, making a blood vessel more permeable. The whole organic crew was on hourly doses of antirads, giving support to their internal workings. It was not enough. Still the radiation soaked in and struck at them. Blood, ichor, sap, or stew of exotic biologies, the fluids that circulated in their bodies changed and grew less capable of supporting life. Physically they grew weaker. Mentally they became cloudy.

Taken out of the environment and rushed to an antirad clinic, like the victims of an industrial accident, most of them still could have been saved.

There was no hope of that. There was no place to take them. No part of the ship was free of penetrating ionizing radiation now, and every hour more and more of the chemistry of their bodies was damaged.

"Ben James, Ben James," sobbed the voice of Doc Chimp.

Pertin roused himself. The thud and screech of the

drive was still loud in his ear. Every time the floor
drove up to meet the cocoon the single huge bruise that
his body had become screamed with pain. Inside his
chest his lungs felt as if they had broken loose and were
being beaten sore against the inside of his rib cage.

He peered blearily out of the cocoon. The chimp was
staring pathetically up at him. The great green plume of
his hat was broken, his fur splotched with dirt and
blood. The rubbery features of his face looked almost
as they always had, except for an open cut along the
flat, sculptured nose.

"What?" Pertin demanded thickly.

"I have to hide, Ben James. The Sheliaks are after
me."

Pertin tried to sit up and could not. "They're not
here to hurt you," he pointed out.

The chimp whimpered, bobbing on all four limbs as
he braced himself against the rocket thrust. "They will!
They're mad, Ben James. They killed the T'Worlie. For
nothing, just killed him. And they almost killed me."

"What were you doing?"

"Nothing! Well, I—I was watching their mating ritual. But that wasn't it . . ."

"You idiot," Pertin groaned. "Look, can you climb
in here with me?"

"No, Ben James, I don't have the strength."

"It's either that or let them catch you."

The chimpanzee whimpered in fear, then abruptly,
on the upsurge of the ship against its shock absorbers,
sprang to the side of the cocoon. Pertin grabbed at him
and pulled him inside just as the next thrust caught
them. Doc Chimp weighed some two hundred pounds
at Earth's surface. The delta-V gave him a momentary
weight of nearly half a ton, all concentrated on Pertin's
shoulder and chest. He grunted explosively. The chimp
was caught with part of his side still across the metal lip
of the cocoon, but he made no sound beyond the steady
sotto-voce mumble of fear.

Pertin tried to make room behind him, in a place

where the cocoon had never been designed to take a load. It tried its mechanical best to give support to the double mass. It was not adequate to the job. Pertin discovered when the next thrust came that his arm was still caught under the chimp. He yelped, managed to free it on the upsurge, discovered it was not broken. He slammed down the privacy curtain, hoping the Sheliaks would not look inside if they came.

"Now," he panted, "what did you say about Nummie?"

"He's dead, Ben James. They killed him. I didn't mean any harm," the chimp sobbed. "You know how the Sheliaks reproduce—by budding, like terrestrial plants. The young ones sprout out of the old ones, and grow until they're mature enough to be detached."

"I know." Pertin had only the vaguest acquaintance with Sheliaks, but everybody knew that much. They didn't have sexes, but their conjugation provided a union that shuffled up the genes.

"Well, that didn't look like fun to me, but I wanted to see. Nummie told me to go away. He couldn't; he was in one of the spare cocoons and couldn't move. But he said they'd be mad." The chimp switched position and Pertin shouted in pain as his upper thigh took part of the chimp's weight on a rocket thrust. "Sorry, Ben James. It was disgusting, the way they did it! Any two of them can get the urge. They sort of melt down and flow together like jelly. All the body cells migrate, pair off, and fuse. Finally they form again into a sort of cactus-shaped vegetable thing that buds off haploid, mobile creatures. Those are the Sheliaks we see."

"You wanted to watch that?" asked Pertin, almost able to laugh in spite of his discomfort, in spite of Nummie, in spite of everything.

"Yes, Ben James. Just for curiosity. And then there's my friend, Fireball. He's the Sheliak who was here all along. He was nice, Ben James. I miss him."

"I didn't know you knew any Sheliaks."

"Not well. But he was with me, helping to guard all of you, and we talked."

"You sound as if he's dead, too."

"Might as well be. That union is a sort of individual suicide. It's something you do for the race, and because your glands push you that way. But it's the end for the individual. It wipes out all conscious memory and individual personality. I guess that's why Fireball couldn't understand our notions of sex.

"Anyway," he said, "it was all right while Fireball was here alone. He wasn't lonely; or anyway, he didn't want any other Sheliaks around. When they're in danger, you see, they can't help conjugating. It's a survival mechanism. The radiation was danger, and he knew that the only way for him to keep alive was to stay away from his own people. When the new ones came aboard he was actually afraid of them. He knew when they came close they were likely to set off a biological process they couldn't control. And when it was over—"

The chimp swallowed. He thrust himself up on an elbow, regardless of the pain, and stared into Pertin's eyes.

"He didn't know me, Ben James! The two new ones that were half him, they came after me. The T'Worlie saw what was happening and tried to stop them—and that's how I got away, while they were killing him. So I ran. But where is there to run to, in this ship?"

When they could move again they found the T'Worlie easily enough. He was floating upside down, purplish drops of blood, perfectly round, floating beside him. The little vibrissae around his sphincter mouth, more like cat's whiskers than anything on a proper earthly bat, were perfectly still. Nummie was rigid. The pattern of five eyes was unmoving. The intricate pattern of blotches of color on his filmy wings was fading.

There was no one else around. "What'll we do with him, Ben James?" the chimp chattered.

"Throw him out in to space, I guess," Pertin said harshly. Normally the mass would be useful in the tachyon receiver, but there were to be no more incoming tachyon transmissions.

It didn't do to think of that. He stared at the T'Worlie. A slow incrustation of thick gel was matting the fluffy surface of Nummie's chest, and where it had once protruded sharply, like a bird's wishbone, it was crushed and concave.

Pertin felt the muscles on his face drawing taut, perhaps partly because of the intense vinegar reek. He said, "Why would the Sheliaks break up equipment?"

The chimpanzee stared at the mess in the room. Bright green and orange transistors and microchips were scattered like jigsaw pieces in the air. "I don't know, Ben James! None of that was that way when I ran out of here. Do you suppose they just lost their temper?"

"Sheliaks don't lose their temper that way. They broke up instruments on purpose. What was coming in before you decided to play Peeping Tom?"

"Oh—" The chimp thought. "More reports on Object Lambda. The density was confirmed. Very low. Like a sparse cloud of interstellar gas."

"We already knew it was Cloud-Cuckoo Land. That couldn't have had any effect on them."

"Something did, Ben James," the chimp cried. "Look, we've got to do something. They'll be looking for me, and—"

"Unless," Pertin said thoughtfully, "it wasn't the Sheliaks who did it. The robot was up to something. And there are still a couple of Purchased People not accounted for. And—"

"Too late!" the chimp howled. "Listen, Ben James! Somebody's coming!"

But it wasn't the Sheliaks who came in on them, it was Aphrodite, the silver pseudogirl, the heavy-planet creature in human form. Her fingers were outstretched toward them, listening, as her great foil wings drove her forward.

Behind her was the Scorpian robot.

They made an eerie pair, the striking orange-eyed girl with her coif of metallic hair and steel-bright body hues, and the mechanical creature shaped like a metal octopus. Its central body was a massive disk, the color of the pseudogirl's flesh, and its silvery tentacles made a fringe of snakes around it. A greenish membrane that bulged above the upper surface of the disk fluttered, producing a drumroll of sound. Pertin's Pmal translator obediently turned it into recognizable words: "DO NOT RESIST. WE WISH YOU TO COME WITH US."

"Where?" he demanded.

There was no answer, at least not in words. Pertin was caught in something like a metal whip that stung a trail of fire around his waist. It was one of the robot's tentacles that had caught him; it pinned his arms, and the pseudogirl launched herself at him, her metal fist catching him full in the face. Floating as he was, the blow was robbed of some of its force, but it doubled him, flung him back against the robot's lash, dazed with pain and sobbing for breath.

He heard a cry of anguish from Doc Chimp, but could not turn to see what was happening. The vinegary smell of the dead T'Worlie penetrated his nostrils, mixing with the tang of his own blood.

"Why?" he croaked, and tried to raise his arms to defend himself as the girl dropped toward him again. She did not answer. She was on him like a great silvery bat, metal feet kicking, shining fists flying. The lights went out. He lost touch with space and time.

Pertin was not wholly unconscious, but he was so near to it, so filled with pain and confusion, that he could hardly remember what happened next. He had a fugitive impression of great shapes whirling around him, then of being carried away while someone behind him sobbed his name, the voice diminishing in the distance.

A long time later he opened his eyes.

He was alone, in a part of the ship he knew only

sketchily. A large open cocoon hung from a wall, and inside it was what looked like one of the Purchased People. Pertin's face was swollen and his eyes not focusing well at all; he squinted, but could not make out the features on the person in the cocoon. It appeared to be male, however, and it appeared to be in the last stages of dissolution.

It moved and looked toward him. A caricature of a smile disturbed the weeks-old beard, and the dry tongue licked the lips. A cracked voice muttered something, the tone hoarse and indistinguishable.

"Who are you? What do you want?" Ben James Pertin demanded.

The figure rasped a sort of hacking cough, that perhaps was meant for a chuckle. It tried again, and this time its words came clear enough—clear, and familiar, in a way that Pertin had not expected.

"I want to talk to you, Ben," it croaked. "We have a lot in common, you know."

Pertin frowned, then his swollen eyes widened. He pushed himself toward the swathed figure, caught himself at the lip of the cocoon, and stared down.

The eyes that looked up at him were pain-filled but very familiar. He was looking into his own, battered, obviously dying face.

Pertin remembered a time, months ago.

He had gone to the tachyon transmitter and lightheartedly enough given his blueprint to the scanners and allowed one self of him to be beamed to the *Aurora*. It had not seemed like an important thing to do. At that time, it was not clear that the *Aurora* was a doomed ship. At that time, he had no one to consult but himself; Zara Doy was still only a casual acquaintance, the new girl from Earth with the pretty face.

"Ben Frank," he whispered.

"Right as rain," croaked the ghastly voice. "And I know about you well enough. You're Ben James Pertin, and you've been aboard two weeks now. Not very thoughtful of you, failing to visit a dying relative."

"But I thought you were dead already! They said—I mean, I wouldn't have had to come, if—"

"Blaming me, Ben James? Well, why shouldn't you? How often have I lain here, blaming you, and me, and all the Ben Pertins there ever were." A spasm of coughing racked him, but he talked right through it. "I wanted them to think I was dead. Only fair, isn't it? They were killing me, and now I've killed their Project Lambda."

"You?"

"With a lot of help. My Sirian friends were the first and best, but there have been plenty since. It was the Sirians who told me you were aboard; you gave one of them quite a start, when he saw you in the instrument room. Wrecked his mission, you did."

Coughing drowned the voice out; the other Ben Pertin convulsively clutched at the cocoon monitor controls. A warning panel lit over the bed. He was very near death; but the cocoon was not yet defeated; it metered colored fluids into the external blood supply that was trying to replace the destroyed blood cells.

"I only have a few minutes," Ben Frank Pertin gasped. "I don't mind. But I'm not finished, Ben James. You have to finish for me. Destroy that probe! I don't want it to succeed; I don't want Sun One to get its orbiting body around Object Lambda."

"But then we— Then we'll all have died in vain!"

"Of course it is in vain! What's the use of it all? A chunk of useless matter—thousands of light-years from anywhere—going nowhere! Do you know how many lives it's cost? I want you to wreck it for me, Ben James, so those fools on Sun One will know better than to try this same stunt another time!"

"But it's not a stunt," Ben James Pertin objected. "It's important. That object is something special, solid but like a cloud—"

"Cloud-Cuckoo Land! It's not worth a single life. Anyway, it's done already, Ben James, my friends are wrecking the probe right now. I only called you here because—"

He paused, coughing terribly. The face that was so much like Ben James' own was aged with the weary agony of radiation death.

"Because," he gasped, "I want some part of me to stay alive. If you keep the tachyon receiver you can live, Ben James. Weeks—maybe months! But once it goes there will be no more food, no more air, no more fuel. I want—"

But what he wanted to say at the last Ben James Pertin would never know. His duplicate suddenly gasped for breath, made a strangling sound and was still.

After a moment Ben James pulled the privacy screen over the face that was his own face and turned to leave.

Halfway to the launch chamber, he ran into the Sheliaks.

They were in pursuit of two beings, one of them the Purchased People woman, the other Doc Chimp. The Sheliaks looked strange, and in a moment Pertin realized why. They were smaller than they had been; essentially they were children now, some of their mass lost when they budded. But their behavior was childish only in its reckless disregard for consequences; it was lethal, as far as their quarry was concerned.

Pertin did not pause to speculate on issues. Doc Chimp was in danger, and he dove to the rescue.

He collided head-on with one of the Sheliaks. It was like tackling a six-foot lump of chilled, damp dough. No bones, no cushioning fat, just a great dense mass of muscular fiber. The Sheliak automatically cupped around him and, linked, they went flying into the wall. The corridor spun around him, a nightmare of blue-green light and red-black shadow and corpse-colored beings.

"Stop!" Pertin roared. "Wait! Listen to me!" But no one wanted to talk. They were all on him, thrusting,

striking, crushing, with whatever offensive weapons
their mobile anatomies gave them. He fought back, using a skill he had never known he had. His hands were
black and slippery with blood, no doubt much of it his
own. Bravely the woman and Doc Chimp had turned
back to fight, but it was three of them against more
than a dozen Sheliaks, and the issue was not in doubt.

What saved them was Aphrodite, the silver pseudogirl. Her carven face remote as an angel's, she drove
toward them with great sweeps of her wings. Coronas of
electrostatic fire haloed her fingers and wingtips; something gun-shaped and deadly was in her hands. The
Sheliaks, all at once and in unison, turned to meet her.
The gun-shaped thing hissed and a white jet cracked
toward them. It passed near enough to Pertin for him to
feel a breath of icy death, but it did not strike him; it
grazed the Sheliak who held him, and at once the being
stiffened and began to drift. Behind them, where the jet
had struck, the wall was hidden with a broad patch of
glittering frost. A cloud of white vapor billowed out
around it.

In the haze Pertin caught sight of Doc Chimp and
the Purchased People woman, momentarily forgotten as
the Sheliaks turned against the stronger foe. The
woman was badly hurt; Doc Chimp was helping her, his
hairy face turned fearfully toward the Sheliaks. Pertin
joined them and the three of them moved inconspicuously away.

When they were two corridors away and the sounds
of battle had diminished they paused and inspected
their injuries. Pertin himself had only added a few
bruises to a total that was already too large to worry
about; the chimp was even more battered, but still oper-
ational. The woman was worst off of any of them. She
was bleeding profusely from, among other places, a
gash on the upper arm; her face was grotesquely puffed,
both eyes blackened; and one leg was bent at an angle
anatomically impossible to a whole bone. But she did
not appear to feel pain. When Pertin spoke to her, she

answered in English: "They don't consider it important. It will not prevent moving about and performing necessary functions."

Doc Chimp was groaning and sobbing in pain. "Those Sheliaks!" he cried, feebly trying to groom his matted fur. "They're wholly out of control, Ben James. They tried again to wreck the probe—may have done it by now, if they've got enough power of concentration to remember what they were doing when we diverted their attention. And if Aphrodite hasn't killed them all."

Pertin said, with a confidence he didn't feel: "She'll stop them. As long as we've got her on our side—"

"On our side!" Doc Chimp cried. "Ben James, you don't know what you're saying. She's worse than they are!"

"But she tried to rescue you."

The Purchased woman said calmly, "That is wrong. She merely wanted to kill the Sheliaks."

"That's right, Ben James! She's against all organic beings now. She's not ionizable. Radiation is only an annoyance to her. The only thing that can kill her is deprivation of energy sources, and that means the tachyon receiver; once it's gone, she will die as soon as the fuel runs out."

Pertin said slowly: "Is it the same with the Scorpian robot?"

The battered face nodded, the stub of the green plume jerking wildly.

"Then," Pertin said, "that means we have to assume all nonorganic beings will feel the same and try to prevent the launch. What about the other organics?"

The Purchased woman recited emotionlessly: "T'Worlie, all dead. Boaty-Bits, more than half destroyed; the remainder too few to make a collective entity intelligent enough to matter. Sirians and Core Stars races, not observed in recent hours and must be presumed dead or neutralized. Sheliaks, destructive and purposeless."

Pertin absorbed the information without shock,

without reaction of any kind, except a strange impulse to laugh. "But—but who does that leave to see that the launch occurs?"

"Nobody!" Doc Chimp cried. "Nobody at all, Ben James—except us!"

FIVE

They reached the launch chamber ahead of the Sheliaks after all. There was no one there.

The capsule, with its tiny bright tachyon crystal at its heart, lay silent and unmoving, connected to the main bulk of the ship only by a jettisonable canopy now. There had been destruction all around it, but it was still intact.

There was less than an hour until launch.

"We'll build barricades," Pertin said. "Anything. Those wrecked instrument boards—the spare plates and braces. Whatever we can move, we'll put it up against the entrance. All we have to do is delay them—"

But they had barely begun when bright silver glinted in the approach corridor, and the silvery pseudogirl came toward them, followed by the tumbling form of the Scorpian robot. They brought up short at the entrance, the robot with one slim tentacle coiled caressingly around the silver girl.

Pertin put his weight behind the channel iron he had been about to emplace at the door and launched it toward the pair. The pseudogirl made a sound that was half a laugh and half the singing of a single piercing note, and the Scorpian uncoiled a long silver sting as they moved aside, easily dodging the missile. The sting reached out and touched Pertin. A blinding light stabbed from it, jolting him with a strong electric shock.

The girl glided in, spreading her now-tattered wings. The stirred air bathed him in a strong scent, ethersweet, with undertones like the pits of peaches. Pertin

71

searched the bright silvery face and found no expression. It was no more human than a doll's. The Scorpian's silver tentacles thrust away the pitiful obstructions, making a sound like an enormous gong, which Pertin's Pmal refused to translate.

The Purchased woman intervened, hurling herself toward the robot, and was brushed heedlessly aside. She struck against the side of the probe ship, a blow that must have been agony to her human nervous system, but she did not cry out. Awkwardly she tried to project herself again into the fight. Pertin, his muscles beginning to relax their spasm, forced himself to join her.

A birdlike trilling from outside indicated that others were coming, and behind the great winged hulk of the pseudogirl Pertin could see black shadow-shapes moving across the dimly lighted shaft, growing rapidly as they approached.

"Oh, no!" Doc Chimp moaned. "Sheliaks and a Sirian!"

The robot's single-minded purpose was not deflected; it floated toward Pertin, green dome pulsing. An elongating tentacle struck out at Pertin like an endless silver snake, not to sting this time but to snare. It wrapped him in slick, chill coils. He fought free, was caught again, and then at last the Scorpian turned to confront the other beings. It arched its stinging jet, but held poised, waiting.

The Sirian was first into the launch chamber, a tapered, blue-scaled torpedo shape fifteen feet long, all pliant wing and shining eye. With a ripple of trailing edges it flashed at the Scorpian.

The sting coiled, jetting white light into the wide blue eye. The Sirian was not defenseless; its own forces gathered the robot's charge and repelled it, sending the jet back at the robot, reinforced and multiplied.

The pseudogirl turned with great strokes of her wings, her three-fingered hand coming up with the gun-shaped something that had killed Sheliaks. Desperately Pertin twisted to intercept her. Her wings were sadly battered now, but still gave her superior mobility; he missed her on the first try and crashed against a wall. Half blind with his own blood, flowing ink-black in the greenish light, he doubled his legs under him and launched himself at her again.

The gun-shaped thing swung to meet him. It clicked in the pseudogirl's bright silver hand, and the white jet hissed at him. He heard a brittle crackling sound in the air, and felt the cold breath of death.

But the jet had missed, and he was on her. With one hand he swung at her wrist. It was like striking a crowbar with his bare hand, but it jarred the weapon loose; and just then the battle between Scorpian and Sirian reached its climax.

The Sirian's triply potent return jet struck a vital place in the great green dome of the robot. It exploded. The mellow booming sound the robot made became a hollow jangle. The tentacles writhed and recoiled. It sprawled in the air, a grotesque huddle of tortured metal, spilling green fire and drops of an acid that sizzled and burned where they struck.

If robots have life, that life was gone; it was dead.

The silvery girl abandoned the fight with Pertin. With a great stroke of her wings she propelled herself to the robot, hovered over it, wailing an unearthly sound.

And the great blue eye of the Sirian turned toward Pertin. Behind it the Sheliaks, late on the scene but ready for battle, were elongating their wrinkled necks toward him.

Pertin cried desperately: "Wait! They—they were misleading you. They were trying to prevent the launch, to save their own lives!"

The eye hesitated.

"We're dead already," he croaked. "Nothing can help us now, not any organic creature. The radiation will kill us before long, even the Sheliaks. But the robot and the girl—"

He could hear his voice translating and hissing or singing out of the aliens' Pmals.

"The robot," he repeated, "and the altered copy that looks like a terrestrial female—they weren't radiation-vulnerable. They could go on indefinitely. But the rest of us—if we let them succeed in stopping the launch, then we will die for nothing!"

The eye paused, irresolute.

Then the foremost of the Sheliaks cried: "Fool! We too are not radiation-vulnerable! We simply need to conjugate, and be born again. But we must have the tachyon receiver, and if you try to keep us from it you must die!"

And the three tapered teardrop shapes, like a school of sharks in formation, plunged toward them, blazing with their own crimson light.

The Sirian eye irresolutely turned toward them, then back toward Pertin; then, with decision, whirled to confront them.

Contemptuously the Sheliaks changed course to meet it. The leading Sheliak widened a ruff of flesh like an instant air brake and stopped in the air, flowed with a dazzle of color, narrowed a neck toward the Sirian eye.

The thin neck spat a stream of yellow fluid. It struck the Sirian eye and clung, acid, adhesive, agonizing. The Sirian made an unearthly wailing noise at the sudden pain of the attack against which it had no built-in defenses. The great blue eye turned milky white; the horse-huge body knotted itself in agony.

But it still had strength for a final blow. It fired the jet of energy that had destroyed the robot against the Sheliaks.

Electrical energy paralyzed their muscular systems; heat seared the life from them. They died instantly, all three of them. But it was the last effort of the Sirian. All its stored energy had gone into that pulse. The reflected cascade of burning energy came bouncing back upon them all, bathed the silvery girl and sent her reeling soundlessly into a wall, to collapse into an ungainly contorted mass that didn't move. Pertin was farther away and partly shielded by what was left of the robot; even so, it lanced his skin with pain.

But he was alive.

Slowly, and very painfully, he caught a holdfast on the wall, steadied himself while he looked around.

The Purchased-People woman was dead, either bled empty or caught in that last furious bolt. The Sirian eye floated aimlessly, broken and no longer moving, a milky ooze coming from its body. The robot was destroyed; the pseudogirl was drifting impotently away; the Sheliaks were cinders.

The chamber was filled with the stench of many different kinds of death, but Pertin was still alive.

Suddenly remembering, he cried, "Doc Chimp!"

The ape was out of sight. Furiously Pertin ransacked the chamber, and found him at last, wedged between the wall of the probe and the ship's canopy, not quite dead but very unconscious.

Pertin looked down at him sadly and affectionately. It was nearly time to launch the probe, and the question in Pertin's mind was: Is it better to wake him up, or to let him sleep as the probe is launched, the canopy jettisoned, and all the air in the chamber puffed instantly and murderously away into space?

The question was taken out of his hand as the ape stirred, moaned softly, and opened his eyes. He looked up at Ben James Pertin and said thickly, "The probe?"

"It's all right," Pertin said. "We'll have to launch it by hand."

"When, Ben James?"

Pertin checked the time. "Just a few minutes now," he said.

The ape grinned painfully. "That's good to know, Ben James," he said. "No more problems. No more aches and pains. I always thought I'd be afraid of dying, but you know? To tell you the truth, I'm kind of looking forward to it."

* * *

The process that animated the body of the silvery pseudogirl was more like electrophoresis than chemistry, but it was vulnerable to attack. It was damaged now.

But she was not dead. The great wings were broken and useless, but her limbs still moved, the inappropriate angel face still showed its bleak, proud expression.

She was in great pain; that is to say, all the sensory nets of her edited body were transmitting messages of malfunction, damage, and warning. She did not perceive them as a human perceives a toothache, a sensation so blinding that it can lead to suicide; but they did not interfere with the few pleasure-bound processes left to her: reminiscence, forevision, contemplation. In the sense that these messages were pain, she had experienced pain from the moment she floated out of the tachyon receiver on *Aurora*. All edited members of her race did. There was no way to rearrange their structures into forms viable in atmosphere and low-G that was comfortable for them.

Time was when Aphrodite had experienced pain only infrequently, and in ways that were soon mended. Time was when she had lain with her sisters in the icy methane slush of her native planet, absorbing energy from the radioactive elements that swam about them, growing, learning from the tutorials of her orthofather, competing in the endless elimination battles of her race that finally won her her choice of assignments, and ultimately led her to the *Aurora* and its imminent doom. Her race was not greatly interested in astronomy; they had known almost nothing of it until the first T'Worlie probe survived the crushing pressures of their atmosphere and brought them into contact. From the surface of their enormous planet, there were no stars to be seen. Even their aircraft never reached an altitude beyond dense yellow-gray clouds.

What brought her to *Aurora* was the trait that her whole upbringing had trained into her: the competitive need to go farther and do more. It was not goal-oriented. It gained nothing from victories except the opportunity for further victories. And the only victory now open to Aphrodite was to survive; and there was but one way to do it—by preventing the launching of the probe.

She calculated she had strength enough left to destroy the two organic creatures in her way, but only just; and only if she acted now.

It was Pertin who saw her first: he froze with his hand on the release lever, and it was Doc Chimp who acted. He flung himself on the pseudogirl. "Hurry up, Ben James!" he shouted. "She's too strong for me—" And his voice stopped, punctuated with a screech of pain as the silvery arm thrust him away like a cannon shot. The chimp went flying into the floating wreckage of the Scorpian robot. The soft, frail dome of the skull, so cleverly mutated nearly into the shape of man's own, impaled itself on a steel shard, and the thoughtful, considering brain was destroyed.

Pertin hardly even saw it. He was past the point for sorrow. It would be easy to let the pseudogirl destroy him. At least one life would be saved, her own. His no longer counted. He could hope for a few days, a week or two at the most, of being able to move and breathe. But what would it be like? Increasing pain. Hopeless fear. Regret. Envy—

He pressed the lever just as her fingers touched him.

The instant sharp slap of the explosion was the last sound he ever heard.

At the second Ben James Pertin pressed the release, explosive shears cut the aft end of the ship free. The canopy flew out and away. The air puffed into emptiness. The probe rocket dropped free and began to align itself with the now near great disk of Object Lambda.

The first thing Pertin felt was the sharp pain of the explosion, then the second, longer, more deadly pain as the air pressure dropped to instant zero and his own blood and body fluids, the air in his own lungs, the

gases dissolved in his blood tried to expand to fill the
enormous emptiness all around. He caught a glimpse of
the silvery girl, arms, legs, and broken wings flailing, as
she shot past him, careened off the jagged edge of metal
where the shears had cut the probe satellite free, and
ricocheted out into emptiness. If she made a sound, he
could not hear it. There was no longer a way for him to
hear sound. There was no longer a continuous medium
of air to carry it.

He had just a glimpse of the huge near surface of
Object Lambda—the body he had called "Cuckoo"—
as it hung like a great dull circle in the empty sky, cutting off one spiral limb of his own, eternally lost, Galaxy.

He did not see the orienting jets of the satellite spurt
carefully controlled measures of flame to position it for
its final thrust. He did not see the great violet flare of
the fusion rockets that began to slow it. He could not
see any of that, because by then he was dead.

Neither he nor anyone else in the probe ship saw the
great series of flares as the satellite fought to slow itself.
Aurora flew on, back toward the Galaxy, without
power, containing only the least flickerings of life for a
few of its beings. The probe left it as it drew more and
more rapidly away. The distance between them was
millions of miles before the satellite made its first me-
teoric contact with the outer layers of that anomalously
thick atmosphere around Cuckoo.

It was a spectacle worth watching, if there had been
eyes left in *Aurora* to see. The satellite plunged through
a carefully planned chord of the atmosphere. It's abla-
tive surface burned and tore away in a flare like all the
Fourth of July fireworks in man's history going off at
once. But there was none to see, not Sirian eye nor
Sheliak sensors, not T'Worlie or Earthman or alien
of any kind; where life remained at all, it lacked strength
for curiosity, and it would not remain very long.

Fifty thousand years later *Aurora* might pass near

some sun of an outstretched spiral arm. But by then it would no longer matter to anyone, except as a historical curiosity from a time about which no one cared any longer.

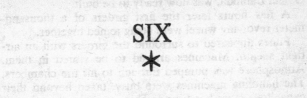

SIX

*

Some days later, the sensors on Sun One reported that the probe was in a stable orbit. The beings on Sun One responded with pleasure; everyone was delighted that the project was a success.

Now stable, the probe began to do the work for which it had been designed.

The complex H-bomb sequencing units and the small, strong pressure-plate shock absorbers fell away, responding to remote controls from Sun One. They would never be used again.

The tachyon-receiving unit began to emit a stream of tiny metallic shards, none larger than a few inches in its greatest measure.

When some hundreds of them were through, floating like a metallic mist around the drone, a quick small machine came through and began to catch them and link them together. Time passed, hours and then days. A queer boxlike shape took form and became a larger tachyon receiver, ready for action.

From tens of thousands of light-years away an angular, crystalline machine flashed along the tachyon patterns and emerged in the new receiver. It was not alive. Was not even a robot, or a proxy like the Purchased People. It was simply an automatic machine that sensed certain potentials and charges, double-checked the strength of the materials and the solidity of the joints, directed the hummingbird-sized construction machine to correct a few faults, and then reported that Cuckoo

Station, the orbiting body around what had been called Object Lambda, was now ready to be built.

A few hours later the first girders of a thousand-meter revolving wheel were being joined together.

Plates appeared to surround the girders with an airtight sheath. Machines arrived to be stored in them. Atmosphere was pumped through to fill the chambers. The handling machines were busy, taxed beyond their capacities; more handling machines were sent, and soon the orbiting station was whole, supplied, and being-rated.

The first living beings appeared. A Sheliak, naked to the cold of intergalactic space—but for the brief time of its transition to the orbiting wheel unharmed by it. A dozen T'Worlie in a single elastic air bubble, scurrying into the protection of the orbital wheel. There were Sirians, reptilian Aldebaranians, a hive of Boaty-Bits, and, at the last, a couple of humans.

One of them was named Ben Linc Pertin.

He floated out of the tachyon receiver in his pressure suit, his thruster unit ready in his hands.

He did not use it at once; he paused a moment, to look around.

The first thing he did was to stare down at the enormous flat surface of Cuckoo, so near, so huge, so incredible as it hung like an endless shield in the sky.

The second was to look back to where the Galaxy lay, sparkling like the sea of stars it was.

He could not see the doomship, but he knew it must be somewhere in his line of sight. There were no signals from it anymore. There was no way of detecting it, and would not be for tens of thousands of years.

He stared for a moment, then half shrugged. "Poor bastards," he whispered, and turned and drove toward the wheel awaiting him.

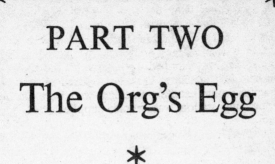

PART TWO

The Org's Egg

*

ONE

The mountain was a friendly mountain. It had been growing for half a billion years, as mountains naturally did. Its slow cells fed on rain and air and windblown dust, compacting them into a core of solid quartz.

On other planets, Earth for example, mountains also grew, but in a different way. Terrestrial mountains were thrust up from below by the slow violence of shifting continental crusts and the shock of volcanic eruptions. Here mountains grew more gently.

A boy, whose name was Fifteenth, lived on this mountain with his people. When he was little it was his whole world and he had not imagined anything beyond it. Now he was nearly grown. From time to time he looked beyond the mountain, but always came back to it. It was home.

It was not all hospitable. Its summit was a rounded crown, carved with winding fissures, glowing with a blue bioluminescence brighter than the storms that often boiled around it. Lower down, where the winds were now too warm and dry, its surface film of shining life was tattered into drying shreds. With the life-coat dying, the age-eaten stone beneath was caving away from the vertical cliffs, adding black and shattered masses to the boulder slopes below, where the wild orgs nested. The boy never went that high. It was too dangerous.

But lower still, there was home! The dead stuff of the mountain had rotted into rich black soil that spread in delta-plains and marshes all around its foot. Floods

from its stormy heights ran down to water the forests
and mosslands that reached all the way to the grassy flat-
land where the people ranged to find food and trophies,
and bring them back to the sweet slopes of the mountain.

Fifteenth's people were nomadic wingmen. From the
heights on the side of the mountain they could launch
themselves into always-present orographic updrafts, and
spiral out of them to overfly the green rainpaths of the
plain. There were roots and fruits, waterholes and
game. When they found what they wanted they
swooped down and possessed it. It was a good life. It
was the only life Fifteenth had known, but it was not
good enough.

And when he was just coming bearded, he looked
around the camp of his people and sat in thought for a
long time, testing a thought that had come to him. He
looked out across the flat plains to that other distant,
seemingly barren mountain that his people called Knife-
in-the-Sky. It was hard to see in the uncertain light
from the plains and the few forested parts of its slopes.
The boy's people had never seen daylight, or for that
matter night; they marked the passing of time by their
own body cycles or by changes in the trees and animals,
since they had no other clock on a world that showed
nothing in its sky but clouds and, rarely, some faint
misty distant gleam that looked like a swirl of muted
silvery fire. But even when they could not see Knife-in-
the-Sky they knew it was there. For every org on the
boy's own mountain there were a thousand on Knife-in-
the-Sky. On his own mountain their clutches were
scant, and often the eggs produced weaklings; but always there were new orgs coming from Knife-in-the-
Sky to replenish the stocks. The boy sat staring at the
distant jagged peak for many thousands of breaths, and
then he went to tell his brother that he had resolved to
leave his people, to cross the plain, to climb Knife-in-
the-Sky and steal a wild org's egg.

"You are young," his brother said wearily and

fretfully, "and you are foolish. Other youths have gone org-hunting. They do not come back."

Fifteenth stood stubbornly silent, hanging his head. His brother was the head of his clan, the clan in which fourteen other males were older and therefore more powerful than himself. The boy did not want to show disrespect to his brother by disagreeing, but he could not make himself promise to give up his plan.

"Only those whose minds are on the ground hunt orgs," his brother warned.

The boy still did not speak. They were standing outside his brother's new tent, pitched in the yellow light of a clump of fire-trees. His brother's new wife was singing in the tent, grinding grain for their next meal. From beyond the fire-trees the slow clang of a blacksmith's anvil rang; that was the boy's cousin, Second.

The brother carefully worked his awl through a double thickness of leather before speaking again. Then he looked up. "If you stay with us, I will share my skills with you," he offered.

The boy showed his astonishment. Their father had been a wingwright. As was proper, his skills had come down to the eldest of his sons. With a new wife, First would surely have sons of his own before long, and to give wingwright skills to Fifteenth would be depriving his own get of what was rightly theirs. "I thank you," the boy said. "But I will go."

"Knife-in-the-Sky is farther than it looks," his brother said. "Why go there when there are orgs here, if you are determined to die?"

"There are better orgs on Knife-in-the-Sky. I have never seen their lairs there. I know what they are here."

"From your mother," First said gloomily. "Of course. But there are more orgs and stronger orgs there, and they take care of their eggs. Besides—"

He looked up from the harness he was mending and scowled across at the jagged distant mountain.

"Besides the orgs, there are the Watchers."

"Why should the Watchers bother me?"

"They do not tell us why!" His brother looked up angrily and incautiously, pricked his finger with an awl, and grimaced with pain. He put the finger in his mouth and said around it, "They live beyond the mountains. They ride in the sky in machines the size of twenty orgs, and attack all creatures that don't obey them. And there are new Watchers now. Little ones. No one knows what they may do."

"I've never seen a Watcher," the boy said.

"Not on the mountain. But to get to Knife-in-the-Sky you must cross the plain and marshland. You cannot do it all by wing. You must walk for many sleeps. I'm afraid the Watchers will find you."

"But if they do not," the boy said, "I will come back riding an org."

"You—riding an org!" The brother took his finger out of his mouth and spat blood. "You've never seen an org close up."

"My mother did," the boy said.

He turned and scowled across the plains toward Knife-in-the-Sky. He was a strong young man, tall even among his people, who averaged better than seven feet in height. If he had been on Earth he would have weighed no more than a hundred and sixty pounds—here much less—he looked not like a reed but a whip.

He looked a great deal like his mother—his father's second wife, whom his father had stolen away from another band. She had been a First Man's daughter, and her father had pursued them on a tamed org, until the fleeing couple set fire to dried grass and escaped under the smoke. She had handed on her lore of org-training to the boy: where the eggs were found, how the hatchlings could be tamed.

The time had come for him to use that knowledge, because he was of an age to use it—and for another reason. For the girl who had become his brother's new wife had been the girl Fifteenth himself had wanted.

The brother picked up his awl again. "If you have to be a fool—" He shrugged and suddenly grinned. "I'll make a new harness for you."

And so, for many meals, the boy hunted meat while his brother made the harness. The dark-eyed girl who had become his brother's wife helped him smoke the meat, and if her presence near him was a steady pain he never showed it, and if she knew she never told.

When the harness was finished and fitted he loaded himself and the three of them trudged up the friendly mountain toward the finest of the launching places. There where the slope fell steeply away for a thousand feet, the gentle, cradling updraft never failed. From this cliff edge one could circle and soar more than a mile into the thick, sweet air of their world, and launch one-self many sleeps away across the plain in a single flight.

They stood and stared at Knife-in-the-Sky, and then the dark-haired girl caught her breath and cried, "A fire in the clouds! Look!"

Before them, even higher than Knife-in-the-Sky, a lance of silvery light was extending itself in a soaring arc down through the bright, living clouds. Neither the boy nor his brother was frightened, although it was a strange thing to them; their world knew nothing of meteorites, since near them there was nothing small enough to fall into their air. It was not unique. It was rare.

The brother muttered, "There was such a flame a hundred sleeps ago, and after that the small Watchers appeared."

"Has anyone been harmed by a small Watcher?" the boy demanded.

The brother shook his head no, though what he meant was "not yet."

"Then I will not fear if there are more. Good-bye," the boy said, kissed them both, grasped his buttocks with his hands, and leaped headfirst into the air. When he was well clear of the rock he swept his arms up in the sinuous stroke of the wingman, extended the filmy

wings of scraped leather, and flapped and soared until
his brother and the girl were all but invisible to him,
tiny, staring figures no larger than pebbles.

And then he turned out of the updraft and stroked
through the air toward Knife-in-the-Sky.

He did not look behind him.

Even if he had looked, he might not have seen that
something shared the air with him, a cube of metal,
bright on all its faces, brighter still with lights and lenses
on the face toward him. It was no larger than Fifteenth's fist and a long way behind as it stolidly
punched a passage through the air, borne on magnetic
forces of which none of the boy's people had ever
heard. The boy did know it was there. He was not
meant to.

TWO

A long distance away in terms of the boy's world—but only a step in astronomical distances—a man named Ben Linc Pertin watched a holographic virtual image of the flying boy and turned away, shaking his head. "They're skinny and funny-looking," he said, "but by God they're human. Figure that for me, Venus."

The girl beside him was not a girl. She did not look like a human girl except in the way that a statue does; she was silvery metal, thixotropic, anisotropic, tamed by the science of her people to flow and move like flesh. On her home world Venus had not looked human at all; for that matter she had not been female, because her race had not bothered with sexual distinctions in its development. She said, "Not only human beings live on Cuckoo, Ben Linc. We have already found Sheliaks and Boaty-Bits, or beings genetically parallel to them. And we have only begun to look."

"None of your folks, though," Ben Linc observed cheerfully. "Guess you weren't popular."

"As to that, Ben Linc, how could you tell?"

He grinned. Venus was an edited form, specially tailored to operate well in the near Earth-normal environment of Cuckoo Station.

"Well," he said, "I suppose we might as well retransmit these tapes. I think we need help, Venus. More equipment, more survey scouts. And more beings. I think it's about time we sent people down to Cuckoo. What do you say?"

The silvery girl was silent for a moment. Ben Linc knew that, through her Pmal translator, she was communicating with FARLINK, the computer that processed all the manifold information-handling procedures on the orbiter called Cuckoo Station.

FARLINK was the station's nerve center. It processed the tachyonic transmissions that replicated new personnel for the station. It coordinated the reports from the drones they sent down to the surface of the strange object itself. It stored their cumulative data and solved their research problems; and it sent their findings— such as they were—back to Sun One.

Its main terminal was a ring-shaped console inside the hollow hemisphere where Pertin, the silvery girl, and other beings were working. The beings on duty sat inside the console, or rested or clung or stood there as their anatomies dictated, with input devices within reach of their manipulative organs. The output flashed and shimmered on the screens that lined the dome, translated into the visual symbols of half a hundred cultures.

Ben Linc became impatient. "What's the matter, Venus?"

She did not move but her expression, as far as she could be said to have one, seemed to cloud. "There is difficulty," she said.

"Difficulty?" That seemed unlikely! FARLINK was as close to perfect as any machine ever made. Many tachyonic channels linked it to the banks of the even larger computers and research teams back on Sun One, and it had its own built-in power sources. And yet—

And yet abruptly, before his very eyes, the myriad screens suddenly flickered and went black!

There was an instant rumble of consternation. Cries and hoots and clangs of shock rang out all around the ring. From the console position nearest his own a scorched-fur scent of T'Worlie dismay came from the bat-headed, butterfly-winged being named Nammie.

"What the devil!" he cried. The screens were black

for only a second; then they glowed with the green computer symbols that spelled out the same message in half a hundred languages:

"REGRET INTERRUPTION. INTERFERENCE DISTORTING INCOMING SIGNALS. ORIGIN OF INTERFERENCE NOT KNOWN."

Venus whispered, "But we've never had any interference before . . ."

Pertin had no answer. Suddenly he felt very lonely. The tachyonic channels were their only bridge of thought and communication across that gulf of space that was too vast for anything material to cross. With the bridge broken, the thirty thousand light-years between all of them and all of their diverse homes became terribly real.

The T'Worlie beside him was fluttering on frantic wings above its console position, stabbing at the keys and whistling at its mike. After a moment it rose from the keyboard and turned its five-eyed face to him.

"Mode emergency!" it shrilled. "Query implications of signal distortion."

"I wish I knew," Pertin said, shaking his head.

"Propose conjecture! Assume sentient masters of Cuckoo. Query: Have they discovered us? Are they initiating contact? Query probable intentions."

"I don't know, Nammie. What about DFing? Do we know where the source comes from?"

The T'Worlie spun and punched a combination; and all the myriad screens lighted up:

"SOURCE UNKNOWN. DF PROGRAM INITIATED."

And then abruptly the green symbols shimmered off the screen. Patterns of color flashed and vanished in the deep tanks that were their three-D vision screens. A new message appeared:

"INTERFERENCE FADING. STAND BY. SIGNAL RECEPTION RESUMING."

The Sun One sign burned itself onto the screens: a red disk inside a thin green ellipse—the artificial satellite called Sun One, inside the Galaxy itself. Before it appeared the tall, glowing cone of a Sheliak official, back at Sun One. He was speaking, apparently oblivious to the interruption, while his translator turned his soft hooting into Earth English on Ben Linc's screen. Green symbols overrode the image for a moment:

"INTERFERENCE HAS CEASED. SOURCE NOT TRACKED."

Venus and Ben Linc looked at each other.

"What was that all about?" he demanded.

Slowly she shook her silvery head. "At any rate, it's over." All around the dome, beings were resuming their interrupted chores. "One moment, Ben Linc," she added gravely; and then, "Yes, we have concurrence. We authorize you to transmit a call for additional survey forces."

Ben Linc Pertin nodded and cued in the tachyon transmitter. Carefully he began to phrase the report that the supervelocity tachyons would flash toward the distant Galaxy, to the artificial planet called Sun One—where all the races of the Galaxy maintained the headquarters that had launched this survey party—and from there on to the home planets of scores of kinds of beings. His own words might sooner or later reach his own world, Earth.

Ben Linc wondered if somehow, back on Earth, that original Ben Pertin who had volunteered for tachyon transmission long before might hear the voice of his double, and if so what he might think.

But that was not profitable wondering. Behind it lay too much pain, too much loss, too many regrets for what could never be undone. Behind it lay the memory of the girl he had married on Sun One. Zara had not lost her husband; but Ben, her husband, in this copy at least, had lost his wife forever. And it hurt.

THREE

*

Although the boy named Fifteenth was strong,
launching himself from the ground was very hard work,
only for emergencies. When at last he began to run out
of strength on his first long flight across the plain toward Knife-in-the-Sky he was careful to choose a spot
where hillocks gave him a small height advantage for
the next launch. A tall tree would have been better, but
here there were only fire-trees and bee-trees, and neither was any good for climbing. When you climbed fire-
trees no matter how careful you were some of the fire
clung to your skin and, although it did not seem to do
immediate harm, after a time you sickened and died.
And bee-trees, of course, were guarded by their bees.
These were not really bees in any sense, but they shared
with Earthly bees a disposition to assault invaders en
masse, so the boy avoided them.

He did not sleep on his first landing, only ate from
the stocks he carried, rested drowsily for a thousand
breaths, and then launched himself again. It was unsat-
isfying flying over the marshes that he soon encountered. There were few updrafts, and only weak ones, to
climb in. Nearer home, generations of wingmen had located reliable springs of rising air in many places—
where the lowest slopes of the mountain shaped the
wind, or where for some reason the ground was always
warm. But he was at the edge of the known world already, as far as his people were concerned. He could
recognize some helpful signs. Nearly always fire-trees
meant rising air, not because the trees themselves were

warm but because they only grew in warm soil. But the stands of fire-trees here in the marshes were spindly and infrequent. Better than nothing. Not very good.

So he climbed mostly with the power of his lean, long arms and chest muscles, and flying was steady work. Better than walking. Still, not good.

It did not matter. The boy's purpose held, and after every rest or meal or sleep he launched himself again and drove on toward Knife-in-the-Sky.

He had known that mountain all his life, but he hadn't known how far it was. He slept twenty-three times crossing the alternating marsh and flatlands past the edge of the grass, and eighteen times more crossing what was pure marsh, where he could rest only on hillocks and the steamy mist that rose around him while he slept was malodorous and cloying. Each time he knotted the count into the cord around his throat when he woke, and looked toward Knife-in-the-Sky; and still it seemed no larger.

Beyond the marshes he crossed an endless carpet of thick, bright moss that had a queerly sharp smell which he associated with the electrical storms that rolled around the upper reaches of his mountain—but he had no name for "ozone." Something in the air above the mossland made him sneeze. The moss bore no fruit and it gave him no game. He counted twenty-eight sleeps on his way across it, and came out giddy with hunger and thirst.

He came down, with the last of his strength, on the bank of a shallow river that rimmed the moss world. Flying off again would be hard work, but it couldn't be helped. He knelt and drank the black water until he began to feel ill, and then looked for food in the forest on the far bank. Its plants were club-shaped and leafless, shining with their own cold light like dwarfed, warped fire-trees. Shining daggers of thorns guarded the hard red nuts they bore. He picked a few doubtfully, and looked farther. But there was none of the game he knew from the grasslands near his home, none of the fleet four-legged herd animals, or the horned, two-legged hoppers. His arrows killed a small weakly flying thing that fed on the nuts, but its flesh was tasteless and dry. He roasted some of the nuts, and felt sicker after eating them than he had before.

He summoned the strength to pitch his wings together to make a tent, pegged against one of the club-shaped trees. He rolled inside, curled up in a ball, and tried to sleep. It was not easy. The boy had never known what insomnia was, but he had heard old people speak of it sometimes and now he understood what they meant. He was drained and aching. For the first time he began to wonder if he were not as crazy as his brother had said. His brains truly felt as if they were bound to the ground. His thoughts could not rise and fly over him; they were limited to fear and misery and depression.

After a time he decided that he must eat, no matter what, and rose again.

Here in the marshes the sky was darker than on the slopes of his mountain; there were fewer fire-trees, and the light from the steely bright moss on the far side of the river was of little help. The boy had never heard of concepts like "day" or "night." He had never seen a sun in his sky, or for that matter a moon or stars. There were none to be seen, except for the occasional rare coils of silvery haze that, he had no way of knowing, were distant galaxies. One time was as good as another to sleep, or to eat, or to hunt. But he was not used to being hungry or ill.

It made him feel dizzy and faint, and when he crawled out of his wing-tent and saw the bright cube that whirled away out of sight he thought at first it was the imagining of sickness.

Sick as he was, his brain cleared almost at once. Once or twice before, in the long flights over grass and marsh and moss, he had thought he had glimpsed something small and bright and far behind. But it had always hung just at the threshold of visibility. He knew that the

Watchers traveled in huge things that were bright and shiny. But this did not seem very large, nor did it ever come closer. He had heard of the small new Watchers that his brother had told him about. Was this one of them? He could not say.

All he could be sure of was that it had not harmed him so far, at least, and certainly there would never be a better chance to do him harm than while he lay shaking and weak in the wing-tent.

It gave him much to think about, but he could think without fear, for somehow he did not believe that this small Watcher intended to hurt him.

Curiously, the effort of thinking, perhaps also the sense that some sort of creature was not far away, even if hiding, seemed to sharpen his mind and his will. He stood up, drank again from the river, and began to search for the sprays of flame-bright red bloom he had seen from the air. These marked a thick-rooted plant. When he found them he dug out roots, and found among them nests of blood-red worms that, he thought, he had heard the older wingmen of his people describe as edible in bad times.

The roots were sweet and white and good, the worms less good. They were gritty and revolting raw, but he made a fire and soon learned to clean them of their digestive sacs before broiling them. He made his first satiating meal in many sleeps, rolled back into the wing-tent, and slept soundly and well. He stayed by the river bank for three more sleeps, and then felt strong enough to pack himself with roots and smoked worms and go on again.

He flew steadily and low, saving his wasted energy, careful with the now-worn bands of his harness. He strained his neck with watching, ceaselessly scanning the sky all around for orgs, or Watchers, or for another sight of the small Watcher that had fled from him by the river—all the time searching the forest for food, studying the horizon for signs of updrafts that might help him.

The dully glowing forests sloped sharply upward now. He slept seven times in a belt of fog and rain. With Knife-in-the-Sky now lost in the lowering sky his target was gone. He set his course as much as he could by following the upward slopes. When those signs failed, or were doubtful, he drew from his harness the one gift his mother had given him that had been her father's.

The crystal-cased object that glittered like the small Watcher was the size of the boy's thumb. Inside it a needle spun about, but ever seemed to quiver toward a single direction with the end that was brighter than the other. His mother had not known much about it, except that the wingmen of her people used the devices to mark the direction of flight when landmarks failed.

The air grew cooler as he climbed. When he camped for one sleep on a moss-grown rock he woke shivering and chilled. He crept stiffly from beneath his tented wings and found the low clouds gone.

He looked up and caught his breath.

Knife-in-the-Sky filled all the world ahead. The forests lifted toward it forever, rising piles of pale brown and gray and ivory, splashed with vast black masses of fallen stone.

So high he had to stretch his neck to look, the mountain itself rose out of those broken boulders. Walls of dead rock marched up and at the top of that unclimbable wall, higher than he could imagine, the jagged summit slashed across the rippling colors of the sky.

He studied that summit for a long time, looking for orgs while the damp wind that blew down the slopes of the mountain numbed him with unexpected cold. He knew they were there. They were always there, when they were not sweeping down to the lower slopes and the marsh and the grasslands and forests, seeking their prey. Perhaps those distant black spots, so hard to distinguish from the motes of dust that one sees on the surface of one's own eye, were orgs; he could not tell. Whatever, they were still a long way off. He stepped back to see more clearly over that giddy wall, felt a sudden gust as he was caught off stride; and the ground slid away under him. He grabbed wildly for the anchor rope that secured his tented wings, but his chilled fingers slid off it. The wind spun him off the rock; he flailed his arms, trying to get his balance; the moss was slippery, the cold had made him clumsy and he went sprawling over the edge.

The fall was only twenty times his own height—say, a hundred and fifty feet by Earth measures—so there was no real danger. Even without wings he could glide to some extent, as Earthly sky divers used to direct their fall before allowing their chutes to open. He picked out a landing spot where a bank of crimson moss promised some cushion, stretched out his arms, writhed with his body, spun around like a cat dropped from a table, and landed not too badly, considering the sluggishness of his muscles from the cold. A pink cloud of spores rose around his plowing feet and half blinded him. He sprawled, sneezing and choking, and then stood up and looked around.

The clouds below had shifted, and he could see across the great bowl of marsh and plain almost to the slopes of his own mountain. Past the brown and yellow slopes beneath him, the moss world made an endless sea; past it, the marshes, overhung with cloud, traced with thin black lines of rivers. In the hollows white fog lay.

He had not realized home was so far, but he could spare no thought for it. He turned and looked up the rock to where his tented wings and supplies were. Without wings he could not fly, but he could still climb; unfortunately, the rock was very steep and he could not trust his stiffened fingers to seek out holds in its crevices. He would have to climb the long way around.

The boy had no lack of practice in climbing, but as a wingman he disliked it very much. Without wings it could be dangerous. The combination of low gravity and dense atmosphere that his world possessed made the lifting of mass easy, but unbalanced the equation of wind versus inertia; caught by a gust on a vertical face, it was quite possible he could be flung so far out that even the slow acceleration of his world would crush him when he struck ground again. So he sought an easy way and sprang carefully from point to point, and was concentrating so hard on his task that he almost did not see the small Watcher as it swooped past his head and then spun away upward toward the place where his gear waited for him.

The boy shrank back into a crevice in the moss and waited for attack.

The attack did not come. Actually, he had not thought it would; this small Watcher for some reason did not seem menacing to him. And yet what could it be doing with his gear? He could hear nothing. He could see nothing—then, in a flash, he saw something startling: a bright flare of golden light that washed the side of the mountain and disappeared in a moment.

Cautiously the boy eased his way out of the little fold in the terrain and stretched himself to peer upward. He listened; he looked; he smelled; he reached out with all of his senses toward the top of the rock, but there was nothing.

He knelt on folded legs for a hundred breaths, considering. Strictly speaking, there was nothing on the rock that he could not do without. Food, spear, bow, wings, harness—he could not make them as well as the specialists among his people, but he could make them well enough to get buy. The wings and harness would be the most difficult, but he had seen enough of his brother's work to know that replacing them would not be impossible.

Still . . . the thing was, the gear on the top of the rock was his gear, and he wanted it back.

If the small Watchers were the same as the big ones there would be no question. His only option would be to flee, and that would almost certainly be useless, if his brother's stories were halfway true. But he did not think there was any hostility stored in the glittering little cube he had seen.

So with great daring, very slowly and cautiously at first but then more quickly and openly, the boy made his way around a boss on the mountainside, up and over it, and emerged higher than the rock where he had slept, looking down on it, an easy spring from it.

He had not known what to expect, but he had not expected what he saw.

The cube was no longer just a cube. It hung in air a yard above the moss, not far from his wing-tent, steady as if it were nailed there, not dipping or even trembling in the winds. But it was growing something. From one face of it a glowing, filmy bubble of something was spreading to form a sphere almost the height of the boy—then taller, while he watched.

The sphere stopped growing. The boy looked and pondered, wondering whether to approach. For dozens of breaths nothing happened, unless a shadowy sort of movement inside the sphere was real, and was something happening.

The boy could see his gear, waiting for him. He could detect no harm in the cube or in the bubble.

He did not come to a conscious decision; but in a moment he discovered that his legs were gathering under him and he sprang toward the top of the rock. He turned in air to bring his feet under him, landed well, spun around to face the small Watcher.

And then something did happen. There was another flash of that intense golden explosion of silent light, and for a moment he was blinded. And when he could see again at all he saw that the bubble was burst open, sliced from within, like an org's egg with the hatchling just coming out; and out of it was stepping—what? A man? Short, fat, squat, dark, curiously clothed—but yes, a man!

FOUR
*

The figure that came out of the bubble was twice as broad as the boy, and nearly a head shorter. To the boy it looked like one of his own people, but somehow squashed down and wearing strange bright clothing such as he had never seen before.

The wingmen and their women wore no more than they had to: the harness to hold their wallets and fasten to their wings, a few square inches of cloth or shaved leather for ornament, a few more for modesty.

By the boy's standards, the man was fearsomely over-dressed. His clothing covered nearly all of him. From waist to feet he wore a sort of bright yellow leotard, ending under bright-colored soft boots. From waist to shoulders he wore a sleeveless tunic. His wrists were ornamented with broad, bright-colored bands that looked as if they had the feel of leather, but were colored in blues and greens and mauves; they held little pouches and bright shiny things that glittered and seemed to move. Even the man's head was covered, with a soft cap which (the boy did not know) could come down to protect his eyes against dust or glare, or if need be could shield the entire upper part of him against rain or cold. And that was a bright orange color; taken all in all, the man was queerly and fear-somely garbed, the boy marveled. With such apparel he could never hope to avoid being seen by org or Watcher or game!

His costume and his queer proportions were not all that was queer about him. Even his face was strange.

He was surely much older than the boy, two or three thousand sleeps at least. But his face did not show it. It was not weathered or lined from wind or storm. His teeth were bright and even, as perfect as the boy's own, and far more so than, say, those of the boy's older brother, who had used them to nip off ends of leather for the five thousand sleeps of his adult life.

All this the boy saw in the same photographic glance in which he observed that the man carried no weapon. None at all; neither bow nor knife. Not even a club. Even so, the boy judged, he might not be without danger. His squat frame had the look of strength.

The man took a step toward the boy. It was not menacing. It was comic. The boy had never seen anything like it; the man's step was grotesquely energetic, it propelled him unmeaning into the air. He came down, stumbled, caught himself, fell again in overreaction, and sprawled to the ground. The expression on his broad face was funnier than his ungainly tumbling act itself. The boy could not help laughing. From the ground the man laughed, too.

Then the man stood up, quite carefully, with a wink and exaggerated caution. He spread his hands as if to show he had no weapons. The boy knew that already; he made no move.

The man, slowly and carefully, as if to show that he meant no harm, grasped one wrist with the fingers of the other hand and did something to the shiny baubles on it. Then he spoke to the boy.

When he did, his voice came from two places at once. It came from his mouth in the normal way. Another voice, harsher and more metallic than his own, came stumbling from the bauble on his wrist. The sounds from the thing on his wrist were not the same as the sounds from his mouth, but the boy could understand neither of them. He bent his head in the gesture of negation.

The man looked as if he were irritated with his toy. He touched it again, and spoke once more.

This time the boy thought he caught the suggestion of a word. Strangely, it came from the man's wrist, not his mouth. It sounded rather like the word the boy's people used for "what?" But there was more to it, and the rest was gibberish.

The man shrugged and let his arm fall to his side. Then he grinned, touched his chest, and said a single word. The sound of it was "Ben." The man waited inquiringly, as if expecting a response.

The boy was not sure what was expected of him, other than that the man seemed to want him to speak. The man gestured, pointed to his wrist, and made several other sounds. One sounded like "Pmal," pronounced very slowly and carefully, but what it meant the boy had no idea.

He said slowly, "I don't know what you want me to do."

The man applauded, grinned, motioned for more.

"Well," the boy said, "I am Fifteenth of the men in my people." He paused, a little suspiciously, but the man urged him on. It seemed foolish, but there did not seem to be anything dangerous in it. Hesitantly he went on: "But I am far from my people and no longer one of them," he soliloquized. "So perhaps I can have only a word-name, like an outlaw or a woman. Are you an outlaw? But I am going to get an org's egg. I will hatch it and tame the org. Perhaps I will call myself Org Rider!" he finished, and fell silent, listening to the pleasing sound of the name in his mind's ear.

Excited, the man touched his wrist and spoke again. This time the words from his wrist made sense; they were poorly pronounced, but clearly enough they said: "I am Ben. You are Org Rider!"

From the boy's expression the man saw that communication had begun. His own face reflected joy. He spoke again, and the thing on his wrist stuttered, emitted a few nonsense syllables, and then, very clearly, said: "My people far."

He gestured for the boy to speak on.

But the boy had heard another sound. Frowning, he turned to search the sky.

It was a strangely ominous sound, like the hum of a bee-tree. The boy's first thought was *Org!* Yet the sound was wrong, not the harsh scream his mother had described, but even more fearsome.

Then he saw it: a faint gray glint against the polychrome sky, diving toward them, very fast.

Watcher!

It was like a spearpoint arrowing toward them in the sky; it had no wings, but it moved so fast the boy could hardly realize what was happening. The man heard it, too. Astonishment spread across his broad face. He turned, bounced toward the silently hovering small Watcher, fell clumsily but righted himself and touched it with quick, skillful hands.

At once one face of the small Watcher flared with a bright golden flame, and a bubble began to grow out of it.

The boy did not stand watching this performance. He ran for his weapons. He did not know what good they would be against a Watcher, but he had no other options open to him than to use them.

A bright flash of light from above gave him a split second's warning, then something crashed nearby. Queer sudden yellow flowers bloomed on the black rock, and faded into pale smoke. A sharp reek of burning choked him.

The bubble from the side of the small Watcher had grown tall as the boy now; abruptly it flared brightly gold. Unfortunately for the boy he was staring directly at it when it happened. For a moment he was blinded. Bright lights were out of his experience entirely, except for lightning and the smoky glow of a campfire; the eyes of his people did not have quick recovery mechanisms, since they had no sun in their sky to contend with and no need. He clawed at his eyes in acute pain. He could not distinguish just what was happening.

The man named Ben was clawing at the bubble,

trying to drag out of it some glittering object that had appeared inside. The boy could not recognize it; he could barely see the outlines, could barely see when again there was that sudden crash, and a flash of light behind and above him, and yellow flame and smoke exploded on Ben himself. The boy heard a terrible scream, felt splinters of rock as they tore at his flesh, smelled a queerly hot choking odor that took his breath.

Then blackness drowned him. His bow was in his hand, but he had not had time to raise it, or even see what it was that had killed Ben and was almost killing himself.

Consciousness returned, out of a crazy pain-filled fantasy that was not a dream but a memory. He lay face down on hard, wet gravel. He was shivering to a cold, slow rain.

His first thought was astonishment at being alive, his second to get his wings to wrap around him, covering his nakedness against the rain.

When he tried to move something wrapped around his neck, so tight that he could hardly breathe, tugged him back.

Panic shook him. He tugged at the coil around his neck; it would not loosen. His hand flashed to his knife, but it was gone. He was tied by the neck, like a food-beast awaiting slaughter.

Sitting up more carefully, he saw that he was tied to a great machine, spearhead-shaped, that lay on the gravel. It was mottled in brown and yellow, but under it was the glint of silvery metal.

Ten paces away lay the squat butchered corpse of Ben. A faint pathetic mechanical squeal came from the silvery cube of the small Watcher that had brought him; it would bring no one ever again, for the explosion that had killed Ben had blasted it as well, and it lay sparking feebly, cracked and broken, on the gravel.

"Good to see you awake, boy!"

The booming voice caught Org Rider by surprise. He moved suddenly and was jerked back by the choking coil around his neck. When he caught his balance he saw a man, taller than himself, red-bearded, green-eyed, half grinning, rocking on his feet by the small pile of the boy's weapons and wings.

"Who are you?" the boy demanded.

"Why," the man said, "you can call me Redlaw. You're a long way from home, Fifteenth."

The boy kept off his face the sinking astonishment that this man knew his name. "I am not Fifteenth any-more," he said stubbornly. "My name is Org Rider."

The man's laugh boomed out. "An Org Rider without an org? Your brother was right, boy, you're a fool." Then he said, not unkindly, "Oh, don't be surprised. The Watchers don't only watch. They listen as well. We've been listening to you for a long time."

"How?" the boy cried. "I never saw you before!" The man only shrugged and smiled. "I've never seen any Watcher," the boy said. "And you have never been on our mountain I am certain."

"You're making a wrong assumption," the man said. "I'm not a Watcher. I work for them. As butcher in their galleys"—he gestured at the bloodstained apron he wore—"and sometimes as translator, when they want to know what people like you are saying. But I know you are truthful when you say you've never seen a Watcher, because they don't look a bit like you or me."

"Then where are the Watchers?" Org Rider cried.

"You'll see them soon enough." The man stirred the boy's weapons with a foot, and peered at the boy out of shrewd green eyes. "It's not you they care about, you know," he said suddenly. "It's your dead friend here. What do you know about him?"

"Nothing," Org Rider said proudly, fighting back the pain and dizziness that were tearing at him. Dried blood on his arms and in his hair showed where he had been struck. No one had troubled to do anything about it while he was unconscious. "He appeared from nowhere. I do not know how. I had never seen him before. This is true."

"Oh," Redlaw said, "I believe you. Whether the watchers will or not is something else. But you'll find out—one way or another—because here they come now."

A section out of the middle of the ship dropped flat, to make a wide door and a ramp. Five creatures came flapping out and dropped to the rock around Redlaw, staring from a distance at the boy.

Though they waddled on two legs when they were not flying, they did not look human. They were squat and powerful-looking, like the man who had died so quickly and uselessly. Even more so; they were hardly half the height of Org Rider or Redlaw. But the ways in which they differed from human were extreme.

They wore slick bright armor that looked as if it grew on them, black on their humped backs and red on their bellies; an Earthling would have thought of an insect's chitin, but there were no true insects for comparison in the boy's world. Their armored arms looked thick and muscular, and their wings were yellow-streaked leather—it looked frighteningly like tanned human skin to the boy—that stretched from their arms to their stubby legs. Their faces were beaked. They had no necks. Wide black flexible ears spread out from each side of their beaks. Their multiple eyes were greenish bulges, set on each side of the head, protruding out, behind the ears.

Their hands horrified the boy when he looked at them more closely. For fingers they had short, boneless bundles of what looked like squirming pink foodworms. These twisting worms were palping every seam of his tented wings, every strap of his flying gear.

They emitted a foul odor that struck him in a suffocating wave. It took his breath and stung his eyes, with a sour scent like death-weeds burning. Even Redlaw, who clearly had had opportunity to get used to it, was wrinkling his nose and showing distaste.

The creatures squeaked to each other and then paused, with big ears spread, as if expecting an answer. One of them was holding the needled guide that had been his mother's gift, the direction-showing trinket. The boy shouted: "That's mine! You have no right to rob me!"

"Easy, boy," Redlaw said tightly. "You're very close to being dead right now. Don't push it."

The Watchers squeaked to each other, then once again went through the routine of palping his wings, his garments, his waterskin, his firepot, knife, coils of rope, empty pots. Then they moved, like stumps rocking across the graveled rock, to where the dead man lay. They did not touch him, perhaps from fear. But they squeaked again, this time peremptorily.

Redlaw scowled uneasily, and puckered his lips to whistle some sort of message. It was not much like the squeaks of the Watchers but it was as close as a human could come, Org Rider thought; and the Watchers seemed to understand it. They replied.

Redlaw nodded and turned to the boy. "I've told them what you say. Two of them think you are lying. One thinks you are too stupid to lie. The other two have not yet made up their minds."

The boy was silent, letting that information soak through his brain.

"You see," Redlaw said, "this strange-looking fellow here is very disconcerting to them." He squinted thoughtfully at the racked body that lay staring sightlessly at nothing. "In a way they know that what you say is true. In another way, they are not sure. Why did he come to you, boy? By accident? They'll never believe that."

"I know nothing more than what I've told you," said Org Rider stubbornly. "If I die for it."

"You just might," Redlaw observed mildly, then flinched as a blast of whistling came from the Watchers.

In quite a different tone he demanded: "Why don't you carry the Watchman's eye?"

"What is it?"

"The talisman of their service!" Redlaw touched a sort of medallion he wore around his own neck. "Like this, boy! To show you are their friend and servant, like me!"

"My people are not servants," the boy declared.

"Maybe that used to be true," Redlaw acknowledged. "Your people lived almost out of range. But times are changing. This fellow here is making them change. I think you will go away from here wearing an eye if you go away at all, Org Rider."

A burst of peremptory whistling, and two of the Watchers waddled toward the boy. The yellow coil around his neck tightened, half-strangling him, forcing him to his knees. The man warned: "Don't resist them, boy! It's your life."

The bitter reek set him sneezing even while he gasped for breath. A leather wing slapped him into silence, knocked him down. A hot, hard-armored body fell on him, and those pink, writhing fingers searched his body, prying into mouth and nostrils, anus and ears. The weight, the pain, the indignity, the lack of air all combined to fill the boy with a helpless fury. He could not cope with it, he could only rage inside himself, in pain and fear, until at last the weight came off him and the Watchers took their foul reek away, whistling disagreeably among themselves.

What they were doing was at that moment of no interest to the boy. He was preoccupied inside himself. He had never been so treated. He had never been so helpless, not even when the girl he was interested in had whispered to him that she had pledged to marry his brother, not even when he was tiny and his mother died. Not ever.

In pain and anger, Org Rider was conscious of one certainty. Whatever happened, he would see the Watchers paid for this.

* * *

At length Redlaw's voice boomed: "You can stand up, boy. I've made a deal for you."

He whistled sharply, and the yellow rope fell away from the boy's neck.

"You're to wear the watchman's eye," Redlaw ordered. "It will show them everything you see. If you have any further contact with these funny-looking fellows, they want to know about it."

"What if I refuse?" the boy blazed.

Redlaw scowled. "I don't care what you do!" he shouted. "It's your life." He tapped the square-bladed knife at his waist. "Maybe I didn't tell you that they have a taste for human flesh."

The boy said staunchly, more staunchly than he felt, "I'll throw it away the minute you leave me."

"Tie it to a bubble-seed if you want," Redlaw grumbled. "If they know you do it they'll kill you. If they don't—it's your gamble, not mine."

He paused, looking toward the ship. From the gaping hatch a sixth, and larger, Watcher flapped down. It was darker than the others as well as bigger, its stubby wings almost black. It flew directly to Org Rider and caught him in a reeking hug, clasping something around his neck. "Careful now!" Redlaw shouted, but the boy had already taught himself not to resist. It lasted only a moment, then the large Watcher fell away.

The object was a heavy black globe, twice the size of the ball of Org Rider's thumb. A slick black cord of some sort of leather held it around his neck.

"Our captain asked me to tell you," Redlaw said, "that if you take it off he will do you the honor to eat you himself." He glanced over his shoulder. The captain of the Watchers had already returned to the ship; the others were flapping slowly after him, no longer appearing interested in the boy or in the body.

"Good-bye, Org Rider," the man said, almost reluctantly, as if he had more he wanted to say.

If he had, he did not say it. He turned away and

entered the ship. The hatch closed. At once, a small curved shell tipped down outside the longer shell of the ship. Something whined. A gust of warm wind sent the boy rocking away across the gravel, sliding onto the moss.

The ship rose and slid whining away through the sky. Org Rider watched it until he was sure it was not coming back.

Then he set about gathering his lost gear. None of it was gone, or badly damaged, though it was scattered all over the rock and all of it stank of the death-weed reek of the Watchers.

As soon as he had it, he strapped his harness on, loaded himself with what he had to carry. His torn body was sending messages of pain from the crusted wounds in scalp and arms, and his stomach fought against the clinging reek of the Watchers. He put them out of his mind. He did not even look again at the dead creature who had appeared out of the bubble, or the glittering, broken toy that had brought him.

He turned his back on the campsite that had become so hateful to him, launched himself into the air, turned, and with great, painful strokes continued toward the distant peak of Knife-in-the-Sky. He did not look back.

FIVE

More than a hundred million miles away, far beyond the great broad curve of the horizon, the spinning wheel of the orbiter marched through its endless sweep.

On it Ben Pertin turned away from the monitor screen. The image it showed was as cracked and shattered as the small cube of the monitor itself. All it showed was a ghastly view of Ben's own dead, staring eye, peering emptily forever up into the gaudily clouded sky of Cuckoo.

Ben looked guiltily at the silvery girl he called Venus. He did not think even an alien like her would fail to see the emotions on his face, and he was not proud of those emotions. It was an unsettling thing to see oneself die. The Ben Pertin who had just had his skull smashed and his body blasted on the distant surface of Cuckoo was as much himself as this other body he was inhabiting here, in the orbiting wheel of the survey satellite.

"I'm sorry, Venus," he said.

"Sorry?" she fluted.

He said, "I guess that was a bust. Well, we've learned something from it. First and most important, next time we send somebody down we'd better arm him for bear. No more waiting till he asks for weapons, and trying to get them to him in a hurry."

"Concurred," said Venus. "Also editing appears necessary due to the gravity differential."

"Right. That one-percent gravity is tricky. I—*he* was sprawling all over the place." Ben Linc Pertin managed

115

a smile. "I've never been transmitted in an edited form before," he said. "I don't know how well I like the idea."

"It does not hurt, Ben Linc."

"Of course not."

The silvery girl curled one wing and moved closer to him, studying him carefully. "It is established," she said in her chiming voice, "that my people and Scorpian robots, for example, experience less ego displacement in transmission than do you or, for example, the T'Worlie. Suggestion. One of us can go on the next transmission to the surface of Cuckoo."

"That's an idea. We'll keep it in mind," Ben Linc said. In his heart he knew he didn't want to do it that way. When the next transmission went, he would make it. There were two reasons, one practical, the other not. The practical reason was that, confusing and inexplicable though it was, Earthmen *looked* like the people who roamed this portion of the surface of Cuckoo. With editing, to stretch them out and reduce their musculature, they would look even more so; and the first job of communication with them, building up the store of language that the Pmal translators needed to work, was difficult enough even so. Asking one of these primitives to talk to a robot, or to a T'Worlie, or to a creature like the silvery girl was out of the question.

The other reason was the important one. Ben Linc Pertin had thought it over carefully and, all in all, he had no particular reason to want to go on living.

Ben Pertin was not the first human being in the history of the race to reach that conclusion. It happened often enough, for reasons far more trivial than his own. The thing that graveled Ben Pertin, almost more than the real pains and troubles that infested his head, was that his options were curiously circumscribed. With tachyon transmission, you could die and die and die . . . and still be alive. However many times Ben Pertin let the tachyon scanners memorize his body structure and translate an exact duplicate to the surface of

Cuckoo, and however many times that duplicate met a gory death, he would still be alive in orbit. And he would still be hurting.

Other men in his position could fling their lives away in a reckless gamble against death, and find oblivion. He could not. The only gamble he could take was in a fixed game that he could not lose. It made a mockery of courage . . .

"I said," the silvery girl repeated tonelessly, "the T'Worlie Nammie is speaking to you.'

"Oh, sorry." Ben Linc shook himself into attention and attempted a smile to the butterfly-winged being that hung in the air beside him. "Hi, Nammie. What's new?"

"Theory," the T'Worlie whistled. "FARLINK proposes explication of tachyon interference."

"Really?" Ben Linc was diverted from his internal pain. "What's that?"

"FARLINK identifies sourse of interference as exogenous to Cuckoo. Originates elsewhere. Trace-scanning, locates source as tight-beam signal generated in our own Galaxy. Vector closely equivalent to that of human sun, called Sol."

Pertin frowned blankly at the little bat-winged creature.

"I don't know about that," he muttered blankly. "It doesn't seem reasonable. After all, there is only one tachyon station on Earth capable of this distance and that's locked in to Sun One. Certainly it couldn't interfere with reception here—"

"FARLINK adds," shrilled the T'Worlie, fluttering up and down on its bright butterfly wings, "interfering signal can be identified as mating call of female of human species, beamed from your home world, called Earth, to self, here."

"Ridiculous!" Ben Linc exploded. "Nammie, that's insane! Why—"

He paused as a strong ammonia scent made him

sneeze. "Wait a minute," he said. "What does that smell mean?"

"Query: *Smell,* Ben Linc?"

"The gaseous emission, which registers in my chemical-stimuli-detecting nerve sensors. I know you T'Worlie express emotions chemically."

"It is laughter," the T'Worlie shrilled triumphantly.

"Ah," said Ben Linc, satisfied at last. "Then that was a joke."

"Confirmation," the T'Worlie cried. "Successful one, query?"

"Pretty good. Sorry. You caught me off guard, or I would have laughed, too."

A whiff of etherlike sweetness expressed the T'Worlie analog of hurt. "Regret joke unsuccessful," Nammie piped sadly. "Not all of communication falsified for purposes of humor. True that FARLINK locates source as near Earth in vector, distance not confirmed. Extreme attenuation of signal renders distance estimate undependable."

"Strange," the silvery girl chimed. "Perhaps we should instruct FARLINK to assemble conjectural explanations of this phenomenon."

"You two go ahead," Ben Linc said. "I have to get some sleep."

"We will carry on while you are unconscious," the T'Worlie whistled. Neither he nor Venus slept themselves, and they were critical of human slumber. "Personal conjecture: Whatever explanations, they will complicate our mission."

And indeed they would, thought Ben Linc Pertin as he headed toward his living quarters, out at the higher-gravity shell of the satellite. There should be no random tachyonic transmissions coming in, especially from the Galaxy itself, where all known tachyon sources had been long since identified, located, and compensated for. It was one more irritation in a life that had become increasingly overweighted on the downbeat side.

"What I need," Ben Linc murmured to himself, "is a meal, a bath, and bed. In that order."

There would not be much pleasure there either, to be sure. The meal would be out of a dry-pack and into a microwave oven, and it would taste like it. With only three human beings on the wheel, and a dozen other races with different diets also aboard, there was not much space to waste on epicurean cookery. The bath would be not much better. The wheel was in freefall, so the only way to bathe was through a sort of hosedown from jets inside a thing like a huge bottle, and it was all business, even after you learned how to get clean without inhaling several gallons of water. And the bed, of course, would be solitary.

Ben Pertin hurled himself out of the communications room, in a savage mood. He was the first human being to reach this point in space, tens of thousands of light-years outside the galactic spiral.

He was a conqueror, by any standards the history books could measure.

What he felt like was a victim.

Pertin's "bed" was a cocoon. It felt like a prison. Fed and bathed, he floated in it but could not sleep.

There was a sore place in his mind to which his consciousness always returned, like something caught in a tooth that the tongue cannot resist probing.

That something was himself. Another self: the Ben Pertin from which he had been copied. That Ben Pertin was forty thousand light-years away, in the artificial satellite that hung in the Orion gas cloud and was called Sun One. To Ben Linc Pertin, he seemed both farther, in the sense of being something unattainable, and closer than his own skin.

That other Ben Pertin—Ben Charles—would be enjoying the domestic pleasures of marriage, as well as an interesting and productive career with all the amenities Sun One offered its citizens. Lucky man, thought Ben Linc, hating him.

Yet that man too was himself. Only a couple of months earlier they had been not only identical but coincident. That was before Ben Linc had come here. He remembered perfectly well what had happened. He had got up that morning out of the arms of his new bride, kissed her good-bye, but only as any suburban commuter kisses his wife good-bye at the station, and entered into the tachyon-transmission chamber on Sun One.

There the tachyon beams had scanned his body, built up a pattern of atoms and molecules and transmitted that pattern on the super-speed waves of the tachyons, the particles whose *lower* limiting velocity is the speed of light. And that pattern had been received here, on the orbiting wheel that spun around the strange astronomical object called Cuckoo, forty thousand light-years away. And here it had been reconstructed, atom for atom and link for link.

So on Sun One, one Ben Pertin had walked out of the chamber, in no way different than he had gone in. He had done whatever he had had to do in the balance of that working day, and at the end of it returned again to Zara, his/their wife.

But on the wheel, another Ben Pertin had floated out of the receiving chamber and had felt the instant shock of knowing that he had lost the gamble. He was the one on the wheel, which he looked at with some curiosity but not much pleasure.

If you had put the two Ben Pertins side by side, no clue could have told you which was "original" and which "copy." Both were originals. Neither was a copy—except in some abstract, irrelevant sense that meant nothing when it was considered that each had a complete store of everything Ben Pertin had ever had, from DNA linkage to the last, most evanescent, half-gone memory of infancy.

There was only one real difference: one was *there*, the other was *here*. One was living a normal life on Sun

One. The other was doing a necessary job, without joy, on the orbiter, which he would never leave.

That was the paradox of tachyon transmission: since it was only a pattern that was transmitted, the object being transmitted remained unchanged. No matter how often you left, you always stayed behind.

Ben Linc Pertin tossed angrily against the restraining web of his cocoon. That was the damned unfair part of it! his mind cried. Why couldn't Zara join him?

It would cost her nothing! Like him, one of her would walk out of the tachyon chamber on Sun One, the other would be here. They would be together. He would be no longer alone . . .

He groaned resentfully, angrily, petulantly.

The worst part of his resentment was that, in the end, it was directed against himself. It was his own fault that Zara was not here now. It was he who had persuaded her not to come with him at first, not until the orbiter had been made more comfortable. She had wanted to come. But she had listened to him, finally agreed, promised to come later.

Lying deceitful promise! Now she not only had not come, she would not even answer his tachyon messages. Not for weeks! First he had suggested she might come—then asked outright—finally pleaded. No answer.

When Ben Linc Pertin finally fell asleep, his dreams were harsh and punitive.

He woke in time for an all-hands review of the material gathered on Cuckoo.

In all, there were forty-one beings living on the orbiter at that moment, counting collective entities as a single creature. They fit nicely into a cylindrical chamber not much more than fifteen feet across, partly because most of them were rather smaller than human beings, mostly because in free-fall, placement was volumetric rather than planar. The sole T'Worlie acted as sort of general chairman for the meeting. Out of the bat's head perched on his butterflylike body he squeaked a short sentence, and all around the room the Pmal translators of the various beings rendered it into their own languages:

"I will display the information gathered so far on Cuckoo."

In the center of the chamber a stereostage display quickened into life. It showed a deep red sphere, floating in nothingness. There was no hint of size, because there was nothing nearby to compare it with; but the voice accompaniment to the display began to give the values for its physical characteristics, and all the Pmal translators faithfully relayed the information to their owners. Radius, slightly under one A.U. Mass, about equal to Sol. Density, very low—less than what in some Earthly laboratories was considered a hard vacuum. And yet the thing had a solid surface.

This was a familiar wonder to Ben Linc and the other beings, but they listened anyway. So much about Cuckoo was still unbelievable, even now. Not only did it have a surface, but on that surface creatures lived. The sphere grew and broke off a section, which expanded, turning slowly to present itself to each of the creatures in the room. It grew larger, and they were looking down on a landscape between two enormous mountains, and there was the strangest thing of all. Not only did creatures live there; they were creatures biologically close to some races of the Galaxy itself.

That was impossible.

Cuckoo had never been part of the Galaxy. Its present course was aimed arrow-straight at the Orion arm of the Galaxy. It had clearly been on that course for a very long time, and it had originated somewhere else, from some starcloud other than our own.

Ben Linc Pertin, listening and watching, realized something was touching him. He turned, and it was the woman of the Purchased People who was there as proxy for some water-breathing race from a star on the far side of the Galaxy, always invisible to Earth and never named by it. She said tonelessly, "While you were sleeping, Ben Linc Pertin, this came addressed to you with the last lot of supplies."

He nodded thanks—not to her, heaven knows; the imprisoned personality inside the skull neither expected thanks nor would know what to do with it; but to the distant mollusklike creature that owned her and operated through her body.

He was about to turn back to the hologram, when he realized what the woman had given him. It was a message cassette. There was no reason for anyone to send him a sealed cassette unless it was private; there was only one person who would want to send him a private message.

That person was Zara.

Suddenly Ben Linc wanted nothing so much as he wanted that meeting to end so that he could put that cassette in his private stereostage. But it wouldn't end, and he could not leave, now that the topic had turned to one of his own specialties, the meteorology of Cuckoo. Long since the orbiter had dropped automatic weather stations all along its trail, and they had begun to show tentative patterns for the climatology and airmass movements of the enormous sphere. It was only a beginning. In that immense ocean of air, the seeded stations sketched out only a line, but still Ben Linc had to summarize what was known.

As he finished, the FARLINK screens lit up with an overriding message:

"ATTENTION. PROGRESS REPORTED ON TACHYONIC INTERFERENCE. FOLLOWING SAMPLE ANALYZED."

The computer blanked out, then displayed shaped waves glowing on the screens, followed by endless strings of binary numbers, while bird chirps sounded in the speakers. "Conjecture," whispered the T'Worlie that hung beside him, a vinegary scent of excitement showing that its equivalent of adrenalin was flowing. "Analysis shows message!"

But Nammie's conjecture was wrong. The curved screens flashed again with the all-stations call indicating urgency, then lit up with the message in half a hundred scripts:

"LINGUISTIC ANALYSIS OF THIS SAMPLE NEGATIVE. TECHNICAL STUDIES, HOWEVER, IDENTIFY SIGNAL AS COMMUNICATION OF TUNING DATA FOR TACHYONIC REPLICATION TRANSMISSION. PRESUMPTION: SOME MATTER IS TO BE REPLICATED FROM CUCKOO TO SOURCE."

"Ben Linc," the silvery girl chimed in sudden comprehension, "do you understand what that means? It means we can replicate our own matter at the source of this transmission. We can send a copy of one of us! We can see where this signal comes from, by sending someone there who can report back, in a language we can understand!"

"If he lives long enough," Pertin grunted. He understood the importance of what was being said, but in his personal scale of values there was nothing quite so important as the cassette he had been clutching all this long while in his hand.

And at last he was able to excuse himself, hurl himself through the passages of the orbiter to his private cocoon, squirm in, seal, and then slip the cassette into the sterostage.

A silvery glitter of cloud sprang up before him and condensed into the face and form of Zara, his wife, looking meltingly beautiful and overpoweringly sad.

She gazed at him silently for a moment, as if unsure of what to say. And then—

"Dear Ben," she said, "I don't know how to tell you this. I'm sorry to answer you this way. The truth is, I just can't face you."

She paused, biting her lip.

"You see," she said, "I'm not going to come to join you. I know how disappointed you will feel—disappointed in me, because I promised. But I can't.

"I'm pregnant, dear," she said. She hesitated, and

added, "You know that Ben and I—I mean, *you* and I wanted to have a child. We got permission before—before you left. Well, now we're going to, in about five months.

"So you see I can't come now. It would be one thing for you and me to live on the orbiter and to know that we'll die there. Being together would make all that worthwhile. But not our baby, Ben! I just can't do that.

"Of course, after the baby is born . . . if you still want me—

"Well, we'll talk about it then. I promise you, Ben, dear, I want to be with you. All of me wants to be with all of you! There must be a way!

"But for now I can't see what it is. I—" She hesitated, then said in a rush, "I'm going to stop now, Ben, because I'm going to have to cry. I do love you! Oh, God . . ."

And the image faded and was gone, leaving Ben Linc Pertin more alone than he had ever been.

SIX

*

Org Rider washed his torn garments in a rain pool and spread them on a rock to dry, but the death-weed stench of the Watchers was still in his nostrils. He was out of the storm area now, the rock where the stranger had been killed and where the Watchers had treated him with such contempt far out of sight in the rain clouds. He was cold, and his aches and pains were enormous; but he was alive and free. It was more than he expected.

He fished bare-handed in the pool for horny brown scuttling creatures and kindled a small fire to broil them. They were quite like pond-dwellers he knew from his own mountain, and when they were cooked they tasted as good. He was overpoweringly weary, but he forced himself to catch more of the scuttlers and prop them over the fire to smoke for his pack.

Then he wrapped himself in his wings, and was immediately asleep.

When he awoke the first thing he felt was the black weight of the Watchman's eye against his throat.

His fingers closed around it, and he was close to ripping it off and throwing it in the pool. But it could not harm him while he was wearing it, he thought, and he had not forgotten the warning about what would happen to him if he took it off.

He put it out of his mind. Warm and dry, he filled his waterskin, caught and broiled one more meal of scuttlers, then strapped on his gear and dove out from the hillside to catch the wind.

He was more cautious than ever now, turning unexpectedly to search the sky behind him to see what might be following. Nothing was, neither small Watcher nor ship carrying the repellent creatures who had marked him with the thing around his neck. He was not so far from the rocky, desolate upper reaches of Knife-in-the-Sky that orgs would be unexpected. But he saw nothing like an org . . .

Until it was almost too late.

The far thin scream drew his eyes aloft. A pale brown fleck was dropping out of that high gray haze, sliding down across the long blade of the summit.

It grew as it came toward him, taking shape and color. A slim, winged fish-form of bronze and silver: the body bronze, tapering to a narrow waist behind the stubby wings; the tail and wingtips shining silver. It was beautiful and terrible.

And it was coming toward him.

Org Rider woke out of the trance that held him and realized his danger. This was not a dream, it was a creature that could kill him in a single careless rake of claw or tooth. And he was exposed in the open air, where its speed and skill were far greater than his own.

He dived, flapping desperately, staring over his shoulder to watch it come. It grew so close that he could see the shape of the individual lapped triangular scales, bronze and silver. Its powerful legs unfolded, spreading cruel black talons that stretched toward him. He closed his own wings and arrowed toward a black crevice below, where two great boulders had tumbled together. Even in that moment the beauty of the org choked his throat. To own that power! It was worth the risk of his life . . .

But it seemed his life was already forfeit; his fall was slower than the org's dive. His weapons were useless; the bow hanging from his harness, the spear impotent in this free-fall. Even the knife would only annoy the org, it could not hope to prevail against that wide red mouth spiked with shining fangs.

On impulse, without thought, he snatched the cold hard sphere of the Watchman's eye from his throat. He did not even feel the bite of the thong as it broke free. He flung it into the org's great mouth.

Confused, the creature broke away, lost momentum, soared past and away. It went by with a roar of wind and a strange falling note in its scream. It recovered almost at once, wheeled and returned . . .

But by then Org Rider was deep in the crevice between the boulders.

For many hundreds of breaths the org stayed near the crevice, moaning to itself in anger and frustration, scrabbling at the rock with its claws. Its intelligence was too high to let it come in after him; in the cramped quarters, his spear was a more deadly weapon than its claws. And yet it did not leave.

Its nest had to be nearby. Org Rider knew that nothing else would keep the creature there so long. There was prey in plenty easier to find. Mere hunger did not account for its tenacity.

The thought was like a sniff of dream-fungus, intoxicating, dizzying, a little frightening. Where there was a nest there were eggs. Where there were eggs was one to steal.

Methodically Org Rider unstrapped his wings and lightened his pack. He dared not fly so close to the org's nest. He would have to move fast, and could carry nothing that he did not urgently need. His only way to reach the nest was to thread the maze of spaces between the boulders, where the org might not see him and would hesitate to attack. He wondered briefly what had become of the Watchman's eye. Had the org swallowed it? Was it broken, so that the Watchers might come angry and avenging at any time? He could not tell.

Leaving everything behind except for knife, compass, and a coil of rope, he breathed heavily to charge his muscles, rocked to test his footing, crouched and jumped. He was only in the open for a moment, in a long surge from shelter to shelter. The org was out of sight. He could hear its baffled screaming, but did not see it and assumed it therefore did not see him.

The journey to the top of the boulder pile was long and hard, and beyond it a naked cliff rose above the highest crevice, a dozen times his height.

Org Rider could leap that far; any of his people could. Yet it tested his strength, and he would be exposed while leaping, off balance and vulnerable when he landed. He peered out, saw no org, and leaped without allowing himself time to be afraid.

He soared upward, caught the slippery rock at the rim of the cliff and pulled himself up onto it.

Before him lay a level mile of flat, black rock. In the middle of it rose a rough pink cone.

The org's nest.

Although it was in view, no more than half a dozen long leaps away, it was not yet in reach. A great org hovered over it, scales gleaming in the high blue light of the peak. It had not seen him, but if he approached it would be a matter of moments only. It would never let him reach the nest.

He needed to think. He could not remain in the open for that purpose; he spotted a narrow crevice and scuttled across the flat rock, hugging the ground as inconspicuously as he could.

He drowsed and thought for a long time, and at the end of it the solution to the problem seemed as far away as when he began. It was maddening to have come so far and to fail now. Yet where was the choice? He could stay there for a long time hoping that the guardian org would wander away. That hope was foolish. Far more likely the other org would give up its fruitless sentry duty at the crevice between the boulders or below, and come up to join its mate; and then he would have two to avoid. With two adult orgs nearby it was no longer a question of being able to steal an egg, but of survival. Sooner or later they would find him. And that would be his death.

But as he crouched and drowsed his problem was being solved for him. He did not know it at first. He heard the raucous shrieks of the org, realized tardily that there were two orgs now crying out their rage and resentment, and heard with his mind what his subconscious had been listening to for long moments: a dull, distant *slam, slam, slam* unlike any other sound he had ever heard.

Cautiously Org Rider poked his head out of the crevice and was just in time to see a brilliant flare of golden light.

Dazzled and half-blinded by afterimages, he knew at once that again one of the small Watchers was nearby. Squinting to see what was happening, he saw a naked machine in the air, quartering away from him, emitting the slamming sounds and puffs of smoke. It was curiously ugly, like a stick figure of an org or a person; it had wings, but they did not move, were rigidly extended. And the two orgs were attacking it, screaming in fierce rage. Pieces were falling from it, broken bits that scattered down across the face of the mountain. One seemed to have the shape of a man, and it was from it that the yellow flare had come. But if it was a man he had forgotten his wings and did not know how to hand-soar to guide his landing; he tumbled end over end, disappearing from sight. The machine itself slammed crazily on.

There would never be a better chance.

Blind and caught unawares, Org Rider knew he had to act. He did not stop to think. He was out of the crevice and leaping for the pink cone in less than a breath.

Now was when he needed wings! But he did not have them, and so could only leap, guide himself with his hands, come down with his legs already under him, and leap again. He could hear the distant *slam-slam* of the machine, and the scream of the orgs, but he dared not leap high enough to see what they were doing, lest the orgs see what *he* was doing. At least the sounds were still distant—and he was already tumbling over the rim of the nest.

Built of stones plastered with org manure, it had a good, clean, dry odor, a little like the smell of parching grain. The shallow pink cup held a single egg.

Even in his mad haste, Org Rider took time to look at it, and to feel his heart catch at the sight. Smooth ball, mottled bronze and blue, it was too large for his arms to close around it. The surface felt warm and elastic, yielding slightly when he touched it. It had a friendly feel.

But the yells of the distant parents were not friendly. Gasping with his haste, Org Rider wound and knotted his rope to make a sling for the egg. Its weight was almost nothing, not much greater than his own. He slung it over his shoulder, scrambled to the rim of the nest, and leaped away.

A breeze had freshened, sliding down the mountain; it was at his back, and it made each leap half again as long as before. At the second leap he craned his neck around. Neither orgs nor the queer slamming machine were in sight. He could hear the distant angry baying, but it seemed less furious now. That was not advantageous; it meant the adult orgs were calming down, presumably having destroyed the machine. It would not be long before their fierce parental pugnacity drove them back to the guarding of the nest—and when they found it empty their rage would become incandescent, and all directed at him.

If they could find him.

His life depended wholly on making sure that they did not. He came to the edge of the tableland and leaped straight out, not even looking back.

It took all his skill to guide his descent into the best hiding place he could see. The bulk of the egg was a sail that unbalanced and tumbled him; the one free hand he had for air-swimming was not enough to make much difference. But in the slow, gentle gravity of his home falling could seldom be dangerous, although he was concerned about the safety of the egg. He hit hard when he hit. At the last moment he had thrown himself around to cushion the egg with his own body.

He was—for the moment, at least—safe.

And the egg was his!

He had landed in a vale of boulders, half buried in banks of gray, mossy stuff. A mountain stream purled and cascaded languidly down the slope. Org Rider had chosen the spot for that reason; as soon as he could regain the breath that had been smashed out of him and move he scratched and leaped his way to where a thin, bright ribbon of water leaped out from a sill of rock, and slid and scattered behind it.

What he had hoped for was there—a dry place behind the waterfall. It would do. The sound would drown out any noise he made, even from the keen hearing of the orgs. The spray would carry scent away. The curtain of lazily falling water would screen them from the vision of the parent orgs . . .

"Them."

With a start, Org Rider realized he was already thinking of the egg as if it were grown and mature. He let himself grin with wolfish joy; the worst part was done, that dream would yet come true!

But now he had work to do. Cautiously he ventured out and, one eye on the sky and both ears alert, tore armloads of moss out of the hidden sides of the boulders and carried them back to make a nest for his egg. When at last it lay safe, he took time to rock back on his haunches and inspect it.

It was there, real and true, and truly his. He studied every inch of its blue, bronze-speckled surface, so smooth and warm. It had no crack or flaw. It had not been harmed by the abduction; and, best of all, from its warmth and certain mysterious sounds of movement inside it, it showed every indication of being very near to its hatch time.

His heart filled to bursting with joy and pride, Org Rider sat back and rested for a long moment, planning what next to do.

As near as he could tell, he had come down somewhere near where the cartwheeling figure from the slamming machine had fallen, but a long, long way from where he had left his weapons and supplies. He was in a sort of great natural chimney, with steep rock on all sides. He drank his fill of water from the falls, and it was cold and sweet. He found nuts with queer paperlike shells growing nearby, and though they tasted faintly unripe and he did not want to eat very many of them, they stilled his hunger.

His first step was to try to get his cache.

He crept to the edge of the falls and looked up.

As soon as he was away from the gabble of the falling water, he heard the distant agonized screams of the orgs. They had learned of their loss now, it was clear. The long moaning bellows sounded of rage and the promise of revenge.

But they were far away, perhaps as far as the other edge of the tableland where they had built their nest.

There was a cluster of bee-trees nearby. Org Rider regretted that; the creatures who hived in the trees were dreadful enemies when aroused, and it was known that they had some chemical loathing of orgs. This would perhaps make the adult orgs approach only reluctantly, which was good. But what if they should smell out and attack his egg?

He could not guard against every contingency, he decided with a pang of worry and regret; it was the first time in his life that he had felt like a parent.

Reluctantly (but he had no choice!) he turned his back on the egg, and started out to hunt for better food, his cache, and a good way out of the giant chimney in which they lay.

The boy was gone a long time, longer than he planned, for at one point in his search the adult orgs came wheeling and shrieking overhead and he had to hastily bury himself in the undergrowth beneath a stand of flame-trees. Small creatures like red insects shared his hiding place with him and, although they did not sting, their crawling over his flesh was maddening; but he dared not leave. He lay motionless, half drowsing, for a long, long time, not even able to lift his head to see what was happening when the bellowing screams of the orgs were so close that it seemed certain they had spied him. They had not; of this he was sure, because he was still alive. When they were more distant he dozed again, and he dreamed a frightful dream in which his cherished egg hatched and turned into a black-winged Watcher that stank of death-weed and came at him with a throttling-noose that bore a watchman's eye . . .

He woke trembling, and found the orgs were gone.

He had not located his cache or a way out, but there was food of a sort, succulent stalks from a purple bush that tasted sweet and meaty, some torpid red water-snakes that were dull enough to allow themselves to be caught. He returned to his waterfall feeling cheered and expectant, looking forward to seeing his egg, touching it, listening for its tiny slow heartbeat and the stirring sounds inside it.

With a wary eye out for the orgs he ducked under the lazy waterfall, and shouted with astonishment and anger.

The egg was there, luminously blue in the half-light under the falls. But a creature was crouching over it—a squat man-shape, black-haired and nearly naked, smashing at the egg with a red-smeared rock. The man looked up in fear and astonishment at Org Rider's yell.

And then, for almost the first time in his life, Org Rider felt the creeping terror of superstitious fear. He knew that man; it was the stranger from the small Watcher. He had seen him dead.

SEVEN

Some tens of thousands of light-years away from Cuckoo, on the inner curve of one of the spiral arms of the Galaxy toward which Cuckoo was hurtling, there was a G0-type star of no great intrinsic interest that had in orbit around it the planet Earth.

Earth and its dominant race, humans, were new among the galactic races. They were fully accepted as equal members. The streets of cities like Chicago and Peking were already used to the sight of darting Sheliaks, glittering Scorpian robots, and a hundred other races. Every major city had its own tachyon-transmission center, through which flowed the traffic of many worlds. All the buildings were alike in that they were huge, new, towering over the structures around them, filled with the enormous mass of hardware that met the power requirements of tachyon transmission. Each wore proudly the gauzy spiral that was the emblem of the Galaxy.

Across the tiled flooring of the great concourse of the tachyon center in Old Boston a young woman named Zara Gentry walked with grace and assurance. She had been there before. She had been almost everywhere, for Zara Gentry was a famous stereostage personality, known everywhere for her on-the-spot reportage of the Earth's doings to the Earth's people. She had been everywhere and tried almost everything. She had in fact been herself a volunteer for tachyon transport, several years before. One copy of her lived on Sun One. Another worked and lived in an orbiting station around the planet inhabited by the Boaty-Bits, in the constellation Boötes. Those two she knew of, for they were direct copies sent from Earth. There could well be more. The tachyon duplicates could themselves have been duplicated; there could be a hundred Zaras, or a thousand.

It was strange, Zara reflected, how little she knew about those other selves. They were so much herself, and yet so different; so close to her, and so impossibly far away.

The whole process of tachyon transport was loaded with trauma. She well remembered the quirky fears that had beset her when first she volunteered to be scanned, mapped, blueprinted, and recreated thousands of light-years away. It had been unbelievably scary; she had signed up and called to cancel her signature; signed again and withdrawn again. At the end it was only her conscience that made her go through with it, because by then there had been such an investment of time and training that she could not let it be wasted.

So she had walked into the tachyon-transmission chamber—

And, moments later, walked out again. And it seemed that nothing had happened at all.

She knew with one part of her mind that every atom in her body had been identified and placed in its exact coordinates, and that the blueprint that carried her minutest specifications was even then racing, tachyon-borne, through the Galaxy toward Sun One.

The other part of her mind was wholly occupied with wondering where her date would take her that night for dinner; and that dichotomy had been as frightening as the process itself.

It was frightening and unsettling to think that some-where someone who was exactly, identically *you* was doing things you did not know about, might be terrified or joyous, angry or ill; might even be dead, and you would never know, except as you might hear of what had happened to some former acquaintance. It was frightening and unsettling, but you could not go on being frightened and unsettled forever. So you put it out of your mind. You told yourself that you would keep in touch with your other selves. For a while you did. The two Zaras had exchanged tachyon communications for weeks and months, and then, less frequently, for a year or so. They had even spoken "face to face"—at least, in tachyon-borne stereostage communication.

But all that was now years in the past. When she had sent the second copy of herself to the Boötian planet she had tried to keep in touch with her, also, but that too had trailed off.

And now she was about to expose herself to the trauma for the third time.

Zara grinned to herself, dodging a Purchased Person who carried a hive of Boaty-Bits as she made her way to the elevators. I never learn, she thought good-humoredly.

But it was exciting, you had to admit. Especially this time! This copy of herself was going clear out of the Galaxy entirely, to the strange object identified as Lambda One and more familiarly called Cuckoo. With less fear than anticipation, she rose to the hundred and eighteenth floor and reported for her checkup interview.

The man in charge of her transport was old, tanned, lean, good-looking; he had bushy white eyebrows and a great sweep of white hair like high surf breaking over his forehead. He maintained dignified objectivity in what he said, but they had become friends over the last weeks. "Zara! It's nice to see you again. Well. Tomorrow you make the great leap forward. How do you feel about it?"

On her program Zara would have answered, *"That's a dumb question—look at the psych test profile in my folder. You know how I feel better than I do.*" But she wasn't on her stereostage program; she said, "Well, a little scared. Otherwise fine." And she smiled.

"That's natural enough," he agreed absently, leafing through her folder. "Mmm. Yes." Something in the folder seemed to attract his interest; he stared at it thoughtfully for a long time. Then he raised his head and said again, "Mmm. Yes. Have you seen the legal officer?"

"Not yet," she confessed.

"Oh, but that's very important!" He was upset. "Please don't put it off any longer, Zara. The documents must be signed. You know that the copy of you will be, to all legal intents and purposes, yourself. It can sign your name as well as you can—no," he said, correcting himself ruefully, "not 'it.' 'She.' She is the same as you, Zara. She has an equal right to all your property and is equally obligated with you on the fulfillment of contracts, unless you state clearly *in advance* which of you shall have which property and responsibilities. You must file your statement of settlement at once!"

"I will," she promised. "I have done this before, you know."

"Yes, of course, but each time you create a copy you create the same problem." Then he relented, smiling. "To be sure," he said, "when you come right down to it, the problem is more legal than real. There isn't much chance you'll ever see your copy again, is there? And a half-interest in a condominium in Buzzard's Bay isn't going to mean much to the copy of you that's on Cuckoo. But there is always the chance some question could arise, and so you have to file that statement. Otherwise they won't accept you for transmission."

"Don't make that too tempting," said Zara, not wholly joking.

"Mmm," he said thoughtfully, and made a checkmark on her personality-profile card.

"I really do want to go," she said quickly. "Or at least, I'm going to."

He nodded. It was not an unfamiliar reaction; if the tachyon boards rejected applicants who were doubtful they would never send anyone at all. "I see you've been issued all the cassettes."

"*And* listened to them," she said.

"So you're about as well briefed on Cuckoo as you can get, I imagine. Do you have any questions?"

She said, "Well, those briefings are more distinguished for the questions they raise than the answers they give, aren't they? I mean, nobody seems to know exactly why the object's as funny as it is. The size is all wrong for the mass, and nobody seems to understand how come there are creatures so much like humans and Sheliaks and Boaty-Bits on it."

He grinned. "If we knew things like that, we wouldn't have to send people like you to find them out for you. That's why you're going." He hesitated, looking thoughtfully at her papers. "That in general, of course. But there seems to be some particular reason for you. Do you happen to know why you were requested by name?"

"No, I don't," she said. "And I've wondered. The request came from Sun One, I understand. I have a copy there. I suppose *she's* behind it. But we haven't been in touch lately, so I don't know any more than you do."

"We could send her a message, if you like. You could ask for yourself."

"Oh," Zara said, "actually I'm rather intrigued by the mystery. I'm not fearful about it. That other Zara can't have changed all that much in a couple of years. If she thinks it's a good idea for me to go to Cuckoo, then it probably is. I mean, after all, she is me." She hesitated, then said, "The only thing that does puzzle me is why she doesn't send a copy of herself."

The man said with visible pleasure, "You don't know how glad I am that you asked that. I can answer it. It puzzles me too, so I got her records. The other Zara, you'll be pleased to know, married a man named Ben

Pertin. He's a copy too, of course; his identification is Ben Charles Pertin. And she expects to bear their first child in a couple of months. My impression is that she was anxious enough to go, but not with an unborn baby going along."

"Ah!" said Zara, vastly relieved. "I'm glad for her. What a nice thing to hear about yourself!"

"And you yourself, Mrs. Gentry? I see you're married. Are you planning a family?"

"Why, very likely," she said, "but I'm not pregnant now."

He nodded and closed her folder. "I think that takes care of all the loose ends," he said. "See the legal officer; get a few more shots. Then you'll be all ready to go."

"I'm ready now," Zara Gentry said.

When she was through with the legal officer—an episode which left her with the feeling she had signed a part of herself into slavery—she took the express elevator that dropped her into the physical-training rooms below ground. The *splat* of firearms told her the weapons class was in session. She tarried at the door, looking in at the range. The cassettes had been quite candid about the possibility of physical danger on Cuckoo. Several transportees had already experienced close calls, and two were dead. Besides the known predators—winged creatures like flying seals, armed savages, creatures like Sheliaks gone mad, and others—there were countless trillions of square miles of surface that had been only sketchily photomapped from orbit. What dangers they held no one could tell.

The other thing that troubled Zara in the conscious part of her mind was that the Zara who went to Cuckoo would not be, quite, the Zara Gentry who filled the stereostage receivers on Earth. Cuckoo's surface gravity was so preposterously slight that the first transportees had nearly destroyed themselves leaping about like jumping beans. Her physical attributes would therefore be slightly modified. They had promised that her appearance would not be changed, but she would be a little weaker, a little slower in reaction time. Even so, they said, she would have to watch herself; but it was thought that a little extra strength and speed might be helpful, against the known and unknown dangers of Cuckoo.

The class was ending, and one of the men caught sight of her, grinned, waved, checked his gun with the instructor, and came toward her. "Three bull's-eyes and twelve in the first circle," he said proudly, running a hand though his tousled mop of red hair. He was no taller than Zara, but weighed more than she did, and had muscles like steel and a great barrel chest. He would need a great deal of editing, she thought, leaning forward to be kissed. "I'm all set, dear," she said. "We're due for shots in half an hour, and that's the last."

"Great," her husband said, putting an arm around her. "Cuckoo, here come the Gentrys!"

EIGHT

*

    Org Rider's knife was at the stranger's throat before he could check himself; but the man was so helpless, so battered, that even the white-hot rage that the threat to the egg brought boiling up in him wavered.

The man was both desperate and startled. He brought his arm up, less in a gesture of defense than as pure reflex. He was tremendously strong. His gesture brushed Org Rider's hand and knife away as if they belonged to a child. The violence of his own movement set him lurching against the sheet rock wall behind the waterfall; his head met rock, and he slumped to the ground, stunned.

Org Rider dropped to his knees and embraced the egg fearfully. Its bright curve showed no damage. He pressed an ear against its warm, pliant shell, and heard the even, faint throb of the young org's heart, along with a random skittering noise that, Org Rider knew, meant the creature was close to hatching.

Then he turned to the intruder.

The crawling sensation at his back was still there. There was no doubt of it, the man who lay before him was the man the Watchers had killed. Yet here he was, alive! Cut, scratched, battered—all of those things. But he was not dead, although he had been.

The boy studied him carefully. His clothing was not quite the same as before; the colors were different, and the puff-sleeved tunic he wore was torn and filthy. The bright metallic things on his arms seemed different, but

145

they were the same class of things as he had worn before.

No doubt about it, it was the same man!

It dawned on the boy that this man was the figure he had seen falling from the slamming machine. Perhaps in that there was some sort of explanation; perhaps the machine laid eggs that hatched into identical creatures like this one. He had never heard of such a thing, but he had never heard of a dead man being alive again, either.

Remembering that the man in his previous life had spoken a few intelligible words, Org Rider said carefully, "Are you hungry?"

The man opened his eyes warily. There was no comprehension in them. He stroked the metallic clutter on his wrist with his other hand as if the effort were too much for him, and motioned the boy to speak again.

"Are you hungry?" Org Rider repeated. "I have some food."

The stranger shook his head, but his eyes fell on the pouch of food Org Rider had dropped. He stretched out his hand toward it.

"You are hungry, then," Org Rider said. Quickly he cut a slice of flesh from a watersnake and tried it. The taste was sweetish and good. He put a thin strip of it against the stranger's bearded lips. The man whimpered and sucked at it eagerly.

"It will be better cooked," the boy said, and offered some of the tender purple stalks. The stranger chewed at them while Org Rider whittled a drill, twirled it to light a fire, and set some of the snake meat to roast. It did not take long, and the fragrant scent of roasting meat was as tantalizing to Org Rider as to his guest; they shared the first half-cooked strips contentedly while the rest were cooking.

Then Org Rider forgot the stranger, because the egg made a sound like ripping cloth.

In the nest, the egg was rocking from the thrusts of

some internal eruption. A dark split opened, and spread across the luminous, bronze-flecked blue shell.

Org Rider squatted next to the nest, watching in fascination, urgently needing to help but not knowing how. Inside the egg dull thumping sounds accompanied thrusts against the thick internal membrane. It ripped, and ripped again.

And through the rips the boy could see the dark, wet head of the baby org glistening.

The stranger limped over to watch him, then shrugged and went to the waterfall. He drank thirstily out of the shell of a seed cone, his eyes fixed on the boy and the hatching egg.

The org's head burst through the slit, slick and black. Almost at once it began to dry, changing to a pale, tawny color. The huge eyes opened, the pupils wide and black and mysterious, rimmed with luminous blue. It fixed its gaze at once on the boy.

Fascinated, Org Rider stared back. It seemed to be resting, and he thought its gaze was pleading with him. For what? He could not guess, until he saw that the infant org was laboring for breath and realized that the effort to tear through the membrane was exhausting for it. Org Rider seized the edge of the glistening membrane and hacked at it with his knife.

The rest of the great head came free. The short trunk uncoiled, opened, waved. The hatchling made a faint, strangled, mewing cry, and the odor of its breath came up around the boy, a warm, sharp scent like the nest it had come from, a little like the odor of parching grain. Org Rider leaned forward and wiped from the tip of the infant's trunk a thick brown clot. It was breathing more freely now.

Satisfied, the boy relaxed his attention and realized for the first time that, over the clash of the waterfall, the stranger was shouting at him. Org Rider turned, and saw the man, face savage with fear, pointing toward the sky.

The boy ran out from under the waterfall, and peered

upward. Was it the Org's parents, still hunting their off-spring?

As soon as he was out from under the falls the sound he heard told him it was not: a roaring, familiar whine.

It was the mottled ship of the Watchers, or one so much like it that he could not tell the difference. It was flying low over the pool below the waterfall, its sound magnified by the black walls surrounding him to a shout of distant thunder.

In sudden dread the boy realized he had been seen.

He turned in indecision, peering back into the cave behind the torrent. Would they take the tiny org away from him? Worse—he remembered the warning about the Watchman's eye; and he had thrown it away. Would they punish him?

The gaunt stranger babbled fresh gibberish and pointed again at the sky, and the boy saw that a gray fleck had separated from the ship. The ship flew on, up over the rim of the canyon and away; the fleck dropped toward the pool and in a moment spread great wings and circled gently down toward where they were standing.

Org Rider pushed the stranger back inside the cave, and ran to his org. Its jaws free, it had ripped the luminous membrane off, except for a few rags that still clung stickily. Its tail unfolded, wet and delicate. Its whole body burst out in a rich cloud of that parched-grain fragrance.

It was twice the boy's length, now that its full dimensions had unfolded out of the egg, but it was still an infant, and drained of strength by the struggle to hatch. Its short trunk lifted to sniff him, then it slumped to the damp rock floor of the cave.

The boy began to rub it down with his wadded shirt, drying it and warming it, crooning to it a song he had learned from his mother. Sleepily the org arched its thin body to meet the strokes of his hand, and it's voice seemed to echo the song.

It was out of the question to leave the org, and

impossible to move it. It would be an hour or more before it could fly, and he could not carry it and his food, and still manage the tricky rocks around the falls. He stared desperately at the stranger, wondering how to get him to help.

And then beyond the stranger, in the luminous arch under the edge of the waterfall, another figure appeared.

It was not a watcher; it was human, tall, with a fire-red beard and keen green eyes.

"Redlaw!" the boy gasped.

"Young Org Rider," acknowledged the giant, grinning through the flowing beard. "I see you've got your org after all!"

The giant reached out for the boy's hand. Org Rider drew back instinctively, fingers leaping toward his knife, before he decided the gesture was friendly and allowed Redlaw to shake hands with him. "I followed you here," the giant boomed. "Saw two adult orgs looking more frantic than usual, and wondered if you were what they were worrying about. I see you were!"

The boy grinned, then said, "Followed me? But how? I got rid of the Watchman's eye—"

The giant's laughter boomed. "Clever about it, too, weren't you? We located it—inside an org! And the Watchers aren't going to like it if they see you again, so I recommend you don't let them. So you'll have to get rid of that!" And his finger shot out to point at the compass on the boy's wrist.

"But that was my grandfather's!"

"No doubt. But where he got it, or someone before him, was from the Watchers. It's trade goods, and they can trace you by it as easily as by a Watchman's eye. Made for that purpose."

"But—but," the boy said, "but if that's so, why didn't they come down and kill me?"

"Thank me, boy!" the giant boomed. "I convinced them you'd been eaten by that org. When it came to explaining how one telltale was inside the org and the other here, I really rose to the occasion! Said it had been excreted. But you'll have to take it off before you leave this place, of they'll know you're still alive; org excrement doesn't move from place to place by itself." He peered wonderingly at the stranger, then at the egg. "What's all this?" he demanded.

"My org!" the boy said proudly. "Look, he's hungry!" And ignoring Redlaw for the moment, he ran to slice strips from the water-snake remnants and offer them to the hatchling. It devoured them delightedly, great eyes fixed on the boy. It had preened itself and its external surface was now nearly dry. Most of its body became a pale gold, shading into white along the tips of its tail and its wings. Not yet scaled like the adult orgs, it was covered with a fine velvet that felt like fur but was in fact soft fleshy protuberances that would turn into chitin.

Org Rider fetched water in a seed-cone cup and doled it out to the infant, which slobbered its gratitude and demanded more of the watersnake.

While the boy was tending his org, Redlaw had discovered the stranger. Org Rider paid no attention until the giant called his name.

"We've got to move on, boy," he said. "Take off that compass. Don't break it; they'll know it if you do that. Just leave it here."

"Move on where?" Org Rider asked. "My org shouldn't travel yet—"

"No choice, boy," Redlaw boomed. "This fellow you've got here, he's what the Watchers are looking for. Says his name's Ben Yale Pertin"—he pronounced the alien syllables carefully—"whatever that means. And he's from outside the sky."

"That's insane," Org Rider said seriously. "There's no such place."

Redlaw nodded somberly. "Time was I'd have agreed with you, but the Watchers think there is. They spotted him somehow. It's not you they're looking for right now; it's him. And if we want to keep him alive we've got to get him where they won't look."

"Where's that?" the boy demanded bitterly, slipping the compass off his wrist and gazing at it. "They know where this is. They must know you are here——"

"Not necessarily," the giant boomed, but his voice was thoughtful. "I crawled out through a disposal hatch when they weren't looking. —But you're right about the telltale. When they miss me, they might come zeroing in on it. And I don't know, boy, if the three of us can travel fast enough to get out of range."

"*Four* of us!" The boy turned to look at the org, now sleeping. It stirred and crooned in its sleep, the pliant trunk lifting to sniff toward him. "There's Babe," he said. "I won't leave him."

"Is that his name, Babe?"

"It is now. And he can't travel yet."

"You mean he might travel right away from you, don't you?"

The boy held his ground. "I'm not taking that chance!" he said.

"I don't know, boy," Redlaw said at last. "Our friend here probably can't travel very fast anyway. But we can't just stay here. They won't just kill us, boy, they'll eat us right up, you and me and your org. This other fellow might not be that lucky; they'll want him to talk."

"Talk about what?"

"Where he came from. Weapons. What he's up to, him and his friends that pop up all over." Redlaw looked ill at ease, then suddenly he grinned. "I know! We'll use their own telltale to confuse them! I can move fast enough by myself; I'll take it a good long way down Knife-in-the-Sky and drop it off a cliff somewhere. Let them hunt it there! They won't have any reason to come back here then, and this is as cozy a spot as we'll find." He was already standing, beginning to strap his wings on again. "Keep our friend fed, boy," he said. "Stay out of sight! I'll be back in a thousand breaths or so—if I'm lucky!"

It was more than a thousand breaths. It became fifteen hundred, then two thousand.

Org Rider could have stayed in the cave forever, delighted with watching his hatchling grow stronger every breath; but the growth required food, and he had at last to steal out from under the waterfall and forage. Redlaw had left his cleaver; the boy took it and bounded along the river course to the forest, where huge fat golden moths trailed gray wakes of sickly bittersweet fragrance. The boy despaired of catching one of them without exposing himself, but the trees themselves were sources of food; he leaped to hack off huge seed-cones with the cleaver, split them open and found them full of edible seeds as well as wriggling blind horned grubs, probably those of the moths.

When he came back to the cave behind the waterfall the stranger called Ben Yale Pertin was sleeping again. The boy regarded him with suspicion tinged with fear. He had not forgotten that he had seen this man die once; he did not understand how it was he was alive again, but something about it made the bristles at the back of his neck crawl.

But for the moment Babe was more important. The young org was awake and eager; he drained the water Org Rider brought him, then whimpered and crooned for more food. The grubs went into his capacious maw so fast that before the boy knew it they were gone, and he and his sleeping guest—or captive?—were still unfed. No matter. The humans could go hungry. A new-hatched org had to eat or die.

The stranger woke briefly, just long enough to drink some water, look around for food, find a few scraps, and return to sleep. Org Rider sat with his hatchling, singing softly to it as his mother had taught him. It pleased him immensely as it responded; but it woke again to be fed, and the scraps that were left were

meager. Another thousand breaths later the boy decided
he had to forage once more. At the waterfall's edge he
paused uncertainly, then dived for the shelter of the
vegetation.

At once he realized he was in danger. The sound of
the waterfall had drowned the sound that came from
the sky, the shrieks of the angry adult orgs.

He burrowed under a thick cluster of tough gray-
green vines, inedible and useless to him but not, he discovered, to some tiny biting creatures that disputed pos-
session with him. It was many hundreds of breaths
before he dared venture out.

He stood beside the vines, listening. The shrieks of
the orgs were far away again. But there was something
else; a clattering sound, more like the sound of the
stranger's slamming machine than anything else the boy
could remember hearing, but not much like that, either.

Something appeared over the lip of the canyon and
dropped toward him. As it hit the pebbly fringe of the
pool it made the clattering racket, was followed by
something else like it, and then by the huge form of
Redlaw, dropping easily down toward the boy.

"Hurry!" the giant cried. "There are orgs up the
slope, and a Watcher ship cruising around. Get this stuff
inside!"

"But I've got to find food," the boy protested.

"You won't have a mouth to eat it with if we don't
get under cover," the giant promised grimly. Org Rider
could not argue with that clear wisdom. The clattering
things turned out to be collections of queer metal
shapes, held together by vines. He took one batch, Redlaw the other, and they managed to get them inside the
cave.

Then, panting hard, the giant said proudly: "I found
it, boy! I found his slamming machine! Couldn't carry
the whole thing, it was banged up so bad. But I took all
the loose pieces and brought them back."

From the floor the stranger who called himself Ben
Yale Pertin propped himself on an elbow, staring at the

collection of bits and pieces. He said something in his unintelligible speech and creakingly got to his feet. Dried blood was black on his nearly naked, half-starved body. Org Rider felt compassion for him, mingled with the dread and the anger. Not much of the anger was left, since Babe had not been harmed by the man's attempt to crack the egg and eat it, but there was still a vestigial core of dread.

The man shuffled over in his curious stumbling gait and thumbed through the hardware excitedly. He fumbled out a flat black oblong with a handle and touched it in some way that Org Rider did not understand; it sprang open, revealing queer-shaped shining things that looked like tools. With them the stranger began to assault the bangles he wore on his wrist. Org Rider involuntarily stepped back, remembering how those bangles the other stranger had seemed to speak to him with a voice of their own.

"Go to it, Ben Yale Pertin," Redlaw boomed lustily. "Fix up your gadgets for us! That's what I want you to do!"

"*What* is?" Org Rider demanded.

"Why, I want him to repair those trinkets of his. They're powerful things, boy! Weapons. Machines. I don't understand them, but I know they're something that's never been seen in the world before, and I want them."

"For what?"

"Ah," Redlaw boomed in delight, "for the big job that's ahead of us, son! This funny-looking fellow is our chance to deal with the Watchers. Nothing in the flatworld has a chance to break their power, certainly not your people. Not even me, and I know a good deal more than anyone else you've ever met about weapons and how to use them. But this lad has weapons I mean to have."

Org Rider stared at the scarecrow figure disbelievingly. "He's only a man," he said. "Not much of a man at that. Our potter was bigger than he is, and I beat the potter in fair fight."

"You won't beat this one, boy. He's stronger than you think."

"Stronger than the Watchers?"

"His weapons are! And he'll give them to us, I promise. Or—"

"Or what?" the boy asked, as Redlaw came to a halt.

After a moment the giant finished his thought somberly. "Or we'll kill him and take the weapons away from him," he said.

NINE

When they stepped out of the tachyon-transport chamber, Jon and Zara Gentry were greeted by a female creature, human in shape, but with great angel wings.

"Welcome to Ground Station One," she chimed in a voice like sweet bells. "My name is Valkyrie, and I am pleased to see the first representatives of Planet Earth arrive on the surface of Cuckoo."

Zara looked doubtfully at her husband, then reached out a hand, which Valkyrie took politely. Clearly she had been with human beings in some other environment before coming to Cuckoo; the custom of the handshake did not disturb her at all.

Beyond the silver girl floated a glittering cloud of Boaty-Bits that changed shape like a swarm of diamond bees. Over them, partly obscured by their dazzle, a T'Worlie swam gently in the air. From it came a shrill whistle that Zara's Pmal rendered into, "I identify you, Zara Doy."

Zara looked doubtfully at her husband, who shrugged. "I am Zara *Doy*," she said. "Or was. This is my husband. In our custom I have taken his name and so I am called Zara Gentry now."

The T'Worlie did not respond. In the languid gravity of Cuckoo it did not need to exert itself to fly, it was enough for it to ripple its wings slowly. From it there came a sharp but not unpleasant odor like the pickle jar in a warm pantry.

Neither of the Gentrys had ever seen individual

Boaty-Bits or T'Worlie in the flesh before—if "flesh" was the right word for the Boötians, whose chemistry was not very like organic. They had no difficulty in recognizing them from stereostage pictures, but nothing in the stereoviews had prepared them for the sense of whirling power in the Boaty-Bits, or the acrid odor of the T'Worlie. "My identity," it rapped metallically through the Pmal translator—how quickly, Zara thought, they became accustomed to listening to that rather than the shrill pipings of the T'Worlie itself—"can be described as one Nommie. We did have mutual identification on Sun One, but I perceive you are a different version."

"And I knew you, too," sang the silver girl sweetly. "Will you look around your new home?"

It was a confusing new home. From the inside it was hard to make out a plan, but Zara Gentry had seen stereostage images of it: spherical shells blown out of some transparent golden-hued material, linked together and outfitted to meet the needs of its inhabitants.

They had arrived in the largest of the bubbles, which was elevated above the others. From it Zara and her husband could look out to see a distant flat plain rimmed by mountains. They were themselves on a mountain, for she could see, just outside the bubble, rocky slopes that fell away endlessly. Turning to look out the other side, she saw a shelf of woodland, and then the rest of the mountain rising incredibly toward the sky. Its top was not in sight. Once, as they approached a Sheliak, the shapeless bun exuded a stalk that formed lips and made a sound their Pmal translators rendered as: "It gives joy to encounter you once more."

It was disconcerting to be recognized by creatures she had never seen. Flushing faintly, Zara repeated her apologies for being a different version; it was soon apparent to her that nearly all the beings here were direct copies from individuals on the artificial planetoid called Sun One, where all the races of the Galaxy had representatives to mediate and interpret their differing interests and goals.

After so long a voyage—tens of thousands of light-years—Zara felt she should rest and freshen up. But of course tachyon transport was not tiring. The patterns of their bodies, carried by faster-than-light tachyon particles, had not "really" moved anywhere. When they were in transit they were only concepts, so to speak; they were patterns, and had no more sensation or thought than a schematic diagram. Nevertheless she was fatigued. It was culture shock, she thought: the impact of so much change in so short a time. She pleaded fatigue in any case and without demurrer—no two races of the Galaxy *really* understood each other's foibles—Valkyrie showed them their own quarters.

In the "morning" Zara woke to her first "day" on Cuckoo and incautiously got out of her cocoon as if she were still on Earth. Even edited, her muscles were disproportionate to Cuckoo's needs. She flew off the airbed as if it had exploded, catching her balance at the very last second necessary to keep from crashing into the wall.

The noise roused her husband, in the bunk over her own. He opened his eyes and said, "I dreamed we were on Cuckoo." He looked around and added, "I never had a dream turn out to be true before."

Zara was listening only politely; she had gone at once to their stereostage, to refresh her memory of the place to which they had exiled themselves for the rest of their lives.

Cuckoo was an enormous ball that hung in empty space, forty thousand light-years outside the fringing arms of the Galaxy.

It had been a puzzle for all the Galaxy's scientists since the cruising robot scoutships of the bat-winged T'Worlie first detected it. It was a perfect monad of polar opposites: huge and hard-crusted, yet with an average density not much above that of a total vacuum.

Alone in space in the emptiness between galaxies,
heading toward the Milky Way at a velocity that was a
substantial fraction of c.

There was no such thing as day or night on the surface of Cuckoo. There was no external object bright
enough to light it up. What light there was to see by
came from bright phosphorescing clouds that hung in
its thick air.

It was as big as a solar system, nearly two A.U. in
diameter. Did it rotate? Yes, in a manner of speaking—
to Zara the question was confusing, coming down to rotation relative to what? Relative to the nearest globular
cluster of the Milky Way Galaxy, Cuckoo turned on its
axis once every eight hundred-odd Earth days. To natives of Cuckoo the rotation would have been difficult
to understand and of no importance at all; there was
hardly ever anything to see from the flatlands where
they lived, and even from the high mountains it was
only occasionally that one might catch a glimpse of the
Milky Way. It would take many generations to realize
that that tipped spiral puddle of light rose on one horizon and, over the course of an Earthly year and more,
slowly climbed to its zenith and disappeared below the
western sky. The Milky Way was not the only thing
that could be seen in the sky—M-31 in Andromeda
was quite visible from the mountains, with a little luck,
as were the Magellanic Clouds. But the Milky Way was
by far the biggest and brightest object, occupying nearly
half the sky when fully risen.

None of these were of any use in telling time.
Ground Station One was on galactic arbitrary standard
time, a metrication that cycled at some thirty Earth
hours. Zara found out quickly that it was close enough
to a terrestrial day to be recognizable, different enough
to be disconcerting. It made their first "day" very long.

Even so, there was hardly time enough to do all they
had to do. The briefings on Earth had been intriguing
and even useful; but here in the face of the massive
reality of Cuckoo, swelling all around them, both of the

Gentrys had everything to learn. It was exhausting. They spent hours just in learning to deal with the flimsy gravity of Cuckoo. Even in their down-muscled edited forms, every step sent them flying at first. ("I know I've been trying to lose a few pounds," Jon grinned, "but this is ridiculous.") They had to learn to deal with the representatives of the nine other races in Ground Station One. T'Worlie, Sheliaks, Scorpians, and all, each had its own purposes and needs, and all had as much right to be there as Zara and Jon. More, thought Zara fairly; the galactic culture exchange had been going on for thousands of years before humanity had become aware of it.

And above all they had to learn what was on Cuckoo itself.

There existed, in the central workroom, a three-dimensional stereostage program which, on command, conjured up a slowly spinning image of the body itself. Much of it was blank even yet; the tachyar mapping, scanning the surface of Cuckoo from the orbiting space station, had not completed even one full revolution, and some ninety percent of the surface of Cuckoo had been mapped only at extremely long range or not at all. This did not at first appear. The basic sphere was wholly featureless to the naked eye, except for some blurry discolorations. The program could on command magnify any desired portion. Where the scan was complete, such portions showed seas, mountain ranges, forests, deserts—a thousand different kinds of locales. This one little area that they were now exploring Zara saw with dismay, was only an insignificant point on the globe— yet it stretched half the diameter of Europe! There was simply too much to map. Less detail showed on their globe than the maps of the Elizabethan admirals had showed of the interior of Africa.

Valkyrie was a patient teacher and even-tempered friend. Zara found herself relating to the silvery, winged creature as if she were another human. It was a shock to remind herself that this shape was probably nothing like Val's "real" body, in whatever hellishly inhospitable environment she had lived in on her home world. It had been edited into a more viable form, but Zara knew very well that the shape they saw was not her own.

Fortunately for mankind, most of the races of the Galaxy were close enough to oxygen-breathing, water-based mammals that the consensual common environment, when races met, was usually in an atmosphere human beings could endure. Even races like the Scorpians and the Sheliaks could tolerate it; it was not what they were used to, but it did not matter, since one was robot and the other so protean that it could survive anywhere. For those races to whom oxygen and water were poison, there were two alternatives. They could borrow the bodies of oxygen-tolerating species— humans were very popular for this—by inserting tachyon-coupled transponders into their brains. The bodies were then wholly controlled by the creatures who had taken them over. Zara had seen enough of such men and women, incurable criminals called Purchased People; they were common enough on Earth. The other alternative was to edit the "pattern" transported by the tachyons into some form that could stand air, water, and the temperature limits of the consensual environment. Val's people had chosen that way to go.

To be sure, editing was not uncommon for all races. Zara and Jon themselves were edited. Their physical strength was an actual handicap on Cuckoo, so their new bodies were altered in the physics and chemistry of the musculature to a sort of compromise between what was appropriate to Earth, and what was desirable on Cuckoo, where each of them weighed only a few pounds. At the same time their proportions had been altered, making them taller and thinner, and thus less strange for the natives of Cuckoo.

They were impatient to start to explore the surface of Cuckoo; it was what they were there for. Val apologized, in that voice like the tinkling of sweet bells: their equipment was not yet ready; their flying-belts had to be made to measure, and their new measurements had not been available. They would come soon, she promised. Meanwhile—

Jon halted her. "What I don't know," he said, "is what happened to the other parties that have gone out. I understand they didn't come back. I don't know why."

"They died," Val chimed sweetly.

Zara said, conscious of an unease in her body, "Well, we know that much. We don't know what happened, though." There was something working inside her that she could not quite analyze: a feeling that she should be more terrified—it was death they were talking about—and an opposite, intellectual understanding that said that this life they now had was only an appendage to a "real" life back on Earth, and its death would be only an episode that they "really" might not even ever know. It was fundamentally disturbing, a thought she could not quite deal with and could not wholly suppress.

But Val was answering their questions: "We have dispatched eight individuals to the surface direct from the orbiter, prior to the establishment of this station," she chimed. "All eight have terminated contact with the orbiter. Five are known to be dead. The other three are probably also dead. Six of them were human beings and two Sheliaks—actually," she corrected herself, "one was a human being and one a Sheliak, replicated respectively six and two times."

"Persistent human being," Jon commented grimly. "What killed him?—them?"

"It is not known in all cases," Val said brightly. "Please come." And she spread her great silvery wings and arrowed out of the smaller chamber where they had been talking, into the great central bubble. A Sirian eye was hovering just before a stereostage, patiently studying the scene it portrayed; it did not look around as they came in, but there was a strong sting of ozone in the air. Jon and Zara saw that there was a whole bank of stages beneath the transparent belt that gave them their view out onto the surface of Cuckoo, each with a different scene. Val touched the controls of an unused stage and it filled with a shining silver mist that swirled and hardened into an image of a mountain peak.

"This is the top of the mountain we are on," Val explained. "Observe the bare rocks. Look closely." She waved, and the peak shot nearer so that they could see details. Something that glowed with a faint, unpleasant bluish sheen was clinging to the rock. "That slime," she said, "appears to be a part of a growth process in the mountain. It is violently corrosive—whether through chemical or radioactive reactions we are not sure. The second Sheliak came in contact with it, and literally rotted to death while still in communication."

Zara shuddered. Jon said, "It sounds unpleasant."

Val turned her harshly beautiful stare on him. "It is probably quite undesirable for organic creatures," she agreed. "As you know, Sheliaks do not experience pain in the same way as most sentients. This one was able to describe what was happening until its central nervous system failed entirely. It was not attractive," she finished thoughtfully. Zara wonderingly thought that, whatever the metallic form Val wore as a convenience, in her native state she might well be as frail and delicate, even, as a human.

"There may have been other deaths due to the slime," Val went on. "The three of which we have certain knowledge, however—the other Sheliak and two of the men—were due to flying creatures." She manipulated the controls and displayed an org. "Also," she said, "there are intelligent machine-using creatures of which little is yet known. They may be involved. And, of course, there are analogs of many galactic races. There is no shortage of dangers on Cuckoo. We simply do not yet know what they all are."

Zara Gentry turned slowly, studying the bank of stages. The ones that were in use were panning slowly across a vista of woods, plains, and lakes. These were only monitors, through which the sentients present in Ground Station One could see what was being transmitted to the orbiter and on by tachyon transmission to receivers all through the Galaxy itself, where the images were being recorded and studied. As they watched, one of the stages emitted a harsh electronic squeal for attention. It stopped panning and locked onto something large and winged.

"Found something," Val chimed. "That is one of the flying creatures. The stage is programmed to follow it for a period of time, in case we wish to study it. If not, it will resume scanning shortly. And over there"—she pointed to the stage in front of the Sirian eye—"is what is perhaps the most severe real danger."

The stage revealed a vehicle. Zara asked in astonishment, "The machine users?"

"Yes," the silvery girl agreed. "Those creatures have no analog in the Galaxy. They apparently are evolved autochthons, and may be eligible for participation in the galactic councils. But much of the other life is not native."

She touched the controls again, and displayed a tree that seemed to be emitting a sort of shimmering fog.

Zara looked closer, and gasped in surprise: "Are they bees? No, wait—I think they're Boaty-Bits!"

"Yes," Val chimed. "Boötians. And here is a recording of Sheliaks." She displayed another image, then another and another. "Antarans. Canopan semilizards. Some of these are not to be found in this vicinity, but do exist in other areas of the surface of Cuckoo. Altogether twelve of the sentient races of the Galaxy have been logged on Cuckoo, including—"

And she touched the controls again, and showed the figure of a tall, spare woman in a breechclout, grinding grain.

"Human beings!" Zara Gentry cried. "How did they get here?"

"How did any of them get here?" the silvery girl chimed. "That is a primary mission for us, to find out how that happened. It is definitely established that, however it happened, it was a long time ago: there have been marked evolutionary changes. You can see some physical differences in your own race, no doubt. And some of the species—Canopans and Antarans in particular—have regressed to nonsentient forms, or at least to nonculture forms. The Boötians may retain hive intelligence, we're not sure because we have not been able to communicate and, as you know, they do not under normal circumstances employ artifacts. The only ones we are sure are nonregressed are your own race, and a small colony of Sheliaks, very far from here."

"It's crazy," Jon Gentry said wonderingly.

The silvery girl laughed like sleighbells. "Of course! Isn't that why the object has its name? It was one of your own people, I think, who originally called it 'Cuckoo.'"

Their tailored flying equipment arrived, designed and built on Sun One and transmitted via tachyon transport to them here. The Gentrys strapped it on awkwardly. None of the other sentients in Ground Station One could be of much help. Val had no need of the flying suits, having wings; as had the Sirian eye, the Scorpian robot, and the T'Worlie. In any case the anatomies were so different that the Sirian, for instance, simply could not understand the concept of a belt.

The first items they put on were wings. Zara stroked them between her fingers doubtfully; they were ridiculously tiny, proportionately smaller than the membranes that supported a flying squirrel. "They are only for directional control," Val chimed. "And perhaps for a gentle landing, if for any reason your drive should fail."

Zara was still doubtful. But her husband seemed to accept it, and she looked further. The drive unit itself strapped to their backs. It was simple pulse-jet. It was designed to require only water as "fuel"—not really fuel, but a working medium that would have to be replaced as it was discharged. The actual energy source was a compact star of radioisotopes, which released heat on command. The heat flash-boiled the water. The exploding gas for the jet was only steam. The water was carried in two kidney-shaped flasks of soft plastic strapped around their waists.

"They look very small," Zara said doubtfully.

"The first exploring parties had larger drive equipment," Val chimed. "Some had actual vessels, and they rode inside. It did not keep them alive."

Jon glanced at his wife, and said quickly: "Let's try them out!"

They worked beautifully. The hammering sound of the jet was unpleasantly close to the base of their skulls, but as they gained speed the sound seemed to dwindle behind them.

They returned to the bubble complex rather regretfully; it was a joyous thing to be able to swoop and circle around in the thick air of Cuckoo!

The rest of their equipment was simple enough. Personal necessities: soap, toothbrushes, toilet paper, changes of clothing. Food—not much of it, just iron rations, heavy on protein and vitamins but by no means tempting to the palate or calculated to satisfy a large appetite. "I'm not too crazy about living on that stuff for a week," Jon grunted.

"You need not," Val sang. "You eaters can subsist off the native flora and fauna well enough. You have eaten meals prepared from it already."

"That steak last night?" Zara exclaimed.

"Yes. And the salad. And the beverage. Of course, for myself I need only energy, and I get that from the power packs. But I understand there is as much of the biota here that is edible as there is on your own planet."

That left only one item. With some dismay, Zara hefted a gun that had been custom-built for her hand. "The lower trigger is a projectile," Valkyrie said. "The upper, a laser beam. Lower for food, upper to kill instantly."

"What about you?" Jon demanded.

Valkyrie tolled somberly, "I have my own weapons built in, Jon Gentry. We may need them to defend ourselves. Remember the first eight explorers!" She hung in the air, slowly fanning her wings, regarding them with her bright, silver eyes. "You will need to sleep again," she said. "And when you wake we will begin."

Zara's breath caught in her throat. "So soon?"

"So soon," Val echoed.

When her husband was already in his upper bunk, face turned away from the light and the gentle sounds of his breathing becoming deeper with sleep, Zara Gentry lingered in front of the tiny mirror, stroking her face with cream. She was not looking at herself; she was staring into space and had forgotten what she was doing.

What had made her forget was something she had remembered: that tens of thousands of light-years away, another Zara Gentry was, at that very hour, perhaps making her way through the crowded flyways of New York toward the stereostage studios for her regular nightly appearance. What would she be talking about, this other Zara? Her emotions when she volunteered for tachyon transport to Cuckoo? Her immense relief when she stepped out of the chamber and found she was still on Earth?

Zara absently wiped the cream from her face and rested her chin on her hands, framing the sentences in her mind that that other Zara Gentry would be using to open the broadcast: "Well, friends, I walked out of the chamber and back to Earth"— cut to long shot of the tachyon-transport building, pan of the chamber itself with Zara coming out of it—"and it was queer. Queasy. I don't know how to describe it. I knew that here *I* was. And yet at the same time I was somewhere else: out on the surface of Cuckoo, so far away that I can't even see it with the biggest telescope on Earth, *I* was entering a whole new existence."

She caught herself reaching for the stereostage

recorder, to make a note for the opening of her next broadcast.

There would be no need for that. Not here, not ever here. Whatever else happened, this Zara Gentry was forever doomed to stay on Cuckoo. Oh, perhaps she could physically be carried to the orbiting station in a rocket, if she swung sufficient weight. But that was most unlikely, and that she would ever leave in any other way was impossible.

But after a moment she did reach for the stereostage recorder, and said into it: "For transmission to Zara Day Gentry on Earth. Zara, dear—dear me!—myself, dear . . . I don't know how to address me! But I am here and well. Jon is also well, and in a few hours we are going to begin to explore the surface of Cuckoo. In my edited form I am tall and thin, just as I always wanted to be. And—dear distant self—I can tell you one other thing about me: I am afraid. Not panicky. Not crippled by it. But *scared*."

Scared or not, she went on to give a bright, entertaining ten minute account of what had happened since arriving on Cuckoo.

It was the least a girl could do for herself, she reflected, settling gently into her cocoon. And it was oddly comforting, to know that she would in fact be on the stereostage worldwide one more tme—herself, not just that other Zara Gentry. As she drifted toward sleep she thought that a girl in her position could use all the comfort she could get.

A hundred and twenty degrees of arc around the circumference of Cuckoo swung the orbiter called Cuckoo Station. It was a strange-looking thing, about the size of a three-story house in its main dimensions, but with extensions that shot spindly towers half a mile into space and trailed filmy sheets of laminated metal and plastic for more than three miles around it. It did not look as if it could survive the faintest summer breeze. This was correct. It could not. It never needed to, for Cuckoo

Station had never known an atmosphere around it; it had been created in orbit, out of the tachyon-transport cell dropped by the doomship that had brought the Galaxy's eyes and ears to Cuckoo and then gone on with its dead or dying crew.

The sentients who inhabited Cuckoo Station were quite similar to those on Ground Station One. This was not surprising. Most of those on Ground Station One were duplicated copies from the orbiter itself. One individual who was not duplicated in the station on the surface of Cuckoo was the human being named Ben Linc Pertin. Partly this was because he had already been duplicated enough times on the surface of Cuckoo; he had watched himself die three ways so far, and suspected three others. Partly it was because, for the past few galactic days, he had reported himself sick.

He had felt sick. Sick and despairing. When he reported himself back for duty it was not because he really wanted to get back to his work on the orbiter, it was only because it, or anything, was better than lying in his cocoon and watching stale repeated dramas on the stereostage. He relieved his predecessor on the monitoring detail, a T'Worlie named Nlem, and sucking a bubble of coffee to wake himself up began to reel disinterestedly through the transmissions of the last few days to see if anything had happened.

Something had.

Pertin sat up so abruptly that his motion jerked the bulb of coffee out of his hand. Tfling, the Sirian eye who was conducting some incomprehensible research of its own in the monitor chamber, emitted a staccato ripping sound of electrical energy as it flung itself desperately away from the sprinkling drops of liquid. Pertin's Pmal rang with the harsh, angry accusation: "Danger! Water deleterious! Destructive! Hostile action perceived!"

"Sorry, sorry!" cried Pertin, trying to backtrack the stereo image and at the same time activate the emergency air-purification systems. He managed, but not without further anger from the Sirian—reasonably enough, Pertin knew, but he was not in a mood to be reasonable.

As soon as possible, he spun back to the beginning of the message he had sampled. It had been aimed at Earth, and of course intercepted routinely by the orbiter for information purposes. It was a personal message, and the face of the girl sending it was what had startled him.

It was Zara!

He listened to the whole message, then turned off the stereostage, sick again and dazed.

Zara *Gentry*.

And here on Cuckoo—only light-minutes away!—but with *Jon* Gentry. Her *husband*.

Automatically his hand reached out for the transmission switch: he keyed it to the ground station and croaked: "Orbiter calling, personal communication, please respond."

The station was on its toes—or on whatever passed for toes in a T'Worlie. The creature who responded almost instantly stared out at Ben Linc Pertin and said through its Pmal translator, "Greeting, Ben Linc. I have joy that you are well again."

"Thanks, Nlem," Pertin said. "I want to—"

"It is now Nloom," the T'Worlie said. "Nlem is the version still aboard the orbiter with you. Nleem is the other version transported here."

"Nloom, then, dammit! Please. I have to get a message through right away."

"For whom is your message?"

"For my w—" Ben Linc stopped and swallowed. "For Mrs. Zara Doy Gentry," he croaked. "May I please speak to her at once?"

The T'Worlie, who had known Ben Linc well enough in their time together on the orbiter, stared at him thoughtfully out of its five eyes. Finally the Pmal chirped, "It was my conjecture you would have a message for her."

"Sure I would. Can I speak to her?"

"Negative. She has left with a survey expedition. Their circuits are fully occupied with telemetry and necessary administrative communications at this time. There will however be a direct channel opening in"— the T'Worlie spun in the air to look at something out of Ben Linc's field of view, then spun back to look at him—"in about two and one-half hours. I can then relay a message if you wish."

"I'd rather talk to her direct, Nloom," Pertin pleaded. "Can you patch through then?"

"Affirmative," the T'Worlie chirped, "although that is of course contingent on Zara Doy Gentry's desire to use available time for that purpose." Nloom hung there silently for a moment, and added: "Friend Ben Linc, it is a different version here. She does not know you, I think. What shall I tell her of your desire to speak with her?"

Ben Linc hesitated.

Of course the T'Worlie was right. This Zara had come direct from Earth. If she had heard of his existence at all, it was only casually—someone her Sun One duplicate had met there and married. She did not know him; worse, she herself was married to another man.

What could he say to her?

To that question he had no answer at all.

"I don't know, Nloom," he said dismally. "I guess—I think you'd better forget I called. I have to think this over."

He flipped the switch that dissolved the compassionate stare of the T'Worlie into a silvery mist as the stereostage went blank. He sat there, staring into the empty tank of the stage, seeing nothing, feeling nothing but a wretched, suffocating, overwhelming ache of loss.

TEN

*

That other Ben Pertin, who distinguished himself
with the middle name "Yale," sat, filthy, bruised, and
exhausted, ravenously tearing with his teeth at the flesh
of a kind of watersnake, watching the skinny boy croon
at the monster called an org.

He was delighted that the other human—or near-
human, the one called Redlaw—had found his equipment and brought it to him. But it was badly damaged.
He had managed to repair the Pmal translator enough
to get across a few words to the man and the boy; but it
was not functioning well. All he had been able to understand was that they wanted to use him to fight some
enemies—no doubt the ones they called "Watchers."
Why, he did not know. He also did not know if he had
any freedom of choice about fighting. Was he an ally or
a draftee?

But at least he was alive, and he had not expected
that much when the boy caught him trying to break
open the egg. The first thing Ben Yale tried to get
across through his Pmal translator was an apology for
that. He hadn't known it was a pet. He had only been
hungry. Whether the boy had understood or not, he
could not tell. That lean, sharp Indian face was hard to
read. The boy's words through the spottily functioning
Pmal had hardly been reassuring: "Mine . . . not
kill . . . punish!"

Now the org was perched on a rock, swaying uncertainly as it regarded the watersnake in Ben Yale's

hands. Pertin half-turned, watching the creature over his shoulder. It was still learning to keep its balance. Wings not yet unfolded, it looked ridiculous, like a trunk-faced, big-eyed fish with bird legs.

The exploring trunk reached out toward him, and Ben Yale swore under his breath, tore off a shred of the watersnake and threw it to the org. The boy cried something, which the Pmal clucked over without producing a single intelligible word. From the curtain of spray that concealed the cave, the man named Redlaw said: "He says: 'Meat not spoiled? Not make org sick?'"

Ben Yale shook his head. "It doesn't taste very good, but it doesn't seem to be harming me any," he said. The giant muttered something to the boy, who stared appraisingly at Pertin then, reluctantly, bobbed his head.

"Can give more," the giant said generously through the Pmal.

"I think I'd rather have a drink," said Pertin, not caring whether the translator dealt with it or not. He pushed past the giant, under the shrouding waterfall and out toward the lake.

The boy followed him, carefully scanning the sky. Pertin was not flattered. He knew the boy's concern was not for his own safety, but for fear he might attract the attention of some predator or enemy to the rest of them. Particularly to the org.

Pertin knelt on the gravel beach and leaned forward on his spread hands to drink. The water was cold and good, but it gave him little pleasure.

His position, when he thought it over carefully, was not very happy. The giant, Redlaw, seemed to want to talk only about weapons, and he had none; they had not been in the junk the giant had carried from the wreckage of his ship. To the younger man, Org Rider, he appeared to be only an inconvenience, possibly useful to taste doubtful meat for the org but otherwise a net liability. Neither of them seemed in the least interested in Pertin's reason for being on their world. What he had tried to tell them of the great universe outside had been received by the giant without comment, and by Org Rider, apparently, without understanding; the Pmal translator, in its damaged condition, seemed to function sporadically with Redlaw and almost not at all with the boy.

Ben Yale Pertin stood up and looked around him. He did not even notice the beauty of the scene: the deep, rock-walled valley in which he stood, the lazy waterfall behind him, the cold little lake with water so deep it looked black, the strange, colorful vegetation. Back on the orbiter the prospect of exploring these jungles had seemed interesting, to the extent that anything could interest him more than his own misery and loss without his wife and future. Back on Sun One, when he and Zara had been together, it would have seemed enchanting, a marvelous holiday surrounded by beauty. And farther back still, on Earth, before he had ever submitted to tachyon transmission, when there was still only one of him and that one knew nothing but cities and crowding, this whole scene would have seemed a total fantasy.

Now his eyes did not even register its color or its strangeness. It meant no more to him than a cell.

By the side of the lake Redlaw and the boy were building a fire, roasting nuts they had gathered, muttering to each other, too far away for the Pmal to pick up what they were saying and try to render it into English.

The giant stood up and walked easily toward Pertin. His green eyes were cold and judging. He put his fists on his hips as he stood before Pertin, towering over him nearly two feet, and spoke in his liquid tongue, rapidly and at length.

The Pmal, stammering to keep up, produced bursts of words: "Orgs gone. Watchers gone. Safe to travel. Can now find other slamming machine, other man like you. Can find killing things!"

Ben Yale Pertin kicked a pebble aimlessly into the water. "Travel?" he repeated. "You want me to come with you somewhere, to find another ship with weapons?"

Redlaw nodded vigorously, the bright beard bobbing. "Go soon now, two hundred breaths," the Pmal rattled. "Travel long, hard. You become ready."

Get ready? Pertin looked around him, almost smiling. What was there to do to get ready? What to pack, what to miss? He was ready to go anywhere anytime . . .

But for Ben Yale Pertin where was there to go?

They did not dare fly, and Org Rider's muscles began to ache very soon with the unaccustomed strain of trying to move at ground level, under the cover of the trees. The young org—he called it "Babe," lovingly—wanted desperately to fly, and so Org Rider's task was twice as hard, for sometimes he carried the fledgling, and sometimes kept up a running stream of talk with it, encouraging it to keep hopping along on its wobbly legs, cajoling it back when it attempted to fly. That was what his mother had taught him to do: talk to the infant org, let it know always that you were there. She swore that the orgs could even understand words after a while, like human children. And indeed Babe had already seemed to know what words like "fish" and "water" and "meat" meant.

That was more than the dumpy stranger knew. Org Rider did not like him. He had gotten over the superstitious fear he had felt when he first saw him bending over Babe's unhatched egg; he could not understand how this man could be alive when a dozen sleeps before he had seen him dead. But the puzzle had receded into the back of his mind and lost its power to instill fear. He wanted desperately to ask the man about it, but the clacking machine the stranger talked through did not seem to work well with him, and Redlaw only shrugged and reported that he could not understand what the man had said to him. "The words are clear enough," Redlaw rumbled. "He says it was *another* him. How can there be another? He could not say."

When they had eaten four times they decided to sleep. They were a good distance from the last place they had seen either orgs or Watchers, and so they risked building another fire and roasting more of the green nuts that hung all about them. The stranger moved a little way apart from them and flung himself on the ground; in a moment he began to snore.

Org Rider stroked Babe softly along the gently squirming length of its trunk and listened to what Redlaw was saying about the stranger: "He says he comes from another world. He knows arts the Watchers don't—arts that I think are strange and frightening to them. But he only speaks of these things, he does not have the weapons to prove them." Redlaw scowled at the fire.

"What is 'another world'?" Org Rider asked.

Redlaw shrugged morosely. "What he says about his world is not to be believed. He says it is not flat."

"Not flat? You mean mountainous?"

"No, not mountainous. Round. A little ball, so tiny that men have gone all the way around it."

"That is unlikely," Org Rider agreed.

"What is even more unlikely," continued Redlaw, glowering across the fire at the sleeping stranger, "is that he says our world is also curved like a ball. This is clearly false, but he holds to it. He says that in his place everything is very heavy. A man can't jump much above his own height. And he says, let me see—oh, yes. He says that although there are trees and plants and clouds on his world, they do not glow of their own light. None of them."

"How strange! It must be a gloomy place. How does one see?"

"There is one cloud," Redlaw said. "He does not call it a cloud, but it is in the sky, so what else could it be? It is so bright that its light hurts your eyes, and so high that it looks quite small."

"I have never seen such a thing," Org Rider declared. He peered around, squinting through the leaves at the great flank of Knife-in-the-Sky rising above them. "Where is the way to such a place? Over the mountain?"

"Farther! He says you climb beyond the rain clouds and beyond the flying rocks. He says you come up into a darkness where there is nothing at all. The darkness is bigger than you can imagine—so big that, when you begin to cross it, our flatworld shrinks to a point you can't even see, like an org flying out of sight toward the top of the mountain."

"It is all too strange for me," Org Rider said uneasily, stroking Babe. "If his world is so far away, how is it that he is just a man?"

"He does not know, he says," Redlaw growled. "He says he and his friends came here for learning, and that is one of the things they wish to learn: how it is that he is so like a human person, though from so far away."

"I wish him luck," Org Rider said dubiously. "I saw the machine he came in. It made a great noise in the sky, like slam-bang-bang, slam-bang-bang. But in spite of all the noise, it was slower than the orgs. They ripped the wings off it and tore it apart in the sky. And when the Watchers caught him, he died." Org Rider added thoughtfully, "I do not understand how that can be, either. But I have seen it, so it is so."

Redlaw rumbled impatiently, "It was another like him, he says. Part of that is nonsense, for he says it is him and says it isn't him, both.

"What is not nonsense," he added somberly, "is that he has something the Watchers fear. I must have that from him, or he must die."

They traveled fast and far, and the strain began to tell on all of them. Even Redlaw grew short-tempered and gaunt-faced. In some ways his was the most difficult job of all. Ben Yale Pertin was ill and injured; Org Rider had Babe to care for and often to carry; so it fell to Redlaw to keep alert for Watchers or for wild orgs, and there was never a moment while they were moving when he could relax. When they rested over the campfire they no longer talked amiably, they bickered. It troubled Org Rider that Redlaw seemed sometimes to believe in the stranger's insane stories, and other times to hate and mistrust him. He could not hear the stranger directly; whatever the machine was that Ben Yale Pertin had worn on his armbands, it seemed to respond only to the squeals and whistles of the language of the Watchers, not to normal human speech. So Org Rider could only communicate with him through Redlaw's imperfect understanding, and he was not sure how much was getting across.

Conscience made him try to correct some of the stranger's errors. "I have thought," he told Redlaw gravely, "and Ben Yale Pertin is wrong about our flatworld. It is not round; my mother has told me this. And also I understand how he looks so like us."

Redlaw scowled at him, then guffawed. When he was done laughing he chirped for a moment in the language of the Watchers, and then turned to Org Rider. "Ben Yale wishes to be enlightened, young one," he said, his tone half laughing but not pleasantly. "So do I. Please tell us what your mother has to contribute."

The boy said stubbornly, "It is truth, all people in my tribe agreed to that. The flatworld was made by the makers." He peered into the fire, trying to remember exactly. "My mother used to say they were terrible beings, taller than people, shining with light of their own. They sang death songs, and the songs themselves killed those who displeased them."

He waited for Redlaw to finish translating, chuckling, then went on:

"My people came from seven eggs the makers had made, in a cave down under the bottom of the world. The eggs were guarded by seven keepers, but still they were stolen by the Watchers. The evil creatures first blinded the keepers with death-weed dust, and then stole the eggs for a feast. As our guest would have done with my org," he added carefully.

Redlaw chocked, but managed to translate and

receive a reply. "He apologizes again for that," he reported. "He says he was hungry and did not know better."

Org Rider nodded and went on: "The feast was to be at the top of the Watchman's tower, where the blinded keepers couldn't climb. But the makers were angry, when they found the keepers blinded and the eggs gone. They did not sing their death song, but they sang a special song for the wild orgs. And the orgs heard it as they flew over Knife-in-the-Sky.

"Seven wild orgs dived on the feast, and carried the seven eggs in different directions, all around Knife-in-the-Sky. The orgs hovered over the eggs, keeping them warm. When each egg hatched, it produced a boy and a girl, and two of every creature that is useful to a man.

"But the Watchers spied where the orgs had gone, all but one. One by one, they found the eggs just as they hatched, and devoured the hatchling creatures, and killed the orgs that guarded them.

"But the seventh org they did not kill. It flew out into the shadowworld, where Knife-in-the-Sky hides the flatworld from the Watchman's tower. Here the hatchlings escaped. Green grass sprouted from the droppings of the creatures. The boy baby and the girl baby were nursed by the wild org that had saved them. They grew to be man and woman, and the parents of all our people.

"And what has come to me," Org Rider ended gravely, "is that one of the other eggs did in fact get safely away, and its hatchlings were the parents of Ben Yale Pertin!"

The giant was laughing boisterously. Org Rider paused. "What's the matter?" he demanded.

"What rot, boy!" Redlaw boomed. "Ignorant superstition!"

Org Rider leaped to his feet. "It is as my mother told it to me, Redlaw."

"It is nonsense," Redlaw insisted. "You should spend a few sleeps with the Watchers some time! You'll learn the difference between savage myths and scientific truths. I do not know whose superstitions are worse, yours or Ben Yale Pertin's."

"And what then is truth, all-knowing Redlaw?" the boy demanded stiffly.

"Ah, that I don't know," the giant confessed. "Some of the things Ben Yale Pertin says may have truth in them somewhere. He says our world may be hollow—"

"Hollow!" Org Rider cried scornfully.

"Yes. Does that seem unlikely? It does to me, too, and yet I know there are levels below. The tower of the Watchman guards one of the gates to those levels. I have been there while a captive of the Watchers, and I know. And there is some truth in what your mother told you, too, I think. There are such things as keepers and Watchers, and that is where they live. But—"

He was silent for a time, staring across the fire at the sleeping stranger. Then he stood up.

"It is time to sleep," he said, his voice hardening. "We are wasting time."

Fast and low, they kept going. They were halfway around the thrust of Knife-in-the-Sky's largest bastion, carried by Redlaw's driving purpose. For Org Rider that purpose seemed strange and remote; he could understand Redlaw's burning hatred of the Watchers, who had enslaved him and threatened his life; but now that they were free of the Watchers it seemed pointless to seek revenge. The boy himself was most occupied with his young org, who seemed to grow in size and intelligence and maturity with every breath. When Org Rider woke, the infant org was hopping unsteadily toward him, seeking not food—he was capable of finding his own well enough by then—but affection, the ritual rubdown of his golden fur with a handful of moss. Org Rider did not neglect the duties his mother had described to him. In particular he talked to the org, crooningly, repetitiously, and was rewarded by having Babe repeat some of the words to him. It was not rote replaying, like an earthly parrot's; it was almost like the first experimental use of language of a human child. The org's delicate high-pitched voice could repeat words like "food" when it was hungry, "sleep" when tired, and a dozen others. If it mangled some of the syllables, it nevertheless made itself clear.

Babe's stubby wings began to unfold as the boy groomed them. Tapered triangular fins, they had been molded invisibly into his sleek flanks. They looked almost too thick and too narrow to be useful in flight, but the boy's caressing fingers could feel their muscular power.

When they were fully spread, the boy determined to show Babe how they were used. He climbed a rock, the org hopping after him, spread his arms, and leaped toward another rock, flapping his arms.

To his surprise, Babe understood at once—so quickly that before Org Rider had reached his goal, Babe came sailing over him on quivering wings.

"Oh, good for you, Babe!" the boy shouted in delight. But the delight faded and congealed into panic, as the org kept going, past him and up, up over the sheltering leaves of the forest screen. He wheeled in a climbing spiral and screamed with a sound the boy had never heard him make.

Fear took the boy's breath. Was Babe calling to the wild orgs above the cliffs? He looked back to his companions for help; they were no help—Redlaw sound asleep under a mossy rock, Ben Yale Pertin watching apathetically. Without thinking, Org Rider crouched on the rock and kicked himself into the air, using every bit of strength in his legs and body, leaping a dozen times his own height, straight at the wheeling org.

Babe saw him and joyously dove to meet him. His young clumsiness made them collide, spinning the boy off balance, knocking the breath out of his body. But the org was up to the needs of the moment. Org Rider felt the velvet trunk coil around him protectingly. Strong and supple, it held him, then lifted him to the org's sleek-furred back, just above the rippling wings.

The boy lifted his voice in a shout of breathless triumph. "Now I am truly Org Rider!" he crowed. "Faster, Babe! Faster and higher!" And the org echoed in its piping voice:

"Faster, Babe! Faster, faster!"

Org Rider clung with his knees, fists locked in the golden fur, leaning against the wind of their flight. The throb of wings became a purr as Babe dived across the treetops, climbed again, then wheeled toward a clearing, so close above the yellow-bladed shrubs that the boy saw the giant moths fluttering about in terror. The boy's first alarm became a wild elation. His own wings had never lifted him with such speed or strength. He clapped the org's golden flank and called into the wind. "Good, Babe! Good!"

And the org piped happily, "Good Babe!" as it circled and dived again.

At last the boy found that Babe would respond to voice and tug of fists and kick of heels. Thoughtfully he drove the org back toward the clearing where the giant moths fluttered and cried, "Food, Babe! Eat! Get it!"

"Food Babe!" the org echoed, and showed its understanding by diving at one of the moths to catch it in spread talons. "Home Babe?" it piped questioningly, and Org Rider cried:

"Yes, Babe, home. We'll cook it and eat it. You've earned your food this time!"

They flew high, while the boy searched the flank of the mountain for the place where they had left Redlaw and Ben Yale Pertin. All the trees looked alike to him, all the clearings much the same. He caught a glimpse of something metallic, high above them on an outcropping, but it was not small enough to be Redlaw's cleaver or the stranger's peculiar instruments. He began to feel dismay . . . and then realized that Babe knew better than he; while he was searching the treetops for a clue, the org had already zeroed in on their campsite and was beating toward it powerfully.

When they landed, the boy got off his org's back and said solemnly, "Now I am truly Org Rider, and no longer a boy!"

Redlaw was staring at him with anger, and a touch of wry admiration. "No longer a boy, yes," he rumbled. "But a fool anyway! Listen, Org Rider who is no longer a boy. What do you hear?"

The boy, perplexed, stood still, ears tuned to—what? That distant shrill whistle?

"Do you hear it? Do you see it?" Redlaw demanded. "Over there—beyond the bee-tree. High in the sky!"

The boy looked. He had not heard it, because of the whistle of wind in his own ears, but now he heard it clearly and saw it, too, falling like a thick, blunt spear toward the slope of the mountain. A ship of the Watchers!

"If they saw you," Redlaw muttered, "then, man who is no longer a boy, you will not live to be a man very long."

The sputtering Pmal translator on Ben Yale Pertin's wrist caught only a few words, but they were enough to warn him. The Watchers were nearby.

Pertin did not need to hear more; he had encountered the Watchers. They were the ones who had shot his ship out of the sky of Cuckoo. In any other world they would have killed him, for he had fallen more than a mile to earth; but in Cuckoo's gentle surface gravitation he had survived with only cuts and bruises—and would have missed those if he had been less panicked and in better shape, he knew.

That kind of knowledge was no comfort. Pertin feared the Watchers. He feared dying, even when he welcomed it; there was no kind of future that looked good to him, unless by some miracle Zara should appear and offer a new life here. That was fantasy. Reality was that he would die here, and he would hate it.

The boy, ignoring the danger from the sky, was splitting and skinning the body of the golden-furred creature like a moth, spitting it over the fire. The yellow dust from the creature's fur gave Pertin a fit of sneezing, but soon the aroma of its roasting meat reconciled him to the dust. When it was done, Pertin humbly waited his turn. The best bits went to the org. Redlaw had second choice, then the boy; then last came Pertin. But there was still plenty left, and it was delicious.

By the time they had finished it had begun to rain, great fat slow drops that touched the fire and extinguished it. Gray clouds came dropping in to the tops of the trees.

The red haired giant bounded chuckling and happy over to him, and whistled something that the Pmal translator rendered as: "Rain clouds hide us from Watchers. Now we go! Youth has seen your ship, we find it, get weapons to kill Watchers!"

"But you have been to the wreckage of my ship," Pertin objected, perplexed. "I had no weapons——"

"Not *your* ship, *like-your* ship!" the Pmal crackled in response to the giant's squeals. Pertin gave up the struggle to understand; it did not matter. What mattered was that they were to move again. This time the boy did not need to worry about his org, who flew on above them, so he and the giant, unfettered, made very fast time. It was all Pertin could do to keep up with them. They kept on, and kept on. They did not stop even to eat, only paused long enough to pass Pertin a handful of hard roasted moss nuts, now cold and almost tasteless; he munched them as best he could while they went. Three times they ate, pausing once to drink at a vine-covered stream and to relieve their bowels and bladders, each time hurrying on.

Then Redlaw and the boy stopped and waited for Pertin to struggle up next to him.

"There!" the giant crowed. "Look! Beyond the gray moss, between the boulders. See! What do you see?"

Dizzy with weariness, Pertin tried to focus his eyes. See? Yes, there was something there, something bright that caught his eye.

The glint of light was metal. He glanced at the others, then joined them in a stumbling, hopping run up the gentle slope, and there, half-hidden by purple-flowered moss, was the wreck of a machine.

It was not his ship. It was smaller, and it clearly had been there for a long time. The moss had overgrown it completely, except for a few lengths of metal . . .

Metal? Yes, clearly it was metal. But there was something strange about it. The color was not clean silver, but stained with a watery bluish radiance that look unfamiliar, but vaguely ominous.

He scurried toward it. It must have been a man-carrying machine. Perhaps the machine one of his predecessors had used? He could not say. It was so torn and broken that he could not be sure. He tore at the moss, peering inside through a dark opening rimmed with shattered crystal. A sharp scent stung his nostrils; it did not seem to be coming from the moss, but from the bluish coating on the metal itself. Now that he touched it, it felt slick, slippery, moist—quite repellent . . .

A shrill squeal came from behind him, and his Pmal rapped out: "Do not touch! Not! Not!"

Confused, he stood up. Redlaw and Org Rider were coming toward him, anger and concern on their faces. "What's the matter?"

They looked at him—curiously, they were looking mostly at his hands, it seemed—then at each other. They did not speak for a moment, then Redlaw spoke, his voice oddly gentle. "Clean hands," the Pmal translator rapped. "Wipe on moss. No! No! Do not touch metal!"

He shrugged, not understanding. He seemed to have got some of the blue slime on his fingers. Obediently, he bent and rubbed his hands on the soft gray moss—

What he was rubbing against, he suddenly realized with a heart-stopping sensation of nausea, had the shape and texture of a human skull.

He clawed at the moss. It was a skull! A whole skeleton, in fact, the flesh rotted away, but the bones still queerly dressed, under the moss, in the imperishable plastics of an explorer's jungle garb, red top, orange-and-yellow pants, great white gauntlets, and on the shrunken forearm bones the coils of translator, recorder, direction-finder, timekeeper, and all the other instruments one wore.

The giant spoke, and the Pmal chattered: "Danger! Do not touch stranger bones. Serious! Be warned!"

Pertin looked up at them, aware of the bluish radiance that clung to the bones, aware that it still befouled his fingers, in spite of his efforts to rub them clean.

"Danger?" he repeated dully. "Yes, I suppose so, if you say so. But you're wrong about one thing. They're not a stranger's bones. I know those bones very well, and I know the clothes they wear, too. I ought to. They're mine."

ELEVEN

Far away, around the great bulk of Cuckoo, the orbiter was preparing to transmit its observer along the tachyonic path FARLINK had charted to the source of the interfering transmission in the Galaxy. They still didn't know how far it was, exactly. Roughly in the direction of Earth, yes; but at extragalactic distances, that could mean anywhere from Rigel to Canopus, and farther than that in the line of flight from Cuckoo.

And that was only one of the things they didn't know. Would the transmitted duplicate find breathable air and bearable temperatures when he stepped out of the receiving box?—or sphere, or inflatable bag, or whatever sort of enclosure might contain an uninvited guest; it was only a convenience that made all the inter-communicating galactic races use essentially the same sort of equipment. This wild card might take any form.

"I'm glad I'm not going," Ben Linc Pertin announced gloomily. He didn't sound very glad, even to himself. He found precious little to be glad about these days, and could look forward to not much better.

Venus chimed softly, "I'm glad for you too, Ben Linc. It is less hazardous for an edited form like myself."

Ben Linc Pertin in quick confusion said, "Oh, I'm sorry. I was just thinking—"

"That it was dangerous and unsure, yes. But less so for me. In any event," she continued melodiously, "FARLINK has chosen me and I have consented."

He said miserably, "I am sorry, Venus. I've been

into my own troubles and not thinking about yours. I know how it tears you up to send a self away to suffer or die somewhere; I've done it often enough."

The silvery girl looked at him curiously, "That is so, Ben Linc. But—forgive me—in this form it is less painful. If I were in my own true form I would feel there was more to lose."

"Wait!" the sentient ape named Doc Chimp II said, holding up a hand that contained a banana. "There's a message—"

It was FARLINK. In the recreation room where they were awaiting Venus' time for the Tachyon transmitter there were no screens, but the wall speakers sang out with the computer's electronic voice. "Stand by," it signaled, the Pmal of each being translating the words automatically into its own language.

"Wonder what that is," Doc Chimp mused. "Well, cheers!" And he held up his banana in a sort of toast. Pertin responded with his tumbler of Scotch and water, while the silvery girl sniffed at cloudlets of luminescent mist she sprayed out of an atomizer.

"Orders!" FARLINK'S voice rapped out of the speakers. "The transmission of Replicate 4182, known as Venus, is canceled. A newly detected singularity in the incoming signals has altered the estimate of requirements. Stand by for assignment of replacement."

"Congratulations, Venus," Doc Chimp cried. "That's a last-minute reprieve, if I ever heard one. Wonder who they'll send instead? A Scorpian robot, maybe? A sheliak. Or—"

"Orders," the wall speaker rasped. "The substitute for transmission is required to proceed at once to the tachyon station for replication. He is Replicate 5153, known as Ben Linc Pertin."

"Oh, no," Doc Chimp cried.

"Communication of regret," shrilled the T'Worlie, Nammie.

"I'm sorry, Ben Linc," the silvery girl whispered.

Pertin stood numb. He had not expected it; he did not know how to respond.

"Replicate 5153," FARLINK growled from the wall speakers. "There is the time pressure. Proceed at once for replication!"

"Come on, Ben Linc," Doc Chimp said as gently as he knew how, taking one arm. He gestured to Venus, who took the other; and the two of them walked the unresisting Ben Linc Pertin along the corridors to the radial shaft that led to the tachyon transmitter. He let them. He felt nothing . . .

Nothing while he was on his way to the transmitter.

Nothing (except the sudden surprising hard metal lips of Venus against his own, just before he went inside) as he entered the transmitter and stood through its silent omniscient scan.

Nothing when he looked around, and realized *he* was that *he* who had remained behind.

Nothing, even, while the chimp and the silvery girl escorted him back to the rec room, the T'Worlie fluttering behind. They chattered doubtfully among themselves, then pooled their small quotas of open-choice mass to buy him two more Scotches, doubles. He gulped them down, hardly tasting them. He was still *here*, as nothing had happened. But he was also *there*.

And he could never come back.

Later, he was not sure how much later, there was a final message of progress from FARLINK. "The transmission," the speakers rasped, "has been successful. First acknowledgment of arrival has been received, along with samples for environmental analysis. Unfortunately they are not life-sustaining beyond a fairly short period."

There was a small silence before Doc Chimp said, "Well, anyway, Ben Linc, congratulations. You arrived."

"I arrived," Ben Linc agreed. "And I'm dead."

* * *

Down inside the atmosphere of Cuckoo, nearly two hundred million miles away from the orbiter on Cuckoo's far side, the exploring team was practicing its flying skills.

The expedition, so far, was going well. From their altitude, miles above Ground Station One, miles out from the slope of the enormous mountain, even Cuckoo looked almost small—not the great sweep of its surface, to be sure, but the detail on it: tiny trees, winking bright puddle of lake, silvery thread of river. In the air itself were the curious bright clouds that sailed around, each seeking its own level, seeming to drop spores of some bright seedlings; living glowing things that gave Cuckoo almost the only light it had, bar the glow of plants and animals on the surface itself.

They did not know these glowing clouds to be dangerous, but they gave them a wide berth. Anyway, there was plenty of room in the sky. Not only to travel to a destination, but for pleasure too: Valkyrie and Zara and the T'Worlie took joy in doing loops and barrel rolls, soaring far off from the little procession of Scorpian robot, Sirian eye, and husband, as they chugged sedately along, and returning. Zara found herself laughing from sheer physical joy. She weighed so little in Cuckoo's air that it was almost irrelevant whether she was flying head up or down. She followed the piping, frolicking T'Worlie up in a loop. Below her the great sloping flank of the mountain seemed to subside into a plain; then the plain tipped and became a slope that rose in the other direction, then passed out of sight completely as she topped out her loop and began to come down.

In her earplug communicator her husband's voice, faintly amused and faintly annoyed, said "If you three will please stop playing, we'd better stay close together. This is dangerous territory, you know."

Rebuked, Zara flopped over and flailed her wings to get her bearing. The T'Worlie, used to flight, darted back and hung before her, exuding an odor that she would come to recognize as an expression of rueful embarrassment, like a child caught in the cookie jar.

Zara burst out laughing. She caught sight of the silver girl, far overhead, soaring down toward them with great, strong strokes of her wings. Zara cried: "Come on, Val, Nleem! Race you back to the others!" And she let them signal agreement and start their powerful, effortless flight back toward the sober, sedate members of the party. Then she aimed herself headfirst toward the three distant dots, folded her wings except for a tiny web from wrists to hips for control, and activated her pulse-jet. *Thrump, thrump, thrump, thrump* . . . The radio-isotopes poured heat into measured slugs of water, flashed them into steam, expanded them into the pulse-jet, and she arrowed toward the others at a hundred miles an hour, easily passing the gallant but small T'Worlie, catching up with Valkyrie and leaving her behind a thousand meters from the steady three. Stopping was the problem; she shut off the jet and tried to lose speed by zooming sharply up; but in Cuckoo's wan grip the loss to gravity was so small she found herself looping the loop again, involuntarily, before, laughing and dizzy, she was properly back in line with the rest of the party.

Her husband, in line ahead of her, turned to look disapprovingly at her over his shoulder. "About time you got here," he grumbled.

Zara, who was concentrating on an even, rippling flow of her wings, gave him a docile, absentminded smile. What a butterball he was, she thought dispassionately; even in the stretched-out edited version for Cuckoo, his round body and pipestem legs made him look like a stork. "The Scorpian's getting a strong signal from one of the transponders," Jon added. "That means we are getting near one of our objectives—probably a downed exploring ship."

"How nice," said Zara, winking at the silver girl.

Valkyrie did not wink back; her copy of Earthly human anatomy was not close enough for that. But Zara could hear her chuckle.

Three places ahead of her in line, the Sirian eye raised itself out of the file on its crackling spread of electric forces, and turned to confront her. It had no expression, but she felt reproof in its stare. The tiny sphincter mouth, surrounded by the forty crablike little legs, worked convulsively. Zara could hear no sound from it; Sirians used sound for communication, but the frequencies were far higher than Man's; twenty thousand Hertz was a low basso-profundo note for them. But the Pmal caught it, and rapped reprovingly in her ear: "Estimate: Your use of jet propulsion has increased our risk. Assumption: Such sounds in past have attracted predators. Validation: Air-palping reveals several unidentified traces moving toward us at three hundred and seventeen degrees right ascension, minus six degrees declination."

"Confirmed," the Scorpian robot stated without passion. It did not speak aloud at all. Its talk circuits used radio waves, but the Pmals picked up and faithfully translated the messages.

Zara pressed her elbows into her sides and felt herself begin to drop. It was not what she had intended, but it was better than floundering around while she tried to adjust her telescopic visor. She caught a glimpse of something at the indicated position, realized she was falling farther behind and below the others than she wanted, flapped herself back into position and at last got a clear look at what the Sirian had reported.

There were three of them, all right. But of what? A body gleaming like metallic copper; stubby wings that shone silver at the tips; great claws that were coming out of concealment from under the creatures' body, in anticipation of combat.

For a moment she knew terror; then she heard her husband's voice, triumphant and challenging. "Tally-ho!" he shouted. "I've got 'em!"

And without waiting for comment from the others, he aimed himself and fired his jet.

From directly behind, Zara got the full roar of the pulse jet as it *thrumped* giant smoke rings of steam, thrusting him like an arrow toward the onrushing orgs. There was a confusion of argument that the Pmals were unable to handle, too many beings shouting at once. What they were saying was clear enough, but Jon Gentry was paying no attenion. He had the taste of blood on his lips, and he was on the hunt.

The orgs were wise in warfare. They split up to come at this lone attacker from three directions at once. Against any of the beings that were their natural prey the strategy was winning. Against galactic weapons, it was hopeless.

Gentry's hours on the practice range on Earth had not been wasted. The first spark-hiss that marked the firing of his laser was a miss, but the second found a target. Three times then the cobalt-blue streak of his laser reached out to touch an org. Three times the creature hit screamed, the pain bellow of a tortured beast, and each time the scream was cut off as the blue ray burned through scales and flesh in a split second. Each org flamed briefly, and then tumbled, slowly and ungracefully, toward the mountain flank far below.

Gentry stopped his pulse-jet, and returned to them by wing power alone. As he came close, Zara could hear that he was singing. He swooped past her, touching her with what might have been meant for a caress of affection, but sent her spinning. "Got 'em!" he shouted. "That was worth the whole trip, Zara!"

The silver girl chimed, "It is true that you killed those creatures. I do not think it was wise to attack single-handed, however."

And the Scorpian robot muttered through its Pmal, "Confirm statement as to organic creatures. Propose consequential probability. Premise: Organic creatures are not principal adversaries. Second premise: Use of laser weapons may be counterproductive at this time."

"Ah," Gentry grumbled, "you're just scared—" Illogically, Zara thought with resentment; all the Galaxy knew that Scorpians could not be frightened, since they were not only very nearly physically indestructible but had little emotional attachment to life.

Val chimed: "I suggest we proceed to our objective. I have a strong transponder trace from a point on the mountainside fifteen kilometers away, nearly in direction of flight. The characteristics are compatible with one of the previous exploration ships."

"Propose we go there now," the T'Worlie twittered through the translator.

"Why not?" Jon Gentry said with careless courage. "I think we've seen we can deal with any problems that come up."

Zara dropped back a few meters, looking at her husband curiously. This—what was that old word? machismo?—this kind of behavior was a side of her husband she had not known very well. Of course, on placid Earth there was little occasion for physical conflict, but even so she could hardly reconcile this fire-eyed warrior with the gentle, sedentary, rather dull man she had been married to for three years on Earth. She had never questioned his courage. It had simply never occurred to her to consider it. If she had been aware of it at all, she might have considered it as a sort of mildly disturbing anachronism, like an excess of body hair or a desire for raw meat.

She was jolted out of her reverie by a sudden gabble in the Pmals. Once again several members of the party were speaking at once. The first clear transmission was from Val, who cried: "I think we are in trouble!" And it was confirmed by the Sirian's little sphincter mouth, which squeaked its inaudible message that the Pmal translated as:

"Air palping now registers three new high-speed traces vectoring toward us. Correction. Four traces. Correction. Five, six, six-plus traces. Points of origin

widely separated. Suggest indications are that technological intervention is now occurring."

T'Worlie and humans, plus Val, tried desperately to
see what the Sirian and the Scorpian had detected. Even
for Val, however, they were still out of sight, but Val
confirmed the locating: "I have the trace," she agreed.

"Recommend seeking cover," chattered the Pmal, responding to the Scorpian's signal.

Jon Gentry snorted, "What, run away? Not me!
We've got weapons, let's use them."

Val pealed, "That is countersurvival, Jon Gentry. I
have an alternative proposal. You organics seek cover.
The Scorpian and I will intercept the opponents."

"Concurring," the Scorpian chattered through the
Pmal translator at once.

"No bloody chance!" Jon Gentry blazed. "I guess
you don't know much about Earthmen! Fighting's
nothing strange to us. We came here to carry an equal
share of the load, and that includes fighting. We're not
going to hide behind a bunch of aliens!"

"He *means*," Zara cried quickly, "that we feel an ob-
ligation to help. And honestly, Val—don't you think we
can take care of ourselves?"

The silvery girl swept her great wings up to a point
over her head, thus dropping and turning toward Zara.
"Doubt it very much," she pealed. "Please study the
approaching objects at thirty-four degrees right ascension, eighteen degrees plus declination." She paused
while Zara struggled with her telescopic visor.

"Oh," Zara said at last. "They are—formidable looking, aren't they?"

They were that. Blunt spearpoints, mottled in colors
of bronze and gray that glinted with underlying metal,
they were arrowing toward the galactic party at easily
supersonic speeds. And those were only two. How
many had the Scorpian reported? More than six—

These were not animals or primitives, these were
complex and powerful technological devices, and, Zara

thought with a sinking heart, no doubt armed accordingly.

"I accept offer," the T'Worlie chirped. "Come!" And Nleem stood on his head in the air, and swam his deceptively filmy wings to drive himself straight downward at the forest cover beneath them. There was a spatter of electrical fields, and he was followed by the Sirian eye.

Zara wailed nervously, "Please, Jon! Let's do what Val says." She tried to catch her husband's eye, but he was already higher than she, peering toward the approaching Watcher ships eagerly. "Please?" she coaxed.

"Not a chance!" he snapped. "You go ahead. I'm going to fight this out!"

"Then I'd better stay, too—"

"No way! Damned if you will, Zara! Now get out of the way—there's going to be a fight, and I don't want to have to worry about you getting hurt!"

Angry, and in a way she could not define, afraid—it was not physical fear, it was a deadly feeling that something was changing irrevocably in her life—Zara turned herself over in the air, aimed herself at the rapidly diminishing forms of the T'Worlie and the Sirian, and activated the pulse jet. *Thrump, thrump, thrump,*—the acceleration was terrific. She was catching up on the Sirian and the T'Worlie very rapidly.

Her previous experience had made her cautious. She did not want to overshoot this time; that would mean driving herself into the ground below. She judged the distance as well as she could, allowed the jet to build up speed for a moment, then, when she gauged she had plenty of margin left, cut the pulse and arrowed down on inertia for a few seconds. Then she rotated herself and applied maximum counterthrust with the jet to slow her fall.

Zara had thought she had left herself a large margin on the side of caution. In fact, she had started the counterthrust far too late. It slowed her headlong drop— feebly, tardily; just enough so that when she struck the treetops she was traveling at something like thirty miles an hour.

She hit hard, broke off sprigs and branches, went flying through a tangle of vines that ripped at her skin and bruised her brutally. Every snag hurt her, but every snag slowed her a fraction, so that when she hit the soggy, mossy marsh under the trees she knocked herself unconscious, but lived.

When she came to, she was alone.

She could see very little of the sky, but in it were neither husband nor allies, nor even the enemy ships that had been attacking them; and of the T'Worlie and the Sirian eye that she had been trying to join there was no trace at all.

TWELVE

*

Org Rider involuntarily started to move forward to help Ben Yale Pertin, but Redlaw caught his arm.

"Don't touch him!" the giant rumbled. Then, looking past Org Rider to the stranger, he lowered his voice, adding, "There's nothing you can do for him now. That slime doesn't thrive on vegetation. But it eats flesh. He's done for."

"But—but it's only some kind of sap, or something like that. We can take him to the river, wash it off—"

"You're not hearing me, boy. There's no chance for him at all. If he's lucky, he'll be dead in five sleeps. If he's not, he'll linger on for a dozen. But there's no way to clean him now, and he's death to touch."

Pertin was staring at them, aware they were talking about him, suspicious of what they were saying. He asked a question that Org Rider could not understand, but Redlaw chirped some sort of answer in the whistling screech of the Watchers. Under his breath he said to the boy, "He said those bones were his. What can he mean by that?"

Org Rider said, with the uneasy fascination of horror, "It is as it was before, Redlaw. Remember? He died already, and was alive again. Can it be that he dies many times, and always lives again?"

"If he lives again after that blue slime gets through with him I'll be astonished," the giant rumbled. "Ah, well. We can't help him, but we can feed him. I'll get some food. You build a fire."

"What about the slamming machine?" the boy cried.

The giant nodded somberly. "There it is," he agreed.
"We'll ask Ben Yale Pertin if there are weapons there.
But if they've got that blue slime on them, it will be
ticklish work to find a way to use them."

"Can't we clean them?"

"Ah, yes, clean them. But it's being sure they're
clean that's the hard part. And one single drop of the
blue murder, so tiny you might not even see it, is
enough for death. If you see it anywhere on you, boy,
on toe or finger, wherever, don't wait. If it's on a toe,
lop off the foot! It's miserable work to do, but it's your
life if you don't!"

Numbly, the boy nodded and turned to his org.
"Don't go near him, Babe," he ordered. The soft trunk
squirmed out to touch him reassuringly.

"What I think," ruminated Redlaw, staring at Ben
Yale Pertin, who was scrabbling feverishly in the
wreckage of the ship, "is that this slamming machine is
not his but another's. Identical ships. Maybe identical
people. I think it landed on the living peak of Knife-in-
the-Sky, touched the slime, and then it came down
here. Its occupant, perhaps another Ben Pertin, came
out and touched the slime. When he did that, it was too
late for him."

The boy nodded somberly. "Stay with this one, Redlaw," he said. "Perhaps you can help him. I will get
food." But he felt as he left the org with a cautioning
word and turned into the forest that there was no way
for Redlaw to help Pertin, and that his real reason for
going after food was that he could not bear to see him
doomed thus to die. To die a third time! It was heavy
enough to die once. What courage these people must
have, to die again and again!

He was fortunate almost at once, scouring the wet
black gravel along a sluggish stream, when something
like a buried log humped itself and sprang free of the
black muck. The boy caught his knife and waited; in a
moment he was rewarded, as the "log" ripped suddenly
down the back.

A wild-flower sweetness exploded into the air, and a delicate pink shape thrust and thrust, struggling to escape from its black prison. Org Rider paused, entranced. It was almost too beautiful to kill for food! But he thought of the dying Ben Yale Pertin, and of his org; he had no choice. He waited only until the lacelike wings of black-veined rose unfolded, and the new-hatched creature gripped the sides of the canoelike shell and slowly pulled itself free. Huge luminous eyes, glowing with the rosy red of live coals, gazed blankly at him and were just beginning to focus when he was upon it with his knife, stabbing the new life out of it.

When they had the skinned and gutted body of the butterfly-creature broiling over the low fire Redlaw had made, the giant took him aside. "Here is what I have secured," he said with satisfaction. "Look!" And he offered a handful of gleaming objects to the boy.

Org Rider recoiled. "They're from the slamming machine!" he cried.

"Yes," Redlaw agreed. "But I have taken them out myself, from the interior, where the blue slime did not penetrate. Ben Yale is angry at me because I would not let him touch them. I made him understand that the blue slime is very deadly to us—though I did not say that it was also deadly to him," he added in an undertone.

"What do they do?"

"This," Redlaw said proudly, "is a weapon." He held up a thing shaped like a short seed-cone, with a slim cylinder perched at an angle across its tip. "It is not what I had hoped for," he admitted. "It is only a laser. The Watchers, too, have lasers. Still, it is better than anything we have had so far!

"And this"—he held up a thing like tiny windows, set in an elastic band—"is for far-seeing. Look through it, Org Rider! You will see as far as you can travel in a dozen sleeps!"

The boy took it gingerly. The elastic part clasped his skull gently but firmly as he put it on; the transparent part hung just over his eyebrows. Squinting upward, he caught strange, bent glimpses of the treetops and clouds, like watersnakes seen through the turbulence of a rapid. He shook his head, and the visor popped into place in front of his eyes.

Suddenly the great broad yellow leaves of the tree over his head rushed in on him, and the bright golden clouds beyond swooped down almost within arm's length. Involuntarily he ducked and yelped.

Redlaw guffawed. "Startles you, doesn't it?" he rumbled. "But you'll see Watchers coming at you through that a hundred breaths before your bare eyes will see them, boy. And this thing—Ben Yale Pertin calls it an 'audio log,' whatever that is—listen!" And he touched a switch on it, and a voice—Ben's voice, the boy realized—began to speak from inside the box somewhere. Org Rider could not understand what it said, to be sure; it was in that strange gibberish tongue the stranger used. But it was his voice, beyond doubt.

Redlaw's mood changed. He dropped the audio log to the ground and stared at it angrily. "But there's not what I wanted," he muttered. "Not a weapon that the Watchers don't already have. Not anything that will let us destroy them!"

"Perhaps Ben Pertin does not have any such weapons," Org Rider offered.

"He has them! Or his people do. I'd kill him, if it would make him get them for me! But how can you kill a man who's dying already?" He stared at the squat man, then glanced past him at the woods. "Boy, what's the matter with your org?"

Tardily Org Rider realized that Babe had wandered away from his side, was on the hillside above the wrecked slamming machine. He leaped to his feet, tensely afraid that the org might somehow brush against the blue death. But it was not near the machine and showed no interest in it; something else was engaging its attention. It stood upthrust on its great talons, huge eyes staring frozen into the sky, soft pink trunk squirming upward as to feel what the eyes were looking at.

"What is it?" Org Rider demanded sharply. The org did not even look at him. Then, reflected in the org's eye, he saw a peculiar flash of bright cobalt blue; startled, he looked upward through the leaf canopy and saw, lancing through the sky, a line of cobalt fire that winked, flashed again in a different place, and again. The light was so intense it almost blinded him, who had seen few bright sources of light in his life, but he was almost sure he saw several small dots around the bright blue beams. A distant rushing sound, as of cloth tearing, came to him from where those bright beams flashed, and was repeated again and again. "Lasers!" Redlaw bellowed.

Remembering what he wore, Org Rider jerked the far-seeing visor into place, and after a moment of frantic search, found the magnified images of what was going on above him. A man! A man wearing a queer tree-trunklike thing strapped to his back, pointing something like the weapon Redlaw had showed him; and around and below the man, falling like dead leaves through the sky, two, no three orgs. Dead. Slain by those bright blue bolts.

The boy peered under the glasses, trying to make sense of what he saw, and became aware that there were other dots in the sky. It took him time to find them through the visor, but there they were—four or five creatures, and what strange creatures they were! Something that looked like a winged woman made of silvery metal! A tiny creature with frail wings and a hideous five-eyed head! A thing that looked like an enormous eye, unsupported in the air! A machine, a— what? he could not say for sure, but something that looked like a single great cube of metal with metal attachments hanging from it—also floating unsupported in the air. And with them—

Org Rider caught his breath, steadied the glasses,

and looked again. A woman. A girl. Dressed like Ben
Yale Pertin, or the man who had beamed down the
orgs; but a girl whose pale face and bright eyes were
like no other woman he had ever seen.

He was jolted out of his reverie by Redlaw. "Give
me that far-seer," the giant growled, snatching it off Org
Rider's head. He bounded over to a clearing, jamming
the visor onto his own head, upward. "Blood and
death!" he muttered. "What are those things?" He
lifted the lenses away from his eyes and stared blankly
at the boy. "Did you see them?" he demanded. "Queer
machine things! Animals like nothing I've ever seen!"

Org Rider nodded soberly. He heard the distant
screams of orgs, wondered if they were the three he had
seen killed, the sound reaching them so late because of
distance; then realized it would not be that. These
screams were nearer.

And suddenly the strange sights he had seen in the
sky were driven from his mind, as he heard those wild
screams repeated—less raucously, but closer at hand.
He turned and shouted, "Babe! What are you doing?"

The young org turned the great eyes on him. The
trunk was quivering and snaking out, now toward Org
Rider, now toward the sky. The boy bounded over to
the org, caught it around the neck. "Don't listen,
Babe!" he begged, and the org mimicked, in his own
voice:

"Listen . . . listen . . . listen!"

"Stay, Babe," he coaxed, stroking the org's quivering
head. He could feel a roughness beneath the velvet,
along the ridges over the great staring eyes, and knew
that the hard bronze scales of maturity were beginning
to form there. The shrieks of the wild orgs sounded again,
nearer. "Please, Babe," he begged.

The org's trembling stopped. It froze, staring into the
sky, and the boy saw what its huge eyes had discovered.
Black and narrow and swift against the gray sky, two
orgs were scudding over the treetops, up-mountain,
away from where their fellows had just been slain. And

the cries they were shrilling were of fear and warning.

The drives of his genes and chromosomes were too strong to resist. Babe answered with a hoarse, hooting cry, and launched himself into the air.

The first stroke of his powerful wing struck Org Rider, sent him tumbling across the mossy rock. As the boy picked himself up, Babe paused for an instant high above him. "Please," it screamed, hoarsely mimicking the boy's own voice. "Please . . . please . . ."

And it spun in air and climbed into the bright sky to follow its wild kin.

Alone and desolate, Org Rider stood watching until Babe and the others were out of sight.

THIRTEEN

*

Ben Yale Pertin had not been fooled by the red-haired giant's pitiful attempts to dissemble. He had caught enough of the giant's meaning through the translator to know that, from Redlaw's point of view at least, the blue slime was very bad medicine indeed. Pertin was not unconcerned about that; he was very much concerned indeed, but he also was sure that these barbarians did not know much about medicine. His first concern was to find the medicpac in the wrecked exploration ship. He did not trouble to clean the slime off; not after the first trial at swabbing it from his skin had taught him something new about pain. But he swabbed it with anesthetizing and antiseptic creams from the pac, covered it with self-sealing bandages, and sterilized the whole area with a cleansing spray. The bone-deep itching began to fade away at once, and the pain went with it. Pertin then fished out the bottles of vitamin supplements and swallowed a week's ration at once, before he went looking for proper food. A self-heating can of beef stew, another self-heating can that produced instant black coffee, a can of peaches in thick syrup— he stopped eating at last not because he was no longer hungry, but because he began to think he would burst.

Then he turned his attention to less immediate problems, such as the two barbarians he was with. They seemed much taken with the laser gun, the telescopic visor, and the audio log; well, let the giant play. It did not matter. The log was only a spare. The weapon was more serious, in a way, but as he had been at their

209

mercy for—what? a week? a month? How could one
tell in this place where there was never anything like
day or night—and they had not killed him as yet. Giving them a weapon did not much change anything. Of
course, if he had kept the weapon it would have put the
odds in his favor, he mused. But he still had the bazooka—and his own superiority over these savages . . .

He watched incuriously while Org Rider stroked his
hatchling and the giant puzzled over the hardware, idly
stroking the bandages on arms and legs. They were beginning to tingle again, he realized. That was odd, but
there was no real pain. The only necessary thing was to
get himself in contact with civilization again, whereupon full medical treatment would of course be available.

Unfortunately, this exploring ship was of a different
model from the one he himself had been shot down in,
and although there was a radio he could not make it
work. Batteries run down? That seemed unlikely; most
electrical systems were powered by radioisotopes and
they didn't run down. Broken in the crash? It didn't
seem to be. He came to the conclusion that it was working, after all, but that the frequency on which it was
operating was simply not monitored any longer. He explored further around the craft, and came across the
prime audio log.

Maybe that would give him a clue, he reasoned, and
thumbed it back to the beginning of the record, then
turned it to PLAY.

"Ben Tom Pertin," it whispered in his earplug, "reporting on landing on surface of Cuckoo."

Hearing his own voice in his ears gave him a thrill of
unexpected unease; that voice came from vocal chords
that had once lodged in that blue-smeared skeleton before him. But the voice was going on:

"First entry into atmosphere accomplished without
difficulty; initial target, anomalous formations on top of
mountain. I landed without exiting vehicle because of
low air pressure at this altitude. The top of the mountain

was bare rock, which seemed to be covered by a blue lichen or greasy substance of some sort, which glowed quite brightly. I observed the anomalous formations and have photographed them for transmission. I do not understand them. There appears to be a sort of crater on top of this mountain, although it is clearly not volcanic; there is nothing resembling a lava flow, outgassing, or anything else indicating activity of that sort. On the lips of the crater are some truncated cones which have the appearance of artifacts . . ." There was a click, and then the voice resumed: "At this point the viewports of the vehicle began to cloud over and vision began to be impaired. I do not know the cause of this. Perhaps the temperature differential caused the ports to fog up. As I cannot leave the vehicle I am breaking off this section of the survey to attempt a landing at a lower altitude."

There was another click, and then the voice resumed—but a different, fearful, worried voice now: "Report two: Vision did not improve. I was forced to fly and land by radar, and landed with some difficulty. I do not know if the vehicle is damaged. The blue material appears to be covering the viewports. I will reconnoiter outside and return for further report." *Click* . . .

And then nothing, nothing but the faint distant hiss of the recorder coil unwinding under the scanner heads.

Ben Yale let it run through, hoping against hope for more word, but there was none. He had felt there would not be. He could write the rest of the story himself. He stood at the port of the vehicle, looking out at the great yellow-tipped trees, the marshland and moss, the distant river; and he could imagine that other he standing in that place and looking at that same view, and venturing out to explore this strange new world . . . and never noticing the blue slime that clung to him as he swabbed experimentally at the viewports, or steadied himself against the landing skids. And then, later, trying to get back to the vehicle and medicpacs, and not quite making it—as the skeleton outside attested . . .

Ben Yale scowled, rubbing absently at his bandages, refusing to entertain the unwanted thought that kept popping into his head: suppose this other Ben Pertin *had* used the medicpacs . . . and suppose modern galactic medicine had not been enough to stop the inroads of the blue slime?

Belatedly he became aware of the excitement outside. What were they rattling on about?

He activated the Pmal translator on his arm, and managed to catch a few words of what the giant was shouting. Something about aliens in the sky?

At once Ben Yale was all attention. Now he remembered hearing the *zzzzt* of laser weapons, and the screams of those creatures like the one the boy appeared to keep for a pet. Something was surely going on, but what?

He leaped to the top of the vehicle, staring toward the sky. Yes, there was something there, tantalizingly at the very limit of visibility, something that looked like tiny dots proceeding in file across the broad dome of Cuckoo's heaven. They were terribly near some of the bright clouds in Pertin's line of vision, which made the identification of them even harder; but surely that one creature that glinted so brilliantly had to be one of the winged girls?

And that other—was it human?

He stood benumbed until he heard the screams of wild orgs passing overhead, and remembered to scramble out of sight just in time; he did not want them dining off him! He saw the boy's org join them without any particular interest, and then realized something was going on overhead.

The straight line of beings had broken up. Several were dropping away, the others changing course. He heard the scream of high-speed transport, and caught the distant glint of some sort of air vehicles moving in toward the dissolving party of creatures.

Ben Yale pawed at his forehead, and realized the

visors were gone; the red-haired giant had picked them up, now seemed to be playing with them. Pertin bounded over and grabbed for them.

To his surprise, the giant fled from him as if he were carrying the plague. "Give me my glasses!" Pertin roared, pursuing. The giant ripped off a series of words, which the Pmal struggled over and produced:

"Don't touch! Stay away! I'll kill!"

"They're mine!" Pertin said stubbornly, and, hesitantly, Redlaw glanced at the boy, shrugged, and slowly drew them off his head. He did not hand them directly to Ben Yale but dropped them on the ground and stepped quickly back.

Ben Yale didn't care; he snatched them up and put them on, staring blindly at the sky.

It was so hard to find anything at this extreme distance! Twice he caught a corner of one of the bright clouds, and the magnified light dazzled him. Then he found something, lost it, zeroed in on it again: It was a vessel, like the ones the giant had called "Watcher ships." It looked ugly and dangerous, and it was heading purposefully, at high speed, toward where the party had been sailing along. He sought the party again, with success until he heard the *thrump-thrump-thrump* of a steam rocket. Peering under the glasses, he saw the string of steam puffs the jet left behind, and managed to get the person who was using it in quick focus just a moment before it dropped out of sight.

Before *she* dropped out of sight.

Ben Yale stood transfixed, heedless of the shouts of the boy and the giant, staring emptily in to the now empty sky where he had just seen, diving at breakneck speed for the jungle, the girl he had left behind him on Sun One and had thought never to see again in this life, Zara Doy.

FOURTEEN
*

When Zara realized that she was alone on this strange planet, she was not so much afraid as deeply resentful. She had not had the practice of much physical fear. There was little occasion for it on tamed, human-filled Earth. The sorts of fear she had learned to experience were fear of the unknown, as when she had volunteered for this assignment—and that was more excitement, really—and, from time to time, the fear, or the angry suspicion to be more exact, that some rival was going to damage her standing with the stereo audiences, or that she might fail to perform well in a broadcast.

It was only as time passed, and the only nearby sounds she heard were of stirrings and whisperings in the forest around her, that she began to understand that that quivering in her shoulders, that jumpy need to look around all 360 degrees at once, were the beginnings of terror.

She was not quite alone. She had her communications equipment. She could be in touch with the ground station in any moment. She might even hear, through the Pmal links, some message from her partners, if they happened to come close enough to her. But nothing came from the Pmal, and she drew her hand back a dozen times from the switch that would activate the long-range communicator. Something had drawn those enemy ships toward them—homing on their transmissions? She did not know, but until she felt more sure she was reluctant to risk bringing them back.

And she could hear them, could even catch glimpses from time to time that had to be them, circling low over the treetops, searching. Searching, she felt quite sure, for such of their quarry as had evaded them—like herself.

What had become of the others?

Of only one thing was she sure: in the fight, her side had not triumphed, because there the stranger ships were, roaming boldly around. Val and the Scorpian had lost that battle, and if they survived they too were in hiding.

She thought of her husband and wondered if he had taken part in that fight, or if, at the last moment, he had sheared off and followed after her. There were two conclusions from that thought. If he had followed her, he should be nearby. If he had not, he was probably dead.

At that moment she realized the drone of the enemy ships was no longer distant.

She crept to the edge of a fern-bordered lake, and peered cautiously upward. The drone grew louder, a ceaseless, crushing, killing sound, and something appeared over the trees.

It was long and tapered, with finlike wings at the end and mottled markings that were no doubt a form of camouflage. It poked into the little circle of sky over the lake like a thick, blunt spear.

Zara Gentry cautiously pulled back, away from the black water of the lake, into the doubtful shelter of the trees. The Watcher ship floated out over the lake, supporting itself easily with the thrust of its propulsive jets against the light gravity of Cuckoo. A thin golden snake was trailing below it, slipping around the treetops, dropping into the black water. A snooper device, Zara guessed, and tried to be perfectly still.

The mottled vessel slowed still more, the golden snake growing slack in the water, seeming to writhe around as it sought for something to strike at. Inch by inch Zara crept backward, until she was wholly covered by a patch of great vines with bright blue flowers. She was not alone in her hiding place. Insectlike beings were there too, and welcomed her presence enthusiastically as a source of nourishment.

The mottled ship dropped gently toward the beach and came to rest, not more than fifty yards away. A wide door fell open in its side, and became a gangplank.

Zara could not help gasping at what came out. T'Worlie, Sheliaks, Sirians, and all had not prepared her for the hideousness of the creatures in the ship. An armored, black-beaked, hunchbacked creature waddled out across the lowered platform, and flapped down to the beach on stubby yellow wings.

Zara wriggled uncomfortably, trying to dislodge the small bloodsucking insects, at the same time uneasily conscious of a bad smell of some sort. She could not identify it. Then it hit her hard, and she realized it came from the creature on the beach, a foul odor of carrion and decay, even at this distance strong enough almost to turn her stomach.

The creature flapped awkwardly into the air and flew around the perimeter of the lake. As it came near, Zara willed herself to look down without moving a muscle. The reek was overpowering as the creature flapped overhead.

After a moment she dared to look up, and saw that the Watcher had returned to the beach. It shrilled some sort of message at the unseen crew of the brown-mottled ship, and slowly other creatures like it began to come out of that dark doorway. One by one they vaulted across the flat platform and glided into a ragged line before the first Watcher.

All of them engaged in a colloquy of whistles and screeches, until another appeared from the ship and hopped and flew down to them with what looked like a bundle of white staves or lances, which he passed out to the others. The squat Watcher squealed something, and all of them rose hooting into the air.

Zara realized she was in desperate trouble. This was a search party, no doubt of it, and more likely than not she was the quarry. Perhaps they had seen her dive into the forests here, or perhaps she had given herself away in some other manner. No matter; they were intent on a trail, and at the end of it would be Zara Doy Gentry.

She whimpered in fear, trying to decide what to do. But her choices were so few! She could use the laser weapon at her belt, hoping to kill a few of the creatures before the others killed her. She could try to flee—but where? And with what hope of success? Or she could continue to cower in her bower of vines, being eaten by the tiny biting insects, until the creatures found her. None of those was very attractive . . .

And the time when she would be found did not seem very far away. One of the Watchers was circling near her. She heard it shriek, almost overhead, saw the bright-spotted blackness of its slick hard body, saw the flash of its bright yellow wings. She couldn't tell which way its huge, bulging greenish eyes were looking, but for a moment she thought it had seen her.

But then its great, pliant ears cupped toward something ahead. Squealing, it flapped out of sight, brandishing the long white staff. She caught a gasp of relief—tainted with the creature's evil reek.

She lay quiet, while the hoots and squeals of the searchers kept up an insane dialogue all around her, until finally they seemed to concentrate and grow farther away.

She dared to peer out, and saw that, one by one, they were landing near their vessel again.

Had they given up the search? Were they about to get back in their ship and go away?

She crawled out of the tangle of vines to see. They were in a confused, bickering huddle around the ship. The golden snake that had hung into the water was wriggling insensately about, touching them and recoiling, darting into the underbrush and rushing blindly back. They ignored it. They seemed to reach a conclusion, then, and two of them leaped ponderously back onto the platform and disappeared into the ship.

In a moment they reappeared, bearing great platters of what looked like raw meat. They dropped in their ungainly way to the beach and began to parcel out bits of meat among their fellows.

It was lunchtime, Zara realized. Their table manners—pretending they chose to use a table, which they did not—were atrocious. They bickered and fought over the choicer pieces, throwing the bones and offal carelessly into the woods. The squealing noises did not stop while they ate; they clearly had no compunction about talking with their mouths full, if indeed so gross a species had compunctions about anything.

At that point it occurred to Zara that she had been thinking of them as animals.

But they were not animals. They used advanced technology. They communicated among themselves.

And if she could get a little closer to them, her Pmal translator might be able to pick up enough of their squeals and screeches to give her some idea of what those communications were.

With agonizing care she slipped along the margin of the lake, eyes firmly on the feeding Watchers, until she was less than a dozen yards from the sandy beach where they had landed. She activated the Pmal and held it to her ear. It would take time for it to store up enough speech to be able to deduce meanings, but it should only be a few minutes before it could at least identify and translate a few words . . .

Time was growing short. They were close to finished with their meal. A few of them had evidently been detailed to the task of cleaning up, and were picking up left-over pieces from the platform of the ship. One flapped and waddled toward her.

She became conscious of her exposed position, but the Watcher did not seem interested in exploring the undergrowth; it was only looking for a place to dump its tray of slop. It did so, and turned away.

For just a moment Zara felt a quick thrill of relief. Then she saw what the slop consisted of.

"Dear God!" she moaned aloud, unable to prevent it.

The hooting and squealing rose like a barnyard chorus as the Watchers caught the sound. Hopping and flapping their great yellow wings, they came at her, and the golden snake that had hung from their ship writhed faster than any of them. Before she could move it had slipped across the beach with the sine-wave wriggle of a sidewinder, touched her gently, then locked on her.

She was held so tightly she could hardly breathe, much less run.

But she hadn't been able to run before that, either—not run, and not even stand up. Not since she looked at the trash and offal the creature was throwing away, and saw one rounded bit of waste, melon-sized and bloody, roll languorously toward her and stop . . .

She knew then what these creatures had been feeding on, when she realized that she was looking at the severed head of her husband.

What followed was for Zara a desert of half-understood misery. The choking coils of the golden rope seemed to have intelligence of their own. They wrapped themselves around her, bearable when she was still, tightening cruelly with every move she made to work them off. She was tumbled face-down on the talc-white beach, with the hideous squeals and hoots of the Watchers piping querulously or menacingly all around her, their foul reek choking her nostrils. All that was merely painful. What was unbearable was the memory of the empty, staring eyes of her husband, fixed on eternity. If Zara had been asked to describe her marriage, back on Earth, she would have defended it as a convenient thing that cost little to maintain and, if it gave little in return, was no burden to her. His death had killed no part of herself. But it was pain nevertheless, pain to see this close person destroyed so callously,

used so demeaningly, to stuff the maws of these filthy
creatures.

It was only then that Zara began to realize that she
might share that same fate herself.

She struggled to turn over, free her mouth from the
choking sand. The golden coils punished her, but gasping and panting she managed to flop onto her side.
"Please!" she begged. "I mean you no harm! Give me
that metal thing there—it will let us talk to each other."
And she tried, at terrible cost of agony as the golden
coils remorselessly fought her movements, to point to
the Pmal translator, whispering away to itself on the
sand.

The hideous mask-faces thrust themselves at her,
hooting and whistling. She knew what they said was a
language of a sort, and it was frustration to know that a
few yards away the Pmal was surely translating faithfully every word—but inaudibly, because she had set
the sound so low lest they hear her. "Please!" she
screamed as one came near her with a great curved
cleaver. It paused, seeming to enjoy her fear. The gab-
bling whistles and honks burst like laughter around her.

She closed her eyes, and tried to remember her brief
training. What were her options? Talking was useless,
with the Pmal gone. Her laser weapon was long since
taken away. They had left her only the other instruments strapped to her arms—medicpac, chronometer,
communicator . . .

Communicator!

She took a deep breath, and forced herself to relax.
She lay still as stone for long seconds, remembering
where the transmit switch was on the communicator,
feeling with her body-image senses where her hands
were, where the switch was. There would not be much
freedom of action.

Then she flung herself onto her back, forcing her
hands together, clawing with the fingers of her right
hand for the forearm of her left.

The golden coils responded at once by tightening so

violently that she thought she felt bones snap; but she
had touched the switch! "Help!" she screamed. "This
is Zara Doy Gentry calling! Help! Please! Help me!"

A hundred-odd degrees of arc around the great bulk
of Cuckoo, Ben Linc Pertin was talking to himself.

On his watch duty, desolately killing time while
trying to solve the insoluble problem of what to do
about the wife that was not his, he had observed a curiosity. The comm frequency that had been abandoned
because no transmissions had been received and its
owner, that other avatar of himself named Ben Tom
Pertin, was presumed dead had suddenly come back to
life.

When he first beheld himself he was aghast. This
devastated face, harried, sick, and in pain, was himself!
"Ben Tom!" he cried. "What's the matter?"

- The face in the stereostage reflected annoyance. "I'm
not Ben Tom," it snapped. "And I don't know what
you mean. What's the matter with you people? I've
been trying to call for—I don't know, days!"

"Sorry," Ben Linc Pertin said. "But what do you
mean, you're not Ben Tom?"

The ravaged face split in an unpleasant smile. "Glad
I'm not," he said. "Ben Tom's dead. I'm Ben Yale. Remember? When you—we—volunteered for the sixth
time? Well, that's me. I lost my ship, nearly lost my life.
I've been through hell, Ben Linc! But at that I'm better
off than Ben Tom, because his bones are twenty feet
away from me. This is his ship I've found; my own was
destroyed, communications and all."

"You look as if you've been through hell," Ben Linc
agreed fervently. "What are those bandages?"

The walking skeleton looked incuriously at his arms
and legs. "Oh, some sort of fungus, I think," he said.
"It itches. It hurts, too, but I've blocked it with stuff
from the medicpac. But I imagine I'll need treatment."

"Well," cried Ben Linc, finding something to be
cheerful about for the first time in some days, "I think

I've got good news for you, Ben Yale. We've just been transmitting a new model exploring ship to the ground station. This one's armed and armored, ready for anything, and it's got full ground-to-space capability! We can get it over to you and have you up here in orbit in jig time—as soon as it's ready."

"Fine," Ben Yale said—strangely, thought his duplicate; why wasn't he more excited? But he was looking narrowly at Ben Linc. He said at last tangentially, "Have you heard anything from Zara?"

Ben Linc shook his head. Then he corrected himself. "Yes, as a matter of fact I did," he said. "I don't remember—did you split off before I got her message about not coming because she was pregnant?"

"Pregnant?" Ben Yale demanded. "I don't believe it!"

"Well, it's true. That is—it's true of our Zara. But there's another copy of her—" He stopped. He was not sure how much he wanted to say.

"On Cuckoo, right?" Ben Yale cried. "I knew it! I saw her, Ben Linc! She's in trouble. Not more than five thousand yards from here!"

"Trouble? No, I don't think so . . ." Ben Linc started.

"Don't be a fool, Ben Linc!" his avatar cried. "I tell you, I saw her!"

Ben Linc Pertin hesitated, filled with confusion and a painful mixture of hope and fear. Another Zara, so close? But in danger?

"Stand by," he said. "I'll scan that vector." And his fingers danced over his console to FARLINK, ordering a search for transmissions from a point five thousand yards at twenty-seven degrees from Ben Yale's signal.

From her perch across the console from him, Venus sat quietly regarding Ben Linc Pertin. "What is the matter?" she asked, spraying a tiny violet cloudlet from her atomizer.

He shook his head as the rich menthol scent reached

him. "It's Zara," he said. "Something I don't understand. And one of my replicates down there, looking—well, I don't know what's keeping him alive."

"I ache with your pains," Venus said softly. Though her stare had always seemed blankly opaque, he felt her compassion through it. "So difficult for you, to see yourself. I have at least been spared that. I have no contact with my replicates, save one or two—and then, for one of us to die in this edited form would not be bad."

Distracted, Ben Linc scowled at the console. There was no response to the search, although he could see that the program was functioning. Lately he had found it more and more difficult to distinguish sleep from waking. His sleep was filled with troubled dreams, and his waking life was a nightmare.

The dreams lingered with him, even when he was awake. He shivered, remembering one dream—

"SCAN UNSUCCESSFUL," FARLINK's screen reported. "NO UNIDENTIFIED TRANSMISSIONS FROM AREA."

"Continue," snapped Ben Linc, reinforcing the verbal order with his keyboard.

And he stared into space, remembering that one dream. In it he had been a child again. On Earth. Not the Earth he had left—so many replications before!—but the Earth he imagined, as it had been before the first contact with the Galactic civilizations. He had been sitting at a child's desk, in an upstairs room with an open window, looking out over a sunny yard, reading a book, when something had come in from outside. It had fluttered through the window, lit on the page in front of him. When he raised his hand to slap it it had leaped away, and he saw it was no common fly but a tiny five-eyed bat shape with bright butterfly wings. When he heard it squeaking, and caught its faint vinegar scent, he knew it was a T'Worlie—incongruously there in that pregalactic age, but somehow Earth's first visitor from deep space.

He seized a flyswatter to kill it. Its shrill scream of

protest hurt his ears, and its fear was a carrion reek. Wings whirring, it rose to fly away, but he smashed it on the open page.

For a moment he felt secure in that dream . . .

And then he heard a droning roar from outside. The sun darkened. Shadows filled the window. When he looked out he saw that the sky had turned black with alien beings descending—T'Worlie and Sheliaks, Boaty-Bits and Scorpians, endless processions of a thousand shapes and sizes all arrowing down upon him . . .

He had wakened then briefly, tossed and turned, and drifted off again . . .

To even worse horror.

Now he dreamed that he was his other self, Replicate 5160, at the strange tachyonic station to which he had been transmitted. But his form was no longer human. He had been edited, transformed into a thick metal block, unable to move. He understood at last— attempting to shudder, and failing—the silvery girl's abhorrence of the form into which her own body had been recast to survive in an oxygen atmosphere. His case was worse. He was a chess piece in a three-sided match; he stood on a queer triangular game board, a hapless piece in a game that FARLINK played against two terrible opponents.

One opponent was a bright thing of lambent white flame, writhing and twisting and flickering, without any ordered shape. The other was equally shapeless; but black instead of bright. They reached across the board with curling tongues of bright fire and terrible empty blackness, as if to move their pieces; but Ben Linc could not see their pieces, only the ones on his own side. One was the pseudogirl Venus, her silver body frozen rigid. Another was Zara Doy, alive and moving but imprisoned under a bell jar, pale and gasping, ago- nized for air. A third was Doc Chimp, a lifeless figure in brightly painted metal like a cheap child's toy, hold- ing out a tin cup. The pieces moved, or the board itself moved them, responding to FARLINK's rapped electronic orders; but FARLINK was losing the game. Most of its triangular spaces were already empty. The last move had isolated Ben Linc, far from his companions. A fluttering tentacle of icy blackness stretched out toward him, and he knew that it was going to remove him from the board and then the game would be ultimately, irretrievably lost . . .

"Ben Linc," chimed the voice of the silvery girl, "where are you?"

He came back to the reality of the orbiter and the screen. "Sorry, Venus," he muttered. "I was thinking about . . ." His voice died out, but hers picked up the thought from him:

"About that other Ben Pertin? About Replicate 5160? About all those others of you, Ben Linc?"

He nodded. There had been no other signal from the copy of himself sent back along the tachyon trace to whatever that galactic source of interference had been: one more dead Pertin, he thought; the Universe is getting seriously polluted with my corpses . . .

He sat up abruptly and realized FARLINK was still methodically scanning the surface of Cuckoo for a signal that did not seem to be coming. He sighed and reached from the console to terminate the program—

And at that moment the screen lit up:

"STAND BY! FREQUENCY DETECTED! NO COMMUNICATION AS YET!"

And while his fingers were still poised over the console he heard it. There was no doubt.

On the emergency frequency.

Zara's voice.

And the words:

"Help! This is Zara Doy Gentry calling! Help! Please! Help me!"

In the wrecked survey vessel on the surface, Ben Yale Pertin heard Zara's voice repeated from the orbiter. That voice had traveled nearly half a billion miles, round trip, to get to him, but on the instant flash of tachyon transmission it had taken less time than was measurable. The time the message had taken to travel from the speaker on the satellite to the microphone three yards away that had picked it up was longer than the time for the message to fly on the backs of tachyons through space.

He burst out of the vehicle, limping and rubbing at his bandages, but traveling as fast as ever he had moved in his life. He was not in pain now. He had been steadily doping himself with pills and salves from the medic-pac; he was no longer quite sober or sane. Although the pain of the ulcers under the bandages was blocked, the effects of the blocks were shaking the stability of his mind. All things seemed possible. The entire Universe seemed ready to meet his commands. He scrambled through the undergrowth toward Redlaw and Org Rider, shouting, "My wife! She's in danger! We've got to help her!"

FIFTEEN

*

Org Rider was too full of mourning for the loss of Babe to feel any great concern about the dying stranger's excitement—until Redlaw translated some of what he said.

"I do not understand all," Redlaw said, "but it is a woman of his people and she is a captive of the Watchers. I expect they will eat her," he added, moodily stroking his cleaver. "He wishes us to save her. And he says, too, that if we do this a great ship of his people will come to battle the Watchers for us."

Redlaw paused, uncertain. "I do not know if he is telling the truth," he said. "He is a dying man. Perhaps he has the madness of the dying?"

Org Rider shrugged, but he was thinking about what Redlaw had said. With Babe gone, he was not happy enough to care much about danger. And the woman the stranger spoke about. If she was the one he had seen so briefly as she dashed herself into the treetops—but was that possible? could she have survived that nightmare plunge?—no matter; if it was she, there had been something about her that had appealed powerfully to him.

He said mournfully, "What does it matter if he lies? Let us do as he asks. Where is this woman?"

Redlaw scowled and gestured down the slope of Knife-in-the-Sky. "He says he knows precisely and will show us. But how can he travel? I have seen men before, eaten alive by that blue slime. They do not travel through the jungle! But he is doing it. It is something in those cloths he puts on his ulcers, perhaps, or in those small things he eats and drinks from the metal box. I wish I knew—" Redlaw gazed doubtfully at Ben Yale Pertin, still shouting and gesticulating at them to hurry. "And there is so much more he says that I cannot understand."

"No matter," Org Rider said. "Let us save the woman. For him," he added politely, as an afterthought.

Even so, they were far too slow for Ben Yale's liking; and then the trek through the jungle was longer and harder than they had expected, more than two thousand breaths, because Ben Yale insisted that they wait for him. He chose to carry some great metal thing from the ship that he called "bazooka." It was a wonder he could move at all, even without that weight. Beneath the stained bandages—though he had replaced them just before they left—the blue slime oozed out, always spreading, always etching new ulcers into his flesh. And it was a constant peril to be near him in his clumsy lunging through the trees. A single accidental touch of the blue slime might have meant death for either of them.

But the two thousand breaths were over, and in time they reached a point where they could see the distant black gleam of the tiny lake. There on the far shore loomed the mottled hulk of the Watcher vessel.

Org Rider wished for the far-seeing glasses, but of course they were no longer safe to use: Ben Yale had touched them. He squinted across the lake. With mounting excitement he saw: yes—there she was! The very girl he had seen. Wrapped like the prey of a cord spinner in the golden coils of the Watchers' device, lying helpless on the blinding white sands of the little beach.

Even so, even at that distance, she was beautiful. Disordered as her hair was, it had the reddish glint of far lightning. Something about her made him think of his brother's wife. Yet this girl was more beautiful by far, in spite of the drained pale cast of her face and the terror in her expression.

He glanced at Redlaw, and started to move toward the lake.

The giant stopped him.

"Wait!" he rumbled. "Ben Yale says he has a plan. He says that this 'bazooka' is a weapon. He wishes us to go around the lake, to be ready to attack the Watchers from the forest. He says from here, with this weapon that he has carried, he will destroy the Watcher ship. When he has done that, we are to kill those who survive with his weapon and"—he patted his cleaver—"this one!"

"What weapon does he have that will destroy the ship?" Org Rider demanded suspiciously. "You told me he had no such weapon."

"He lied," the giant growled moodily. "I knew he lied. And perhaps he is lying now, how can I tell? I can understand so little of what he says!"

"What does it matter?" repeated Org Rider, quelling the rising surge of feeling in himself. "Let us do as he asks."

They left Ben Yale just inside the undergrowth, lying on the scarlet moss, peering over the sights of his tree-trunklike weapon, chuckling and muttering to himself in his strange language. And they moved like ghosts through the vegetation, circling around.

They paused fifty yards from the beach. The foul deathweed stench of the Watchers reeked in their nostrils as Org Rider whispered savagely, "How do we know he will destroy the ship? We should have arranged a signal."

"Should have, should have," Redlaw rumbled. "But we didn't, boy." He scowled toward the beach. "If only I were sure of him. I hate like poison to get closer! Those golden ropes of theirs can smell a man, and they never sleep. Still—" He sighed. "I'll try to get them with this thing"—he patted the laser weapon—"and you go after them with your bow. With any luck they'll be disorganized . . ."

He broke off. There was a sharp, flat crack from across the lake and a puff of grayish smoke. Out of the smoke emerged a needlelike metal object lancing across the lake toward the Watcher vessel. It struck, and opened into a bright flower of flame.

Blam.

The sound of the explosion was far louder than they had expected. The mottled vessel of the Watchers seemed to lift off the sand, and fall slowly. Bright flame spouted from the hole that the stranger's weapon had made in its side.

"Curse him," Redlaw howled, "we should have been closer! Do the best you can, boy!" And he loped toward the Watchers, firing with the laser weapon. Sounds like the tearing of paper came from it, and Watchers fell before it.

Org Rider ran to the side of the lake, dropped to one knee, and began launching arrows toward the Watchers. While one was still in the air he was notching and aiming the next. He did not wait to see how successful he was, but out of the corner of one eye he saw one Watcher leap high over the vessel with a startled squeal, an arrow protruding clear through him. Another, squalling and hooting, lay on the ground, tugging at a shaft through his throat, while his drumming feet revolved him in a complete circle around his shoulders.

"They've broken!" Redlaw exulted over his shoulder. "Come on, boy! Let's go in and finish them off!" As he spoke his laser weapon sliced through the golden coils, and another blast from it burned a crisply sizzling hole through a Watcher skull. Now the giant flung the laser to the winds and, screaming as he leaped, bowled in on the Watchers, hacking at them with his cleaver. Org Rider was just behind. The two of them drove the Watchers back like avenging angels. With every stroke of Redlaw's cleaver and the boy's knife a Watcher squealed and fell from their paths.

Zzzzzzat!

The noise was louder than anything Org Rider had ever heard, and for a moment he did not understand what it was.

Then he saw that the Watcher vessel was not, after all, quite dead.

From a round bulge on its top something flashed like lightning, and the great ripping sound lashed at his ears again. The Watcher ship was firing its main armament. Not at them, Org Rider realized—not that there was any question about that; if the laser cannon had been aimed at them they would never have known what hit them—but probing across the lake for the bazooka. *Zzzzzat!,* and a bee-tree went up in smoke, smitten by a lightning bolt. *Zzzzzat!,* and a sudden corridor opened up in a stand of deathweed.

"Grab the girl!" Redlaw bawled. "Let's get out of here before they finish with Pertin and start on us!"

There were still Watchers alive and Org Rider yearned to catch and kill every one; but he knew Redlaw was right. He bounded to the side of the girl. She was just beginning to sit up. The blood had been squeezed out of her limbs for so long she was numbed and tottering.

Org Rider felt almost as dizzy as she was. All this was so terribly new and confusing! The needle-bright light of the laser, the harsh explosions and lightning-bolt sizzling of the long-range battle across the lake were entirely out of his experience, in a life lived in the perpetual pink-gray dawn of Cuckoo. He was not afraid; but he was disoriented.

Still he had to act. He grabbed the girl's arm and pulled her away. She did not resist, except to break free for a moment and pick up a piece of metallic equipment. Then she was with him, bounding as fast as they could into the shelter of the woods, Redlaw close behind. The last Watcher on his feet outside the ship challenged Redlaw, but lost his head and half his trunk to the keen-edged cleaver. Then the giant was beside

them, shouting, "Hurry! We've got to get out of sight!"
The girl could not have understood his words; but she
didn't have to, the need was clear.

At last there was another bazooka shot from across
the lake, and this one was clean and true on the bulge
at the top of the Watcher ship. It blew up in a gout of
flame.

All three of them cheered.

"We did it, boy!" the giant bellowed. "Beat the
Watchers in fair fight! It's the first time it ever happened in all the time of the world!"

Org Rider crowed in pleasure, pummeling the girl's
back as though she were another man. Exultant, laughing, as delighted as he, she clapped him on the shoulder
with a force that sent him spinning.

He picked himself off the ground and looked at her
with new respect. She was no timid, frail maiden! She
was as strong as he. And yet—she seemed more femi-
nine than any woman he had ever seen. More so even
than the girl who had married his brother. A glow of
color began to light her death-pale face, and he found
himself staring into her widening eyes. They were a
bright-flicked brown, like the wild flowers that colored
the grassworld after the rain. Even with the hated reek
of the Watchers still fouling his nostrils he could smell
the faint scent that came from her, a clean sweetness
that swept away the Watchers' fetor and left him with
the fragrance of the rain itself, after the flatworld had
been brown and dry.

"Stop mooning, boy!" Redlaw ordered, laughing as
he said it. "We've beaten one shipload of Watchers, but
they're not through yet. There'll be more. When this
ship doesn't report in, they'll send another to look for
it. If they managed to send off a distress report, that
ship is on its way now!"

Org Rider tore his eyes off the girl. "All right. Which
way?"

The giant gazed about. "We'll have to go back
around the lake," he decided. "First place, we'd best try

to find Ben Yale, if he's still alive. Second, I don't think we can get out this way. That's bare rock up there. We'd be easy targets on it—and I see blue on those rocks, boy; I think it's the slime. We don't want to go near that."

Org Rider nodded and turned to the girl. Speaking as clearly as he could, gesturing to make his meaning plain, he said: "Come. We leave here. Now."

She laughed. She touched the metallic thing she had picked up and spoke, and from the thing came a flat, dead voice that said: "I understand. I agree. And"—to Org Rider even the lifeless metallic tone of the translator could not keep all feeling out of the words—"with all my heart I thank you both."

The boy was enraptured. He recognized the speaking machine; it was the same as Ben Yale's, but whole and working properly. In Ben Yale's conversations with Redlaw he had become accustomed to being excluded; it had not occurred to him that an undamaged machine would make it possible for him to be in one-to-one contact with this wondrous person.

He caught the girl's hand, and they followed Redlaw back toward the lake margin—

And stopped.

From behind the wrecked Watcher vessel a lance of green fire spat out at them.

Redlaw shrieked in agony and spun away, clutching his arm. "Run!" he bawled, setting them an example. They blundered after him, and at every leap Org Rider expected that green fire to burn through their backs.

They stopped almost up against the bare rock wall that cupped that edge of the lake. "There was one still alive," Redlaw gasped, holding the place on his upper arm that had blossomed into a blood-red blister of pain. "It's lucky he fired when he did! If he'd waited he'd have had me clean, and you two as well." He scowled up at the mountain. "We can't go up that way," he muttered. "And we can't go back to the lake, because he's waiting there."

Org Rider risked raising himself to peer around the multiple boles of a flame-tree. He could see the Watcher, broad yellow wings slowly stirring. One was damaged, and dragged; the Watcher had been hurt, too. But he held the thing that looked like a black stick, and spat green flame, without faltering.

"If we can't go forward," Org Rider said, "and can't go back—and can't stay here, because they'll be another Watcher ship before long—then what do we do?"

They waited and watched, but the creature remained steadfastly alert.

"We have no choice," Redlaw groaned at last. "We have to kill him. His gun outranges our weapons, and his bug eyes can see us in every direction. It won't be easy."

Redlaw scowled at his cleaver.

"The only way I see to take him is to rush from all sides. He may kill us all, but I don't think so. One of us will get him. But the other two—"

He hesitated, then he finished: "At least one of the other two will be dead."

"No!" the boy shouted. "Not her. She has suffered enough from the Watchers. You and I can do it, Redlaw!"

The girl, listening, shook her head. She spoke in that pretty, singing voice, and the metal voice from her arm echoed, "I can perform my share. I thank you for your good heart."

Org Rider stared at her and said, "Please don't. I don't know your name—"

She said in her own voice, not through the translator, "Zara." It sounded like music to him as he rehearsed it several times, tasting its flavor.

"Zara. Please, Zara, don't do this. You are not a warrior. Redlaw and I can handle the Watcher."

The giant thundered, "Idiot boy, we can't! Our only hope is three attacks at once. *That* is a faint enough hope—two is suicide!"

The girl spoke, and the Pmal rattled flatly, "It is decided, Org Rider. I again thank you, but now let us act. Tell me what I must do."

The giant rasped, "Come in from behind the ship. Get close to him. The beast has a hard shell, but there are soft joints. One is where his neck would be, if he had a neck. There's a pale stripe above his black hump. Stab him deep in the middle of that, if you can."

Org Rider watched the girl go on her longer, round-about trip with his breath caught in his throat. She would not die! He would see to it. The first one to display himself to the Watcher would surely be the first one fired on; the other two would have a chance at least minutely better. Org Rider determined to be that first one.

But it would be foolish, would even endanger them, for his break to come much before their own. It would simply mean that the Watcher would pick him off quickly, and then have only two foes to confront. So he squirmed to his place and waited, watching the faint ripples in the underbrush that marked the movements of Redlaw and the girl. Could the Watcher see and understand those same ripples? He did not know. He could only hope.

Something was tugging at the back of his mind. What was it?

Then he recognized the growing sound from the sky, and looked up. Down at him dived a great org.

Org Rider froze. It was his death he saw coming. With only the knife left—the bow was long since cast away—he could not prevail against talon and fang. All he could do was stare at its savage splendor. He crouched numbly, waiting for the hooked black talons to strike.

Even in that moment he saw the blue beauty of its huge, hooded eyes, the bright flow of its form, the even sheen of bronze scales shading into the silver flash of its narrowed wings. Wonder at its clean, sleek power made his throat ache. Orgs were better and greater than men! Surely they were more beautiful. It was his death . . . but if he had to perish, here on Knife-in-the-Sky, it was better to be killed by this mighty org than by the waiting Watcher.

But dying that way would not serve Zara . . .

Org Rider leaped to his feet, yelling and bounding toward the Watcher ship.

As he had expected, the Watcher was staring up with his great blind eyes, distracted by the org. Perhaps after the org finished with him it would go for the Watcher next! Org Rider glanced toward the Watcher, husbanding his charges as he nervously waited under the shelter of the ship, then back toward the org.

It screamed again.

The bright wings opened a little, flaring it toward him out of the bottom of the dive, and he saw the scars that marred its lean perfection. A long, dark wound, not fully healed, where the scales had been ripped from its flank. A break in the brightness of one wide wing.

The screaming changed . . . and queerly, became words.

"Babe!" blared the mighty voice of the org, repeating his own voice like a tape under maximum gain. "Babe come back!"

The boy heard his own voice thunder down at him from the sky and could hardly understand. But what the words did not explain the actions did. The org dipped down over him. Its golden-scaled trunk snatched him up into the air, squeezed him almost too hard, flexed to set him on its back above the widened wings.

Then recognition hit him.

It *was* Babe! Changed—older—hurt, but Babe! Scales had replaced the infant fur. The healing scars told of combat. But it was he!

A laser scream spat past his ear and brought him out of his dreaming. He kicked the org strongly and shouted, "Fast, Babe! Over the trees!"

The beast responded instantly, putting the loom of the ship between them and the Watcher. And Org Rider sobbed, "Babe! I'm so glad!" He stroked the bronze scales. Yards below he could see the top of the trees and caught a glimpse of Zara's terrified pale face, staring up at them. What could she be thinking? Had she ever seen an org before? Did she understand that Org Rider was master, not prey?

But looking at her brought him back to the needs of that moment. He wheeled Babe around, low over the treetops, and shouted down: "Now! Let's get him!"

And as he saw the mighty form of Redlaw leap free and begin to run toward the Watcher, he gouged his heels into Babe's scaled side and commanded, "Kill, Babe! The Watcher! Kill him!"

The chaos of the next moments was indescribable. Org Rider heard the shouts of Redlaw and the shriller, fainter cry of the girl. He saw the cleaver glinting in the hands of the giant.

Then he was around the ship and beating back in toward the Watcher.

The black stick crackled. Bright light blasted Org Rider's eyes; a sudden electrical stench choked him. But it had been a miss; he was still alive!

And then they were on top of the Watcher. Babe bellowed as his striking talons ripped the Watcher out from under the hull. They all tumbled in a slow-motion heap, boy, org, and Watcher together. The reek of the squealing Watcher stung his throat as he stabbed and stabbed with his knife to find the death place.

In the end it was Babe that took the last of the life from the Watcher, the great claws simply wrenching the hideous head free of its body. The shrilling scream stuttered and stopped abruptly, and the ugly carcass toppled slowly forward in death.

"We did it!" Org Rider called. "Babe, you're a hero! Babe—"

But the org did not respond.

Shaken, Org Rider lifted his head free and stared. The delicate pink trunk was trembling violently. The huge eyes were dulled. As Org Rider reached out to touch him, Babe screamed in pain.

The Watcher's laser had found its mark after all.

As Redlaw and the girl came running up, Babe fumbled out to touch the boy with his shuddering trunk. The voice that mimicked Org Rider's own said, "Babe go. Babe go . . ."

The light went out of the great eyes, and the org was dead.

Org Rider sat mourning with the great head in his lap, Redlaw and the girl standing helplessly by, until at last Redlaw rumbled, "Sorry, boy, but we've got to get out of here. The Watchers'll be after us any time now."

Org Rider looked up and nodded somberly. "I know." He got up, reaching a hand to the girl. "Are you all right?" She smiled, in both reassurance and compassion; he needed no translator to understand that, or the look of sympathy in her eyes.

There was a sudden scream of high speed from the sky, and all three of them looked upward in instant re-awakened fear.

"Too late!" Redlaw raged. "Friends of hell! There's the Watcher ship on us, while we're standing around like fools! We can't get away now. We'll have to fight—and we've nothing to fight with but the Watcher's own lance!" He dove to the side of the decapitated beast, choking in fury as much as the evil cloud of its deathweed stink.

The girl stopped him.

Her clear voice, repeated through the translator on her arm, said:

"It's all right. It's not a Watcher ship. Look."

Unbelieving, Redlaw and the boy craned their necks to stare upward.

The vehicle that was settling down on them was far larger than any Watcher ship either had ever seen. Even the colors were different: bright silver, crisp black, a flare of yellow-white gas from its underjets.

"They've come to rescue us," Zara said. "We're safe now. All of us."

SIXTEEN

*

In the orbiter Ben Linc Pertin watched in a fever of excitement as the survey ship picked up Zara and her two companions. He stared at her image in pain and wonder. So tall and thin she was, in her edited version! So worn and pale, with the stresses of her battle with the Watchers! He wanted desperately to talk to her, to say words of love and welcome; but although he was hard pressed with grief and loneliness he was not mad, and he understood that their relationship would have to mature in its own way. To him she was his loved and missed wife. To her, coming from an earlier Zara Doy, he was a stranger.

And then there was the solved puzzle of why she called herself "Zara Doy Gentry." She had married someone else! He had scarcely felt that shock when he learned that that husband was dead, fodder for the maws of the Watchers. Shock again! This time a different kind of shock, a reprieve, even if purchased at the cost of a man's life—who could not have been a bad man, Ben Linc told himself with one reasoning part of his mind, for Zara to meet and marry him. But another part of his mind was bursting with joy. How strange for his wife to be a widow and a wooable stranger, all at once!

And suddenly he was exhausted. He had stayed by the communicator for twenty-two hours, past the time of his regular duty, through the new Zara's cry for help, up to the moment of rescue and for some time beyond. Now he had to sleep. He decided against attempting

even to leave a message for this to-be-won Zara, and
headed for his cocoon. There would be time. It was a
long voyage up from Cuckoo and around to where the
orbiter swung, nearly half a billion miles now. It
seemed even longer in the urgency of his anticipation.

Yet there was no way to shorten it. Even with nuclear rockets, the acceleration of the survey ship was
limited to what its rescued passengers could stand. That
was not much. Redlaw and Org Rider had lived all
their lives in the gentle pull of Cuckoo, and even Zara
and Ben Yale Pertin, in their edited versions, could
hardly stand a single gravity of acceleration. For Ben
Yale even that much was dangerous; he had been swept
from the jungle into full medical cocooning, instantly.

Ben Linc fell asleep, thinking of Ben Yale coming up
from Cuckoo, battered and foul with the ulcers of the
blue slime . . . and of that other Ben Pertin, Replicate 5160, lost somewhere at the transmitter of the
tachyon interference, at a point unknown inside the
Galaxy . . . and, above all, of the sweet and smiling
face of Zara Doy, now Zara Gentry, who might some-
time soon be Zara Pertin again . . .

He woke to Doc Chimp screaming in his ear:

"Ben! Ben Linc! Wake up! You've been found,
you're still alive. Oh, wake up, Ben Linc Pertin, there's
a signal from you coming in!"

Heavy with sleep, Ben Linc Pertin stumbled after
Doc Chimp to the terminal dome. His mind was fuzzed
with visions of himself in all his myriad guises. Sometimes he was not sure which he was: the innocent back
on Earth who had never left, the one on Sun One who
was still happily married to Zara Doy and happy father
of her child, any of the dead ones . . . all of them . . .

But one dead one was not dead!

In the dome, the huge image of a haggard human
face was repeated on half a hundred screens, all around
the curve. Half of the face was haggard with dirt and
grime, the other half caked with dark blood; a ragged
wound on the scalp still oozed, untended.

It took Ben Pertin a moment to recognize himself: Replicate 5160.

"See!" Doc Chimp chirped in his ear. "It's you, Ben! Not dead! The message started coming in a few minutes ago. But it's awful bad, Ben Linc; you can't understand a word of it, without the Pmal translators."

Ben Linc was still stupid with sleep. "You mean I'm—he's speaking some other language?"

"Not that, Ben Linc," the chimpanzee said gently. "Look at him! He can hardly talk in any language. The Pmal has to put it into words we can understand. Even then—well, it's in symbol-script, not sounds. He must have had some bad times, Ben Linc."

And it was so: the soiled and battered mouth was moving, but no audible sound came through the wall speakers. Instead bright computer symbols were dancing under each screen:

". . . INCOMPLETELY EXPLORED. IN SHAPE, THIS OBJECT I FOUND MYSELF ON IS A LARGE, FLAT DISK, ROTATING SLOWLY. MAYBE A THOUSAND FEET ACROSS. IT'S SOME SORT OF SPACECRAFT, BUT IT DOES NOT APPEAR TO BE UNDER POWER NOW—MAYBE NOT FOR A VERY LONG TIME.

"THE LEVELS TOWARD THE RIM ARE SEALED AND COLD. VERY COLD. I BELIEVE THE CREW IS HIBERNATING THERE TO WAIT FOR THE NEXT PLANET. ONE PLACE LOOKS LIKE A CONTROL FORM. SPHERICAL. STARS IMAGED ON ITS INSIDE SURFACE, AND A POD HUNG IN THE CENTER FOR THE PILOTS—BUT THERE ARE NO PILOTS THERE. HIBERNATING, I GUESS. I COULD NOT IDENTIFY THE STAR IMAGES, BUT I DID SEE WHAT LOOKED LIKE A REPRESENTATION OF CUCKOO. ONLY IT WAS STRANGE. IT WAS ALL MADE OF METAL. NO SOIL, ROCKS, SEAS, MOUNTAINS—JUST A GREAT SPHERE OF METAL.

"I THINK—"

The bloodied head turned suddenly and vanished from the screen.

For an instant the screens were dark; then shapeless blotches of color flickered over them. FARLINK interposed its own message, in all the tongues of the viewers:

"TRANSMISSION INTERRUPTED. STAND BY."

There was a sudden rush of squeal, cry, shout, and roar from the beings in the terminal room, as each one chattered to its neighbor about the message. Ben Linc, sick at the sight of his destroyed self, muttered, "I don't understand. What is it?"

Venus floated over toward him and filled him in quickly. "Your replicate reported in a few minutes ago, Ben Linc. He was in a ship, but some sort of mechanical device—a robot, but not a fully sentient one, I'm sure—attacked him as he came out of the receiver, and it is only now that he has been able to report."

"Ship?" Ben Linc shook his head, trying to clear it. The source of the distant unidentified tachyon transmission that they had actually intercepted en route to Cuckoo—a ship? There were no ships equipped with tachyon facilities that could possibly have a link with Cuckoo, not anywhere in the known Universe . . .

Of course, there was always the *unknown* Universe, he thought, the muscles of his back crawling.

"And there were representations of many beings there, Ben Linc," the silvery girl went on excitedly. "Your people! Boaty-Bits. Sheliaks. Your replicate thinks that the ship is a sort of advance guard for Cuckoo, sampling inhabited planets, sending specimens back. That would account for— Wait, here it is again!"

The ravaged head shook itself together into view on the screens. It was more horrid than ever; Pertin's replicate had been in another fight. Fresh blood was dribbling down the beard-spiked chin, and the lower front teeth were gone. The hollowed eyes were darting frantically from side to side, as the ruined mouth tried to form soundless words.

"IT'S LOCATED ME AGAIN," the bright words flashed. "UGLY THING. THICK OVAL SLAB, BELTED WITH SENSORS, CRAWLING AND JUMPING ON A FRINGE OF TENTACLES. IT DOESN'T COMMUNICATE, BUT IT HAS JUST

ABOUT KILLED ME. WE'VE BEEN PLAYING HIDE AND
SEEK. NOW *I* THINK IT HAS WON THE GAME, AS SOON AS
IT FINISHES BREAKING THE DOOR DOWN . . .

"ANYWAY, THAT'S MY REPORT. KISS ZARA FOR ME—
IF YOU CAN, BEN LINC. THAT'S ALL FOR—"

And there was no more. The image exploded and
died, and FARLINK underlined it after a moment with:

"TRANSMISSION TERMINATED. NO FURTHER PULSE
FROM SOURCE."

The belt of screens blazed and went blank.

A stir of strain ran around the terminal chamber, and
muted hootings and clangings and shrillings of communication began.

Ben Linc Pertin shook his head slowly, trying to take
it all in. There was so much, all happening so fast. Another death of a double. A real flesh-and-blood Zara on
her way. And on the larger scale, the fantastic mystery
of a scout ship from Cuckoo, sampling inhabited planets.

He tried to tell Nammie and Venus how he felt. He
caught a burnt-fur scent from the T'Worlie that surprised him, until he recognized it.

Fear.

The T'Worlie was afraid of what the message meant.

For a moment Ben Linc allowed himself to share
that fear of the terrible unknown, of the race that must
have built that ship; but thoughts came flooding back,
and his fear melted into anticipation; and that was how
it was with Ben Linc Pertin on the orbiter.

With Ben Yale Pertin on the survey ship, spiraling
around toward the orbiter, things were somewhat different.

They were better than they had been in a long time,
he told himself. The survey ship's medical facilities were
dealing nicely with the blue slime. He spent three days
in the cocoon, while his skin was gently soaked away
and a new one grown on. Then, swathed like a mummy
in circulating-field bandages, he was allowed into the

common room where the others were gathered, his humanoid nurse, a Purchased Person, following after him. "I'm all recovered," he announced.

Somewhat warily, his three companions from the battle against the Watchers welcomed him. They had received medication too, and looked fine—especially Zara, Ben Yale thought greedily, devouring her with his eyes. Redlaw and Org Rider gravely shook his hand, a skill they had just learned. Zara came over and patted his head. She drew back and looked at him. "Not really, I think," she said. "Not *all* recovered. But far better than the last time I saw you."

They and the ship crew had been talking excitedly over the strange message from the orbiter, which had been relayed to them. While the Purchased Person made him comfortable in an open-end hammock, Ben Yale listened. "—explains so much," said the Pmal, speaking for a horse-headed Canopan, the ship's pilot. "Explains why some of you races are duplicated on Cuckoo. That scout ship must have been twenty thousand years sailing through the Galaxy, picking up specimens and sending them back. And of course some got loose and multiplied. They wouldn't know they weren't indigenous."

Org Rider rapped indignantly, "That is our home! Our people have lived there forever—"

The Canopan snickered a whinnying laugh. "No offense," its Pmal said good-naturedly. "But what puzzles me," he went on, "is that picture of Cuckoo the replicate found. All made of metal! But it isn't like that, it's a world. A funny one, but still—"

"Wait," Org Rider cried through his own translator. "Perhaps I know something here! For there is a part of our world that is metal. A desert, that lies far beyond our grassworld, beyond the shadow of Knife-in-the-Sky. My mother heard about it from a chief who owned an org. He tried to cross that metal desert once, looking for another grassworld beyond the reach of the Watchers. He nearly died there."

The other beings looked at Org Rider, who returned their various kinds of gaze steadfastly. "It's true," he said. "It is all bare metal, harder than any axe or knife. There's nothing alive on it. No light except the dim glow of the clouds. The chief flew until his org grew so weak he had to give it all the food they carried for both of them. And then on the way back, trying to return to save their lives, he grew weak too, so weak that it had to carry him in its trunk. And," he cried, remembering more as he spoke, "that is of course how our world began. Everyone knows this! It was a hard bare shell, the first org's egg. Before the makers made their great fire to hatch all things from it."

He paused, puzzled. The beings were making a great variety of sounds, but the Pmals were not translating them into language. They could not; the sounds were laughter.

"But it is true," he insisted.

Zara smiled and gently put her hand in his. "It is puzzling," she said.

Ben Yale Pertin cleared his throat.

"Zara," he called.

It pleased him to see that she released the boy's hand to turn to him. "Yes, Ben Yale?"

He hesitated. How to tell her that she and he had once been married?—*were* married, and having children, on Sun One. He could not think of the right words, and as it was so important to him, and he wanted to be able to touch her, to kiss her, to hold her in his arms when he talked of these things, he temporized and turned what he said a different way. "I'm sorry about—about your loss." He could not bring himself to say, "about your husband's death."

"Thank you," she said. "It was a shock. But I've had a little time to get used to it."

The Purchased Person suddenly spoke, the voice human enough but the thought behind it coming from heaven knew who, heaven knew where. "Had you

considered you could have him again?" it demanded, in
a voice oddly, harshly male.

Zara looked surprised, and Redlaw rumbled, "She
said that before once, when you weren't here. Have
your husband make another copy and send it to you—
whatever that means," he added, knotting his brows
and staring about. Redlaw had never heard the expression "culture shock," but he was well on his way to
drowning in it. Org Rider seemed to accept everything
with grave interest and comfortable admiration; but he
was younger, of course. For Redlaw this sudden exposure to such strangeness was difficult.

Zara said thoughtfully, "Why, that never occurred to
me."

From his cocoon Ben Yale uttered a muffled groan.
Damn that savage! he cursed furiously. Giving her that
idea—

She was speaking again: "He might very well volunteer for replicating again, at that. He was—*is* a kind
person, Jon is. But—"

She looked around and suddenly shook her head,
smiling. "I'm sorry to be bothering you with my personal problems," she said.

"No, no," called Ben Yale, suffering. "We want to
hear. What were you going to say?"

"Well, just that I wouldn't like to ask him to. I know
it doesn't mean anything to be transmitted, in real
terms. You're not any less for having a copy made. But
in psychological terms it does, and you are. Expecially
for Jon. It was hard enough for him to volunteer the
first time. I wouldn't want to put him through it again."

Ben Yale exulted in the cocoon. So Zara would stay
free! Of course, he mused, that did not mean she would
marry *him*. Not *necessarily*. There was always that
other Ben Pertin, Ben Linc, waiting hot-handed on the
orbiter for them to arrive. Ben Yale knew with what
impatience his double would be waiting, and what his
intentions would be; he could not mistake them, because he shared them wholly and exactly. And besides,

he thought, he had time. The survey vessel still had two days to go before it reached the orbiter. It had been three days already—days wasted, he complained to himself; but there had been no way to help it, he had simply been physically unable to court Zara. But now— now things would be different. He closed his eyes, dreaming of how they would come to the orbiter. By then he would be out of his bandages, and rid of this pestilential Purchased Person nurse. He would take her to dinner—no, he thought regretfully, scratch that; there was no place on the orbiter for anything like that. But he would take her aside. In the rec room, at a time when not many others would be around.

She would be grateful to him, he estimated complacently; had he not saved her life? Or at least helped to do so? And she would have the interest women always felt for a hero in him. And he would tell her, very gently and simply, about his love for herself, Zara Doy; and how they had been married, and how much they had loved each other . . .

He scowled. The thought of Ben Linc Pertin intruded. Ben Linc would have almost the same advantages as himself, bar, of course, the couple of days before they got there. But a couple of days might not be enough to awaken her romantic interest.

He nodded to himself, sealed up the end of the cocoon with a quick motion—startling the Purchased Person who stood wide-eyed beside him—and flipped on the stereostage, putting through a call to Ben Linc Pertin on the orbiter.

When he saw himself, or the Ben Linc version of himself, he was startled. So haggard! So sad! For a moment he almost thought it was a replay of that terribly depressing version of himself from the unidentified ship; but then Ben Linc spoke. "Oh, it's you," he muttered. "What do you want?"

Ben Yale said carefully, "I think you know, Ben Linc. It's about Zara."

Ben Linc nodded lifelessly. "Yes. I suppose I should

have expected you to call. I'm sorry, but—well. What can I do? I'll just go on being lonely. I've had plenty of practice—as you know."

Startled, Ben Yale stared at his duplicate. Elation and a nagging, suspicious fear fought with each other in his mind; he struggled to keep his voice level, even as he was wondering what had made Ben Linc give up so easily. "I admire you for taking it so well," he managed to say.

"You do?" Ben Linc looked surprised. Then, slowly, "Well, I kind of admire you, too. I mean, you actually look content, and God knows I can't; I don't feel it. Well, it's too bad we both had to be losers, but maybe it would be even harder if we weren't." And without another word he broke the connection.

Losers?

Ben Yale shook his swathed head, unbelievingly. *Both* of them losers?

And then a sudden fear chilled him, and he opened the end of the cocoon once more and peered out at Zara—

At Zara and Org Rider, sitting quietly, whispering at each other, the boy's hand caught in the girl's two, their shoulders touching.

Losers.

A couple of days had been time enough to awaken her romantic interest, after all.

But not for him.

On Earth astronomers were studying their tachyon transmissions of the object called Cuckoo. Almost invisible in the flood of light from the bright stars Benetnasch and Cor Caroli it swam in toward the center of the Galaxy.

Its course would take it very near the volume of space occupied by Sun and Earth. It was very, very far away. It would not get there for many thousands of years . . .

But it was coming.

About the Authors

Frederik Pohl has been about everything one man can be in the world of science fiction: fan (one of the founders of the fabled Futurians), book and magazine editor, agent, and, above all, writer. As editor of *Galaxy* in the 1960s, he helped set the tone for a decade of SF. His own memorable stories such as *The Space Merchants* (in collaboration with Cyril Kornbluth) have become classics.

Pohl's latest novel is *Beyond the Blue Event Horizon*, a sequel to the Hugo and Nebula Award-winning novel, *Gateway*. He has also written *The Way the Future Was*, a memoir of his forty-five years in science fiction. Frederik Pohl was born in Brooklyn, New York, in 1919, and now lives in New York City.

Jack Williamson began writing science fiction in 1928, before it got that name. With time out for service as an Army Air Forces weather forecaster during World War II, and a more recent career as a college English professor, he has devoted his life to science fiction, and he says he has no regrets.

A Southwesterner, he was born in Arizona of pioneering parents who took him to a Mexican mountain ranch before he was two months old, moved from there to Pecos, Texas, and then, the year he was seven, brought him by covered wagon to the Staked Plains of Eastern New Mexico, where he and his wife, Blanche, still live.

The best-known of his thirty-odd novels is probably *The Humanoids*. He has been honored by the Science Fiction Writers of America with their Grand Master Nebula Award, and he has served for two terms as president of the organization. He taught one of the first college courses in science fiction and has edited a guidebook for science fiction teachers.

Now retired from teaching, he writes on a word processor. His next work, he says, is to be an autobiographical book about his own adventures in science fiction.